D0965524

The CAPTIVE PRINCE

THREE THIEVES · BOOK THREE

Kids Can Press acknowledges the financial support of the Government of Ontario, through the Ontario Media Development Corporation's Ontario Book Initiative; the Ontario Arts Council; the Canada Council for the Arts; and the Government of Canada, through the BPIDP, for our publishing activity.

Published in Canada by
Kids Can Press Ltd.
25 Dockside Drive
Toronto, ON M5A 0B5

Published in the U.S. by
Kids Can Press Ltd.
2250 Military Road
Tonawanda, NY 14150

www.kidscanpress.com

Edited by Karen Li
Designed by Rachel Di Salle and Scott Chantler
Pages lettered with Blambot comic fonts

The hardcover edition of this book is smyth sewn casebound.
The paperback edition of this book is limp sewn with a drawn-on cover.
Manufactured in Buji, Shenzhen, China, in 5/2012 by WKT Company

CM 12 0 9 8 7 6 5 4 3 2 1
CM PA 12 0 9 8 7 6 5 4 3 2 1

Library and Archives Canada Cataloguing in Publication

Chantler, Scott
     The captive prince / Scott Chantler.

(Three thieves ; bk. 3)
ISBN 978-1-55453-776-1 (bound)   ISBN 978-1-55453-777-8 (pbk.)

     I. Title. II. Series: Chantler, Scott. Three thieves ; bk. 3.

PN6733.C53C37 2012   j741.5'971   C2012-900813-3

Kids Can Press is a *C©rus*™ Entertainment company

The CAPTIVE PRINCE

THREE THIEVES · BOOK THREE

Scott Chantler

Kids Can Press

ACT ONE
KIDNAPPED

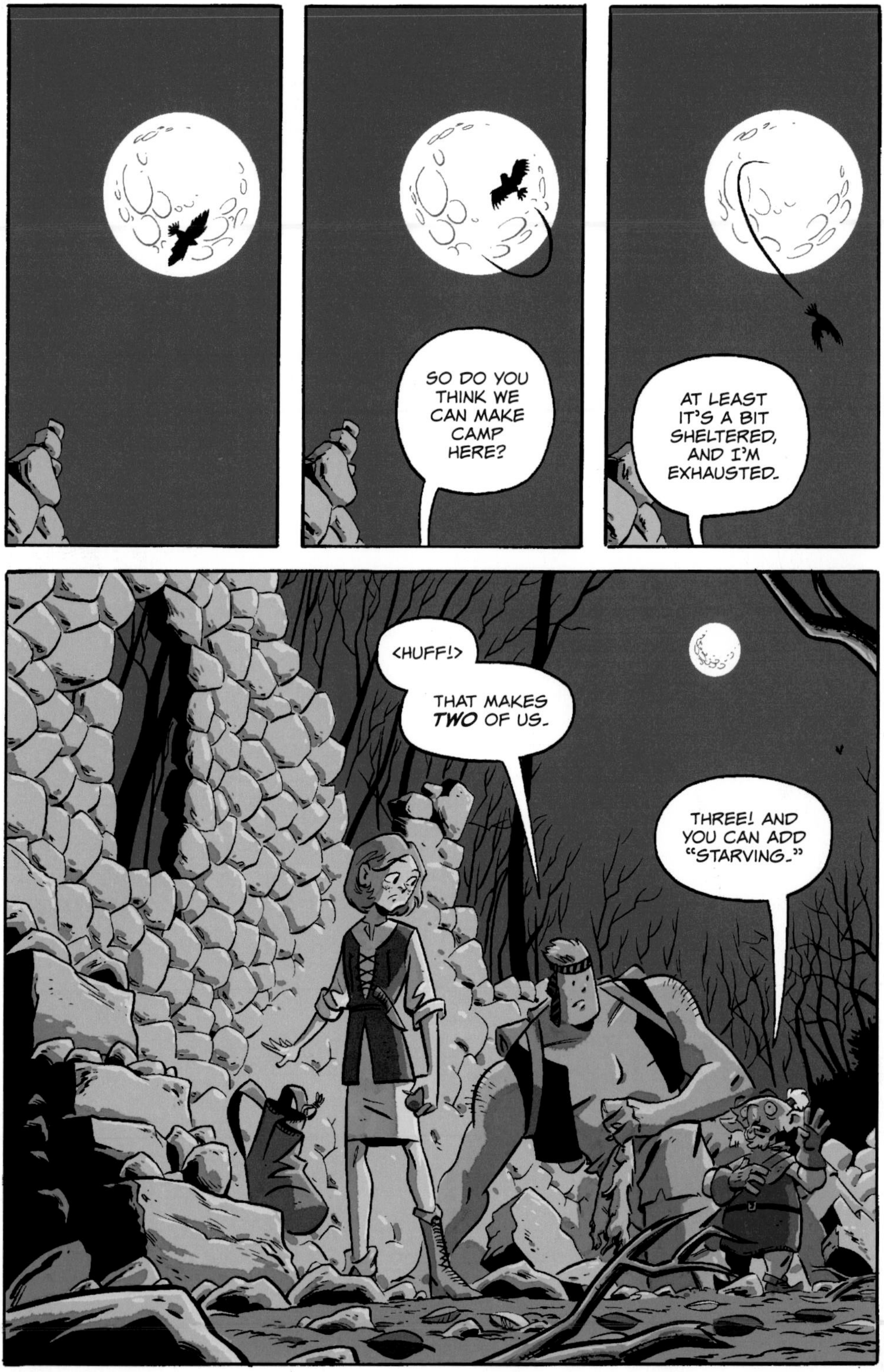
SO DO YOU THINK WE CAN MAKE CAMP HERE?
AT LEAST IT'S A BIT SHELTERED, AND I'M EXHAUSTED.
<HUFF!>
THAT MAKES *TWO* OF US.
THREE! AND YOU CAN ADD "STARVING."

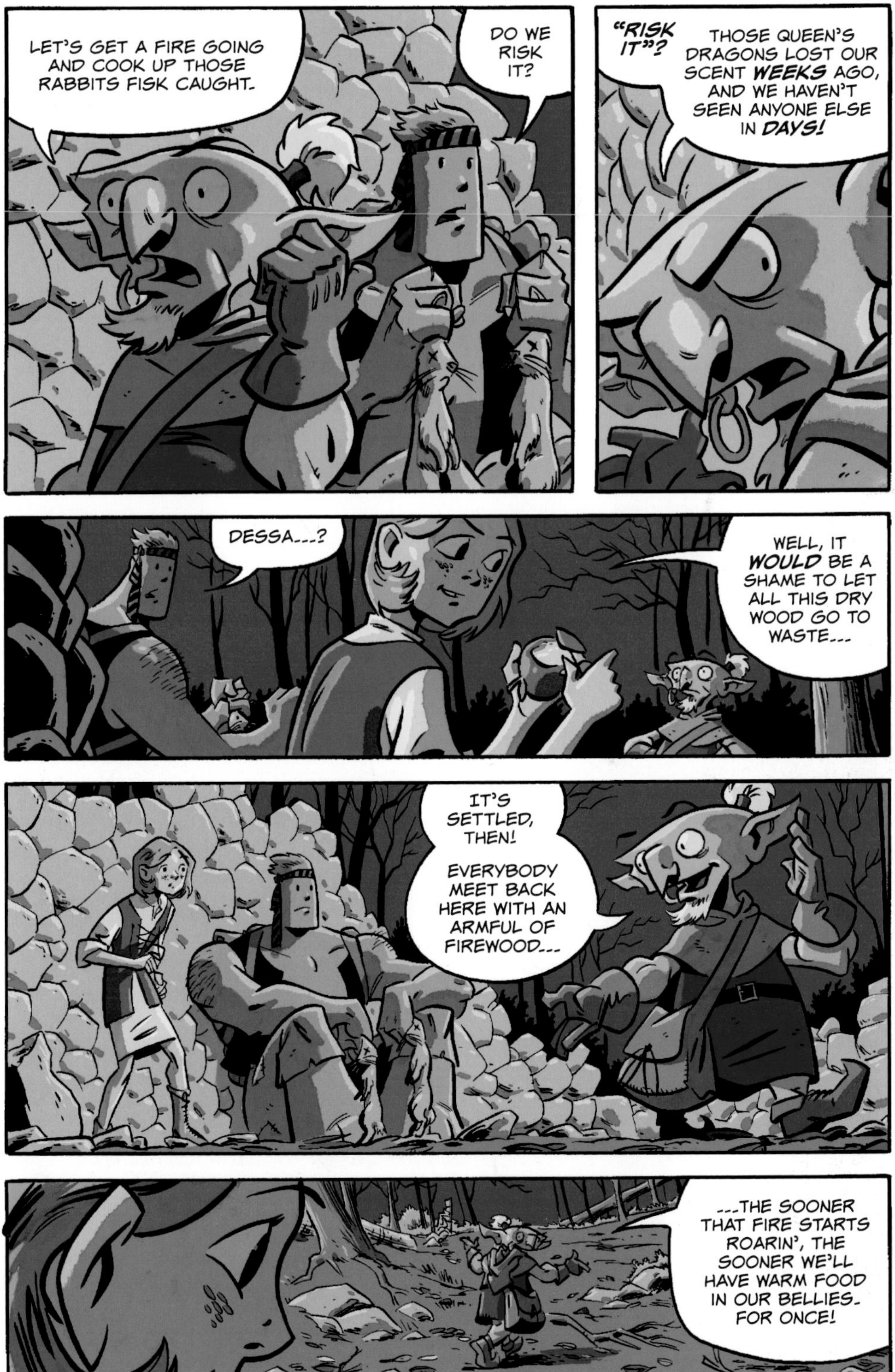
LET'S GET A FIRE GOING AND COOK UP THOSE RABBITS FISK CAUGHT.
DO WE RISK IT?
"RISK IT"?
THOSE QUEEN'S DRAGONS LOST OUR SCENT WEEKS AGO, AND WE HAVEN'T SEEN ANYONE ELSE IN DAYS!
DESSA...?
WELL, IT WOULD BE A SHAME TO LET ALL THIS DRY WOOD GO TO WASTE...
IT'S SETTLED, THEN!
EVERYBODY MEET BACK HERE WITH AN ARMFUL OF FIREWOOD...
...THE SOONER THAT FIRE STARTS ROARIN', THE SOONER WE'LL HAVE WARM FOOD IN OUR BELLIES. FOR ONCE!

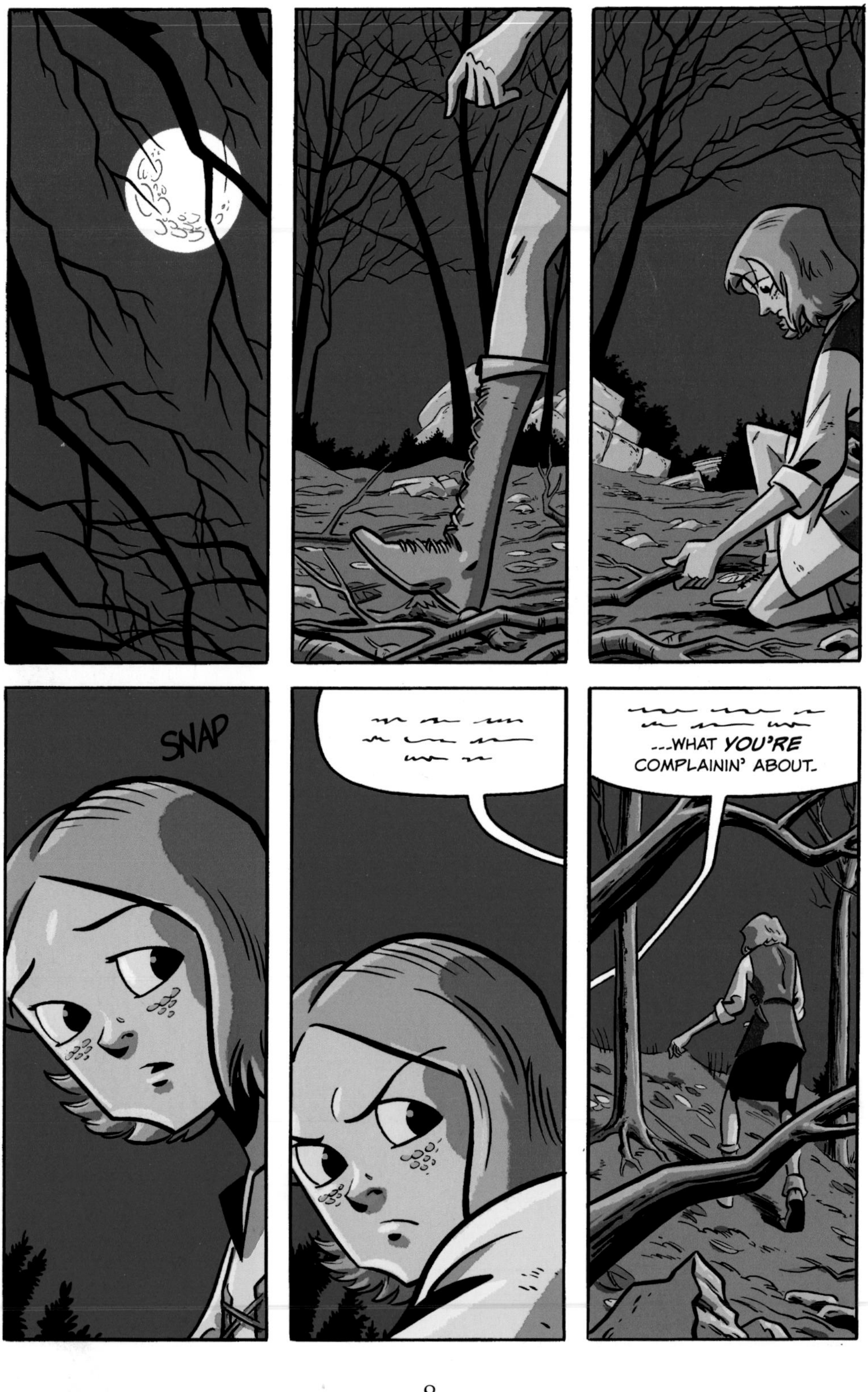

SNAP
...WHAT YOU'RE COMPLAININ' ABOUT.

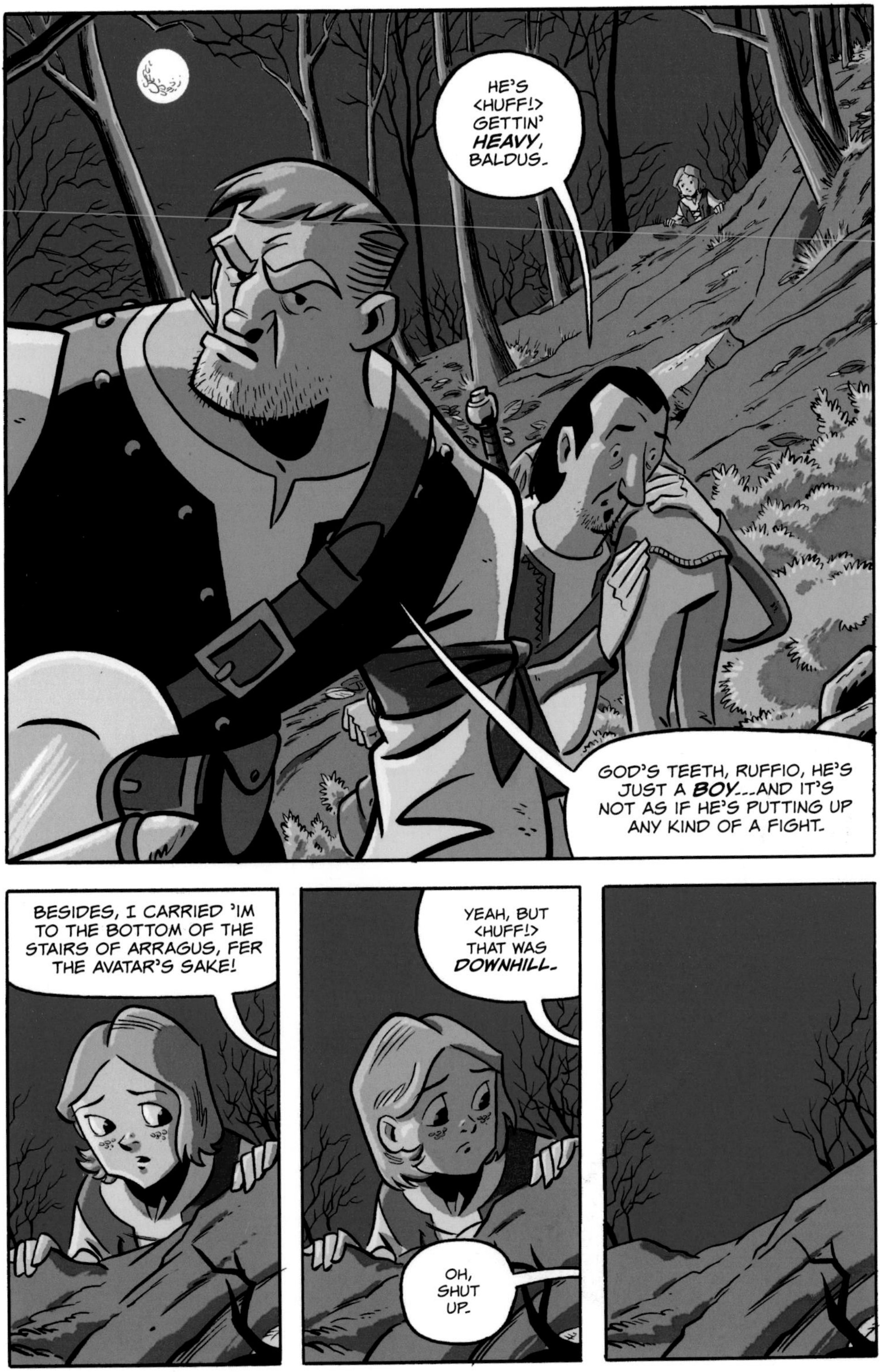
HE'S <HUFF!> GETTIN' HEAVY, BALDUS.
GOD'S TEETH, RUFFIO, HE'S JUST A BOY...AND IT'S NOT AS IF HE'S PUTTING UP ANY KIND OF A FIGHT.
BESIDES, I CARRIED 'IM TO THE BOTTOM OF THE STAIRS OF ARRAGUS, FER THE AVATAR'S SAKE!
YEAH, BUT <HUFF!> THAT WAS DOWNHILL.
OH, SHUT UP.

THAT'S IT...<HUFF!>
...I GOTTA REST.

IF YOU
SAY
SO.

PEOPLE ARE GONNA
COME LOOKIN'
SOON, THOUGH.

I REALIZE
THAT, BALDUS!

BUT WHAT'S THE
POINT TRADIN'
'IM FER ALL THAT
GOLD IF I'M NOT
GONNA BE ALIVE
TO ENJOY IT?!

AND IF YER
SO BLOODY
CONCERNED, WHY
DON'T YOU
CARRY 'IM?!

EH. I'M NOT
THAT CONCERNED.
NOBODY'S GONNA
FIND US IN THESE
PARTS.

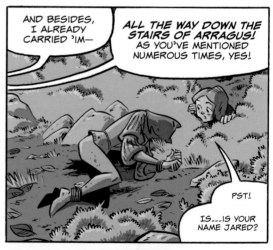

AND BESIDES,
I ALREADY
CARRIED 'IM—

ALL THE WAY DOWN THE
STAIRS OF ARRAGUS!
AS YOU'VE MENTIONED
NUMEROUS TIMES, YES!

PST!

IS...IS YOUR
NAME JARED?

WHAT?
W-WHO'S
THERE?

SHH!

I'M NOT
ONE OF
THEM.

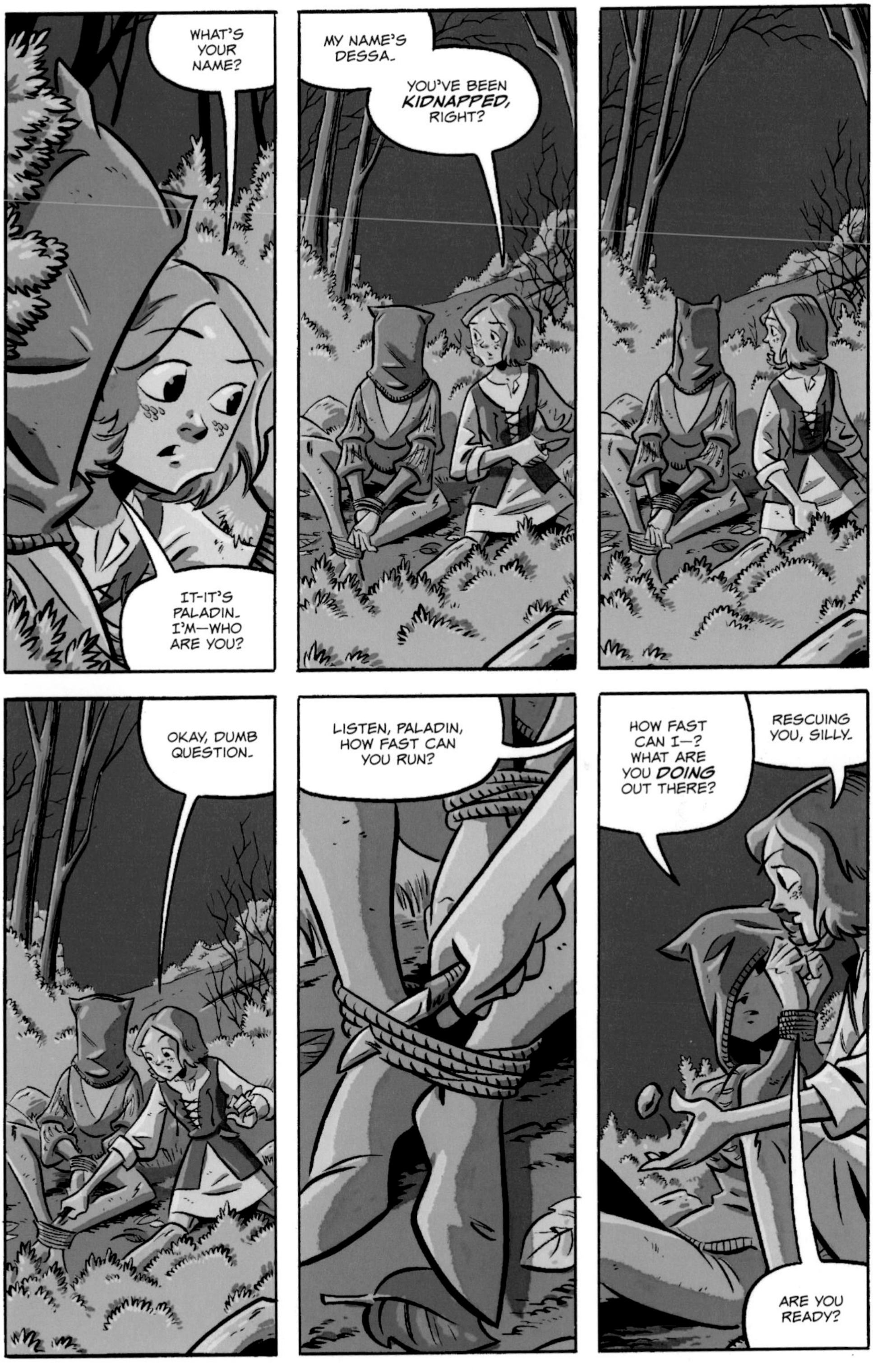
WHAT'S YOUR NAME?
IT-IT'S PALADIN. I'M—WHO ARE YOU?
MY NAME'S DESSA.
YOU'VE BEEN *KIDNAPPED*, RIGHT?
OKAY, DUMB QUESTION.
LISTEN, PALADIN, HOW FAST CAN YOU RUN?
HOW FAST CAN I—? WHAT ARE YOU *DOING* OUT THERE?
RESCUING YOU, SILLY.
ARE YOU READY?

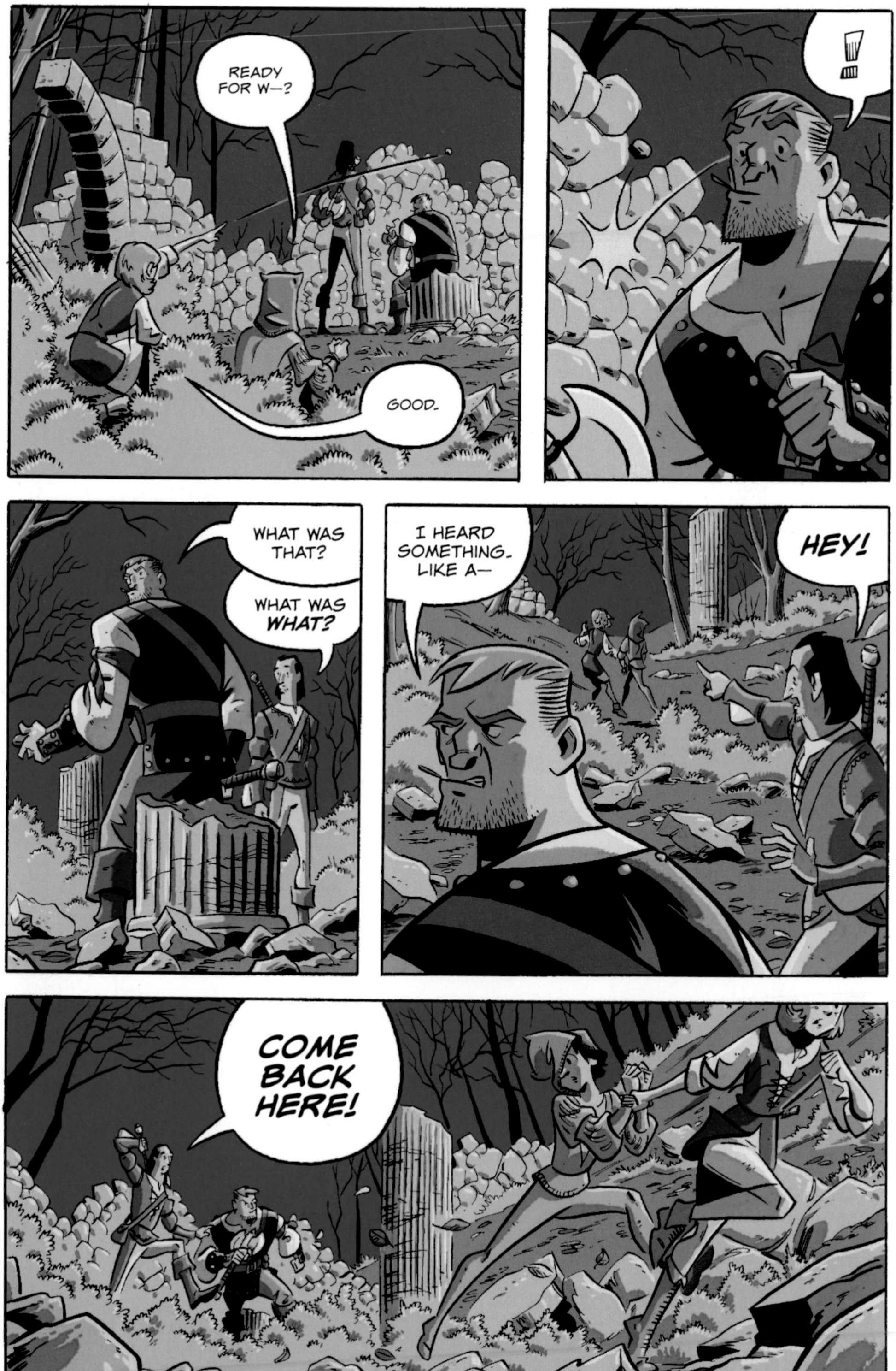
READY FOR W—?
GOOD.
!
WHAT WAS THAT?
WHAT WAS *WHAT?*
I HEARD SOMETHING. LIKE A—
HEY!
COME BACK HERE!

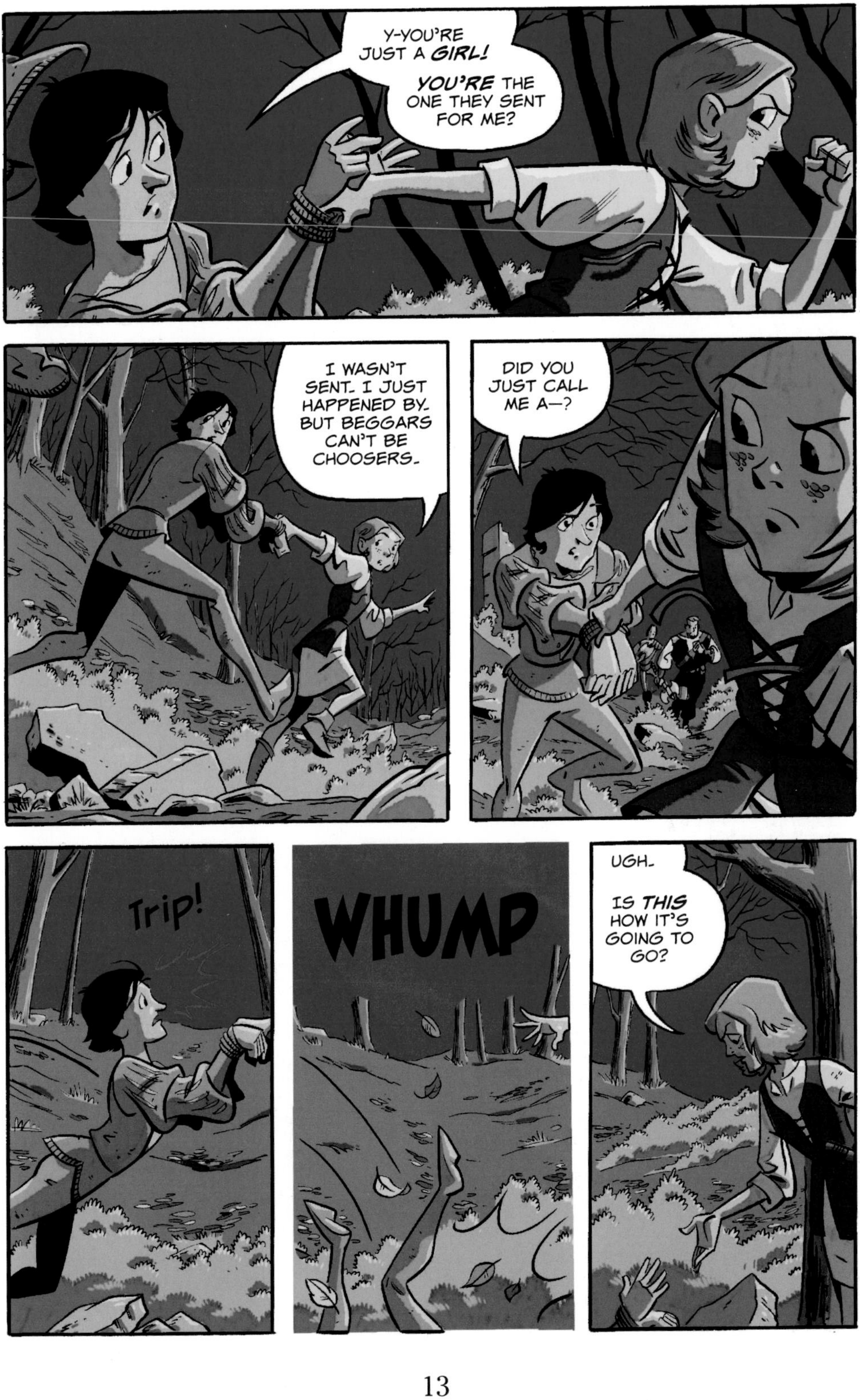
Y-YOU'RE JUST A GIRL!
YOU'RE THE ONE THEY SENT FOR ME?
I WASN'T SENT. I JUST HAPPENED BY. BUT BEGGARS CAN'T BE CHOOSERS.
DID YOU JUST CALL ME A—?
Trip!
WHUMP
UGH.
IS THIS HOW IT'S GOING TO GO?

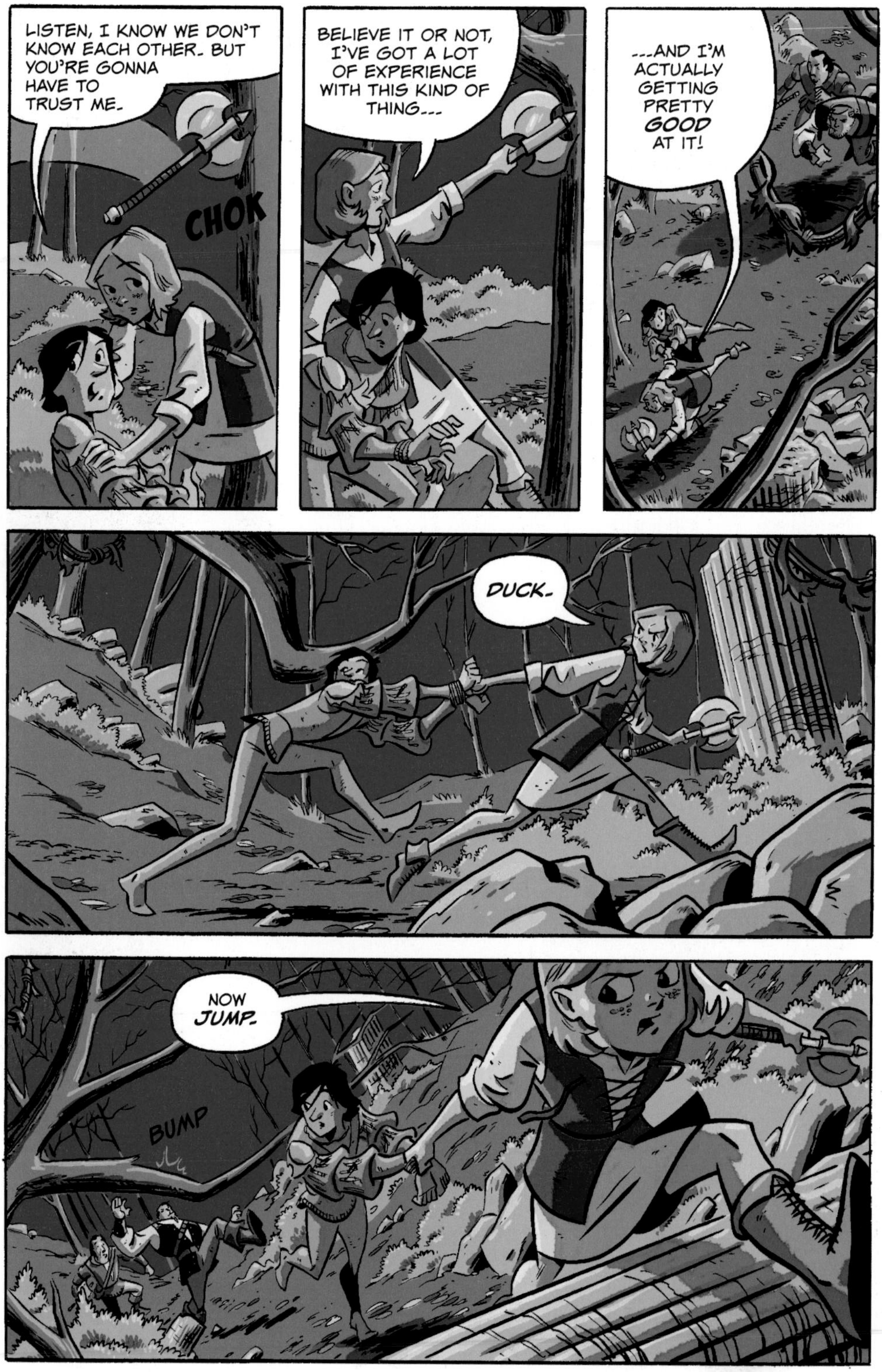
LISTEN, I KNOW WE DON'T KNOW EACH OTHER. BUT YOU'RE GONNA HAVE TO TRUST ME.
CHOK
BELIEVE IT OR NOT, I'VE GOT A LOT OF EXPERIENCE WITH THIS KIND OF THING...
...AND I'M ACTUALLY GETTING PRETTY GOOD AT IT!
DUCK.
NOW JUMP.
BUMP

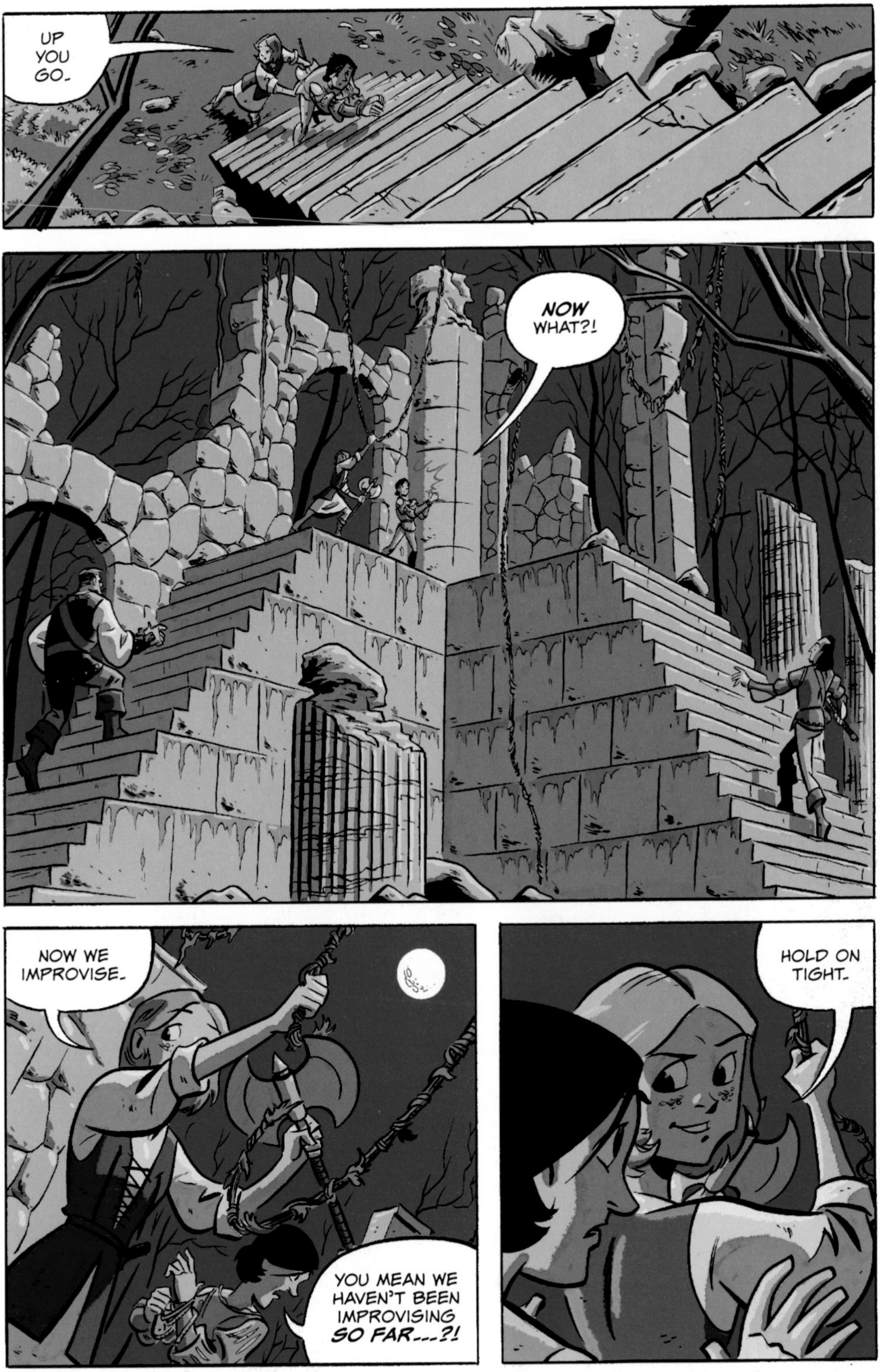
UP YOU GO.
NOW WHAT?!
NOW WE IMPROVISE.
YOU MEAN WE HAVEN'T BEEN IMPROVISING SO FAR...?!
HOLD ON TIGHT.

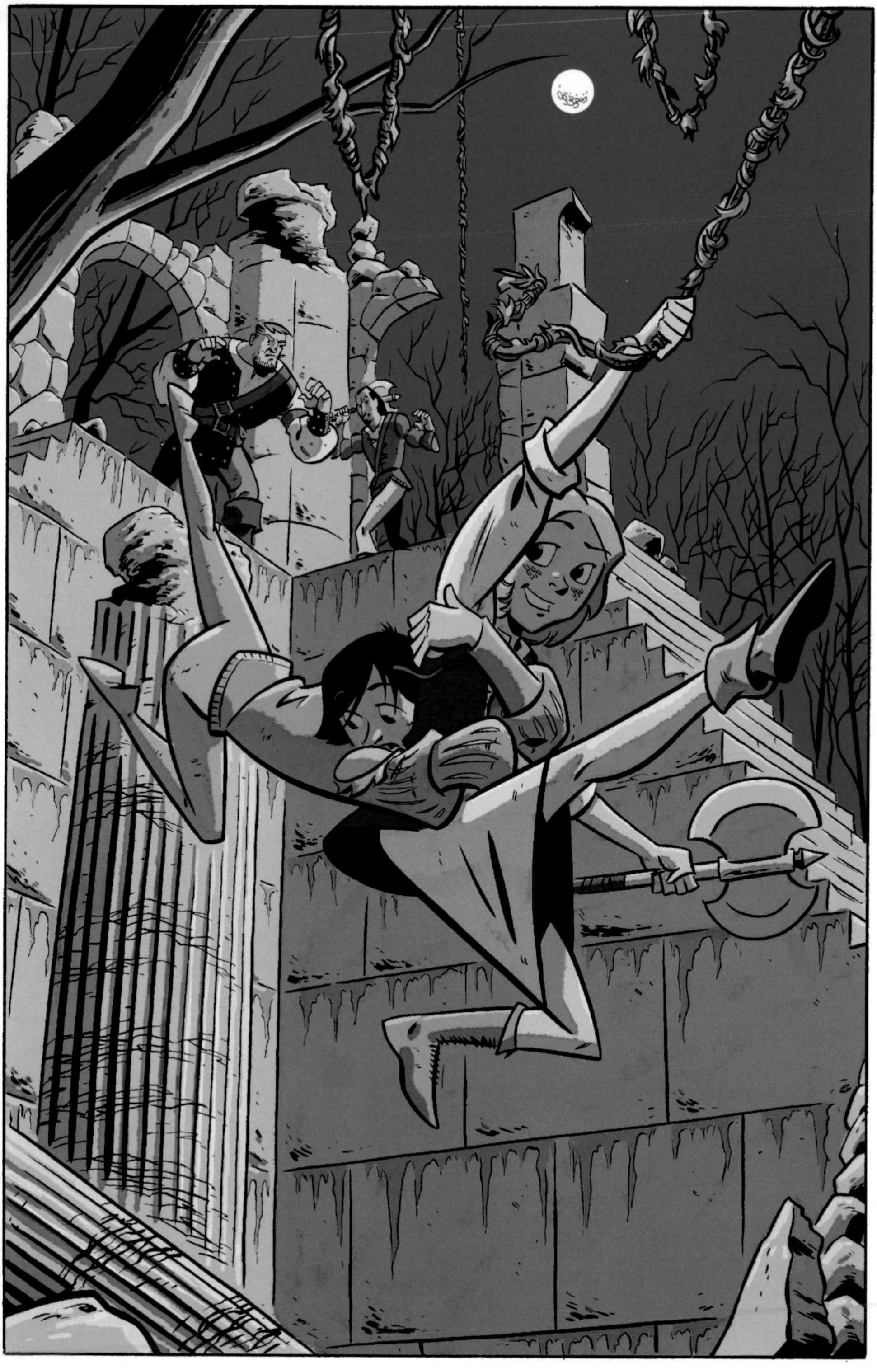

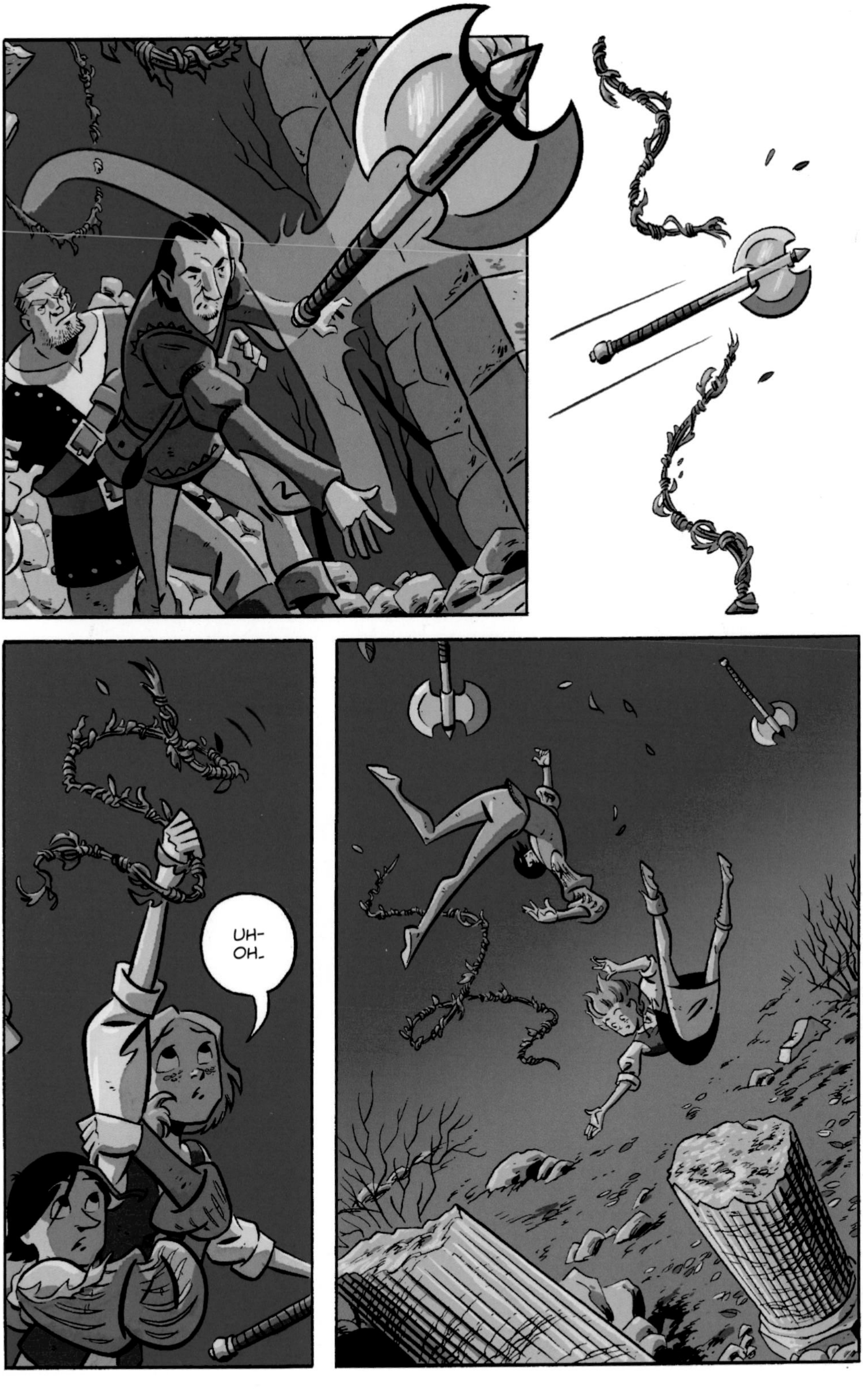
UH-
OH.

THUD

WHUMP

HA!

CRUMBLE
CRUMBLE
CRUMBLE

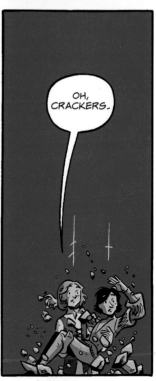

OH, CRACKERS...

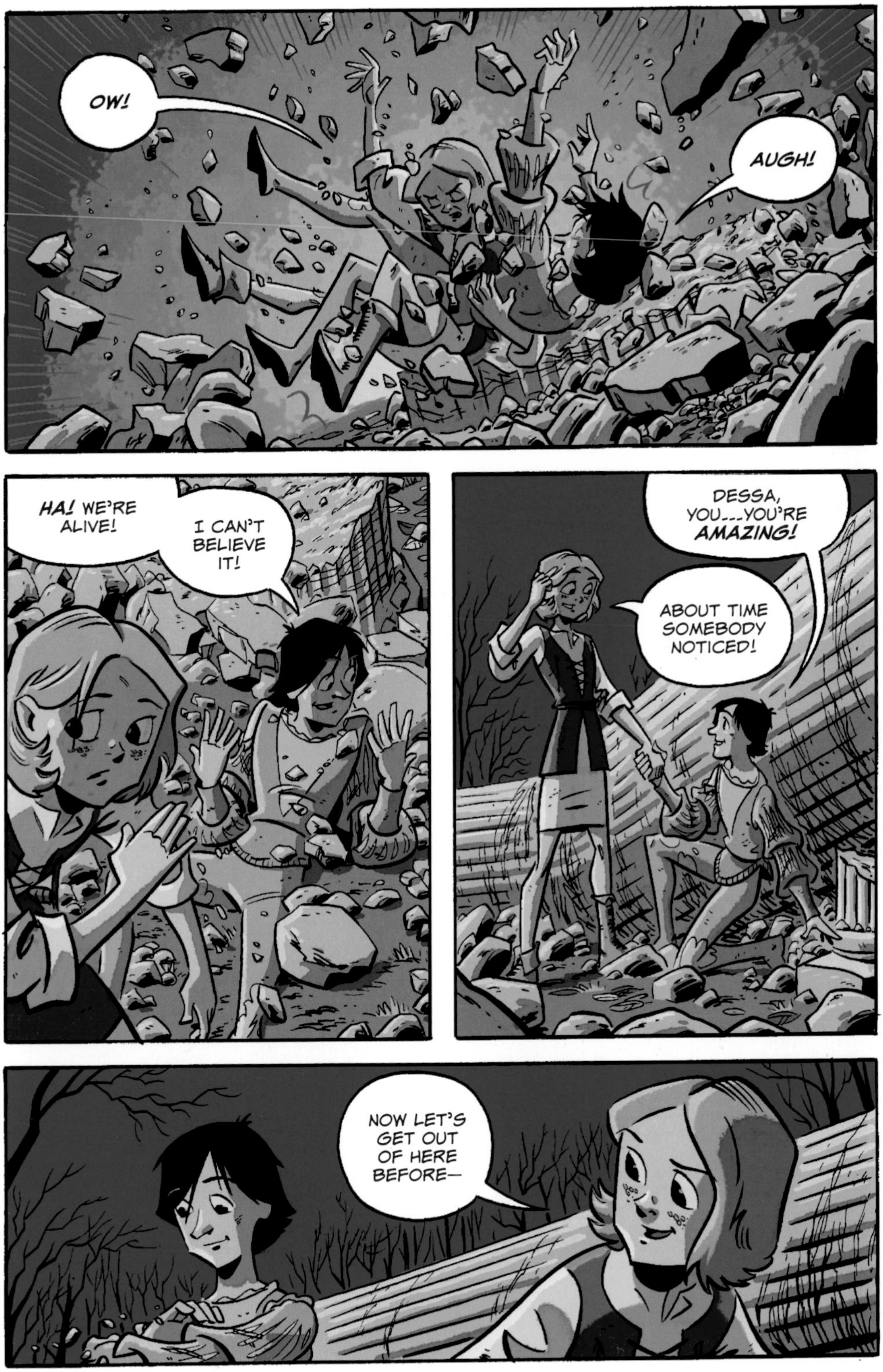
OW!
AUGH!
HA! WE'RE ALIVE!
I CAN'T BELIEVE IT!
DESSA, YOU...YOU'RE AMAZING!
ABOUT TIME SOMEBODY NOTICED!
NOW LET'S GET OUT OF HERE BEFORE—

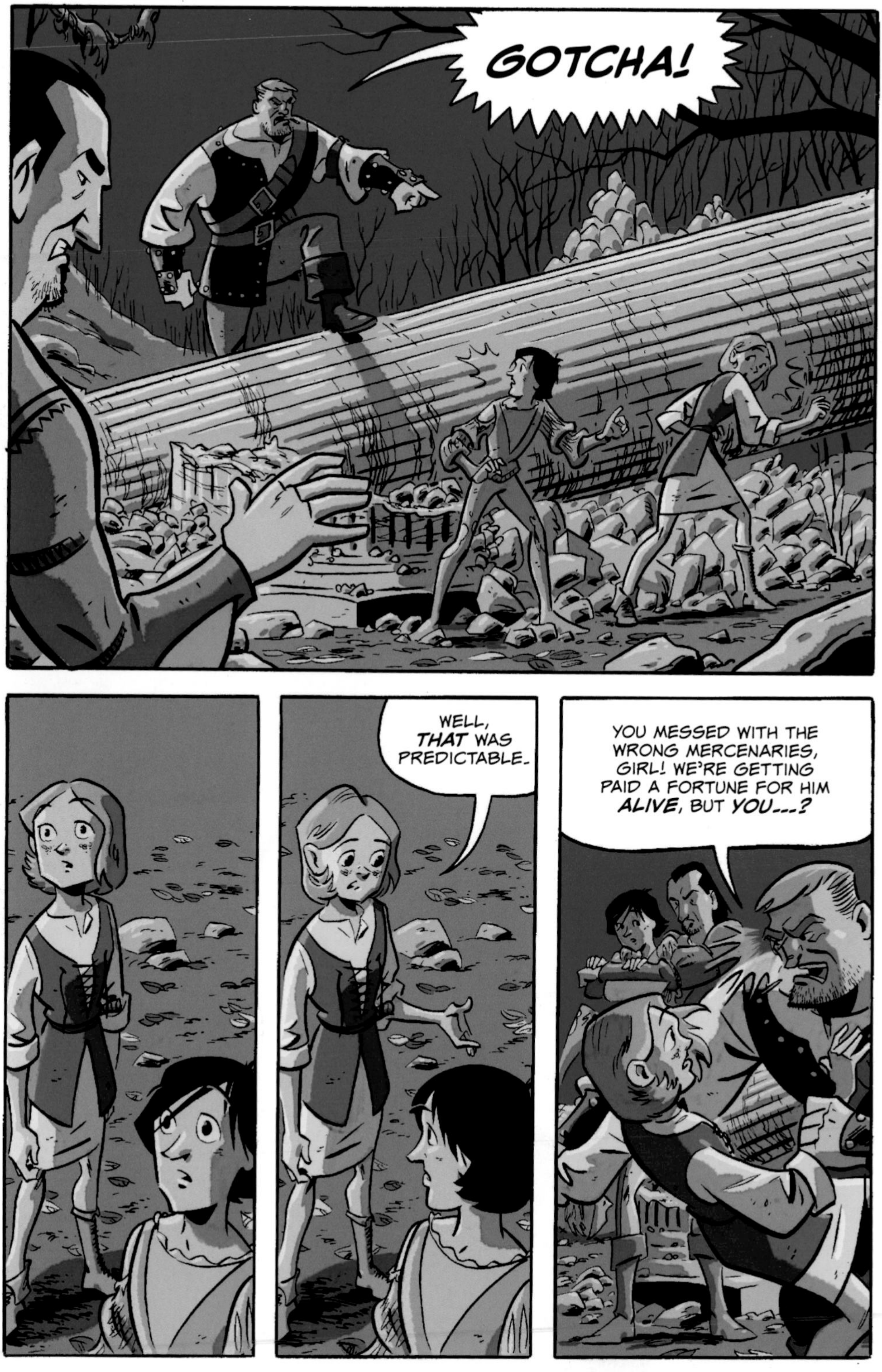
GOTCHA!
WELL, THAT WAS PREDICTABLE.
YOU MESSED WITH THE WRONG MERCENARIES, GIRL! WE'RE GETTING PAID A FORTUNE FOR HIM ALIVE, BUT YOU...?

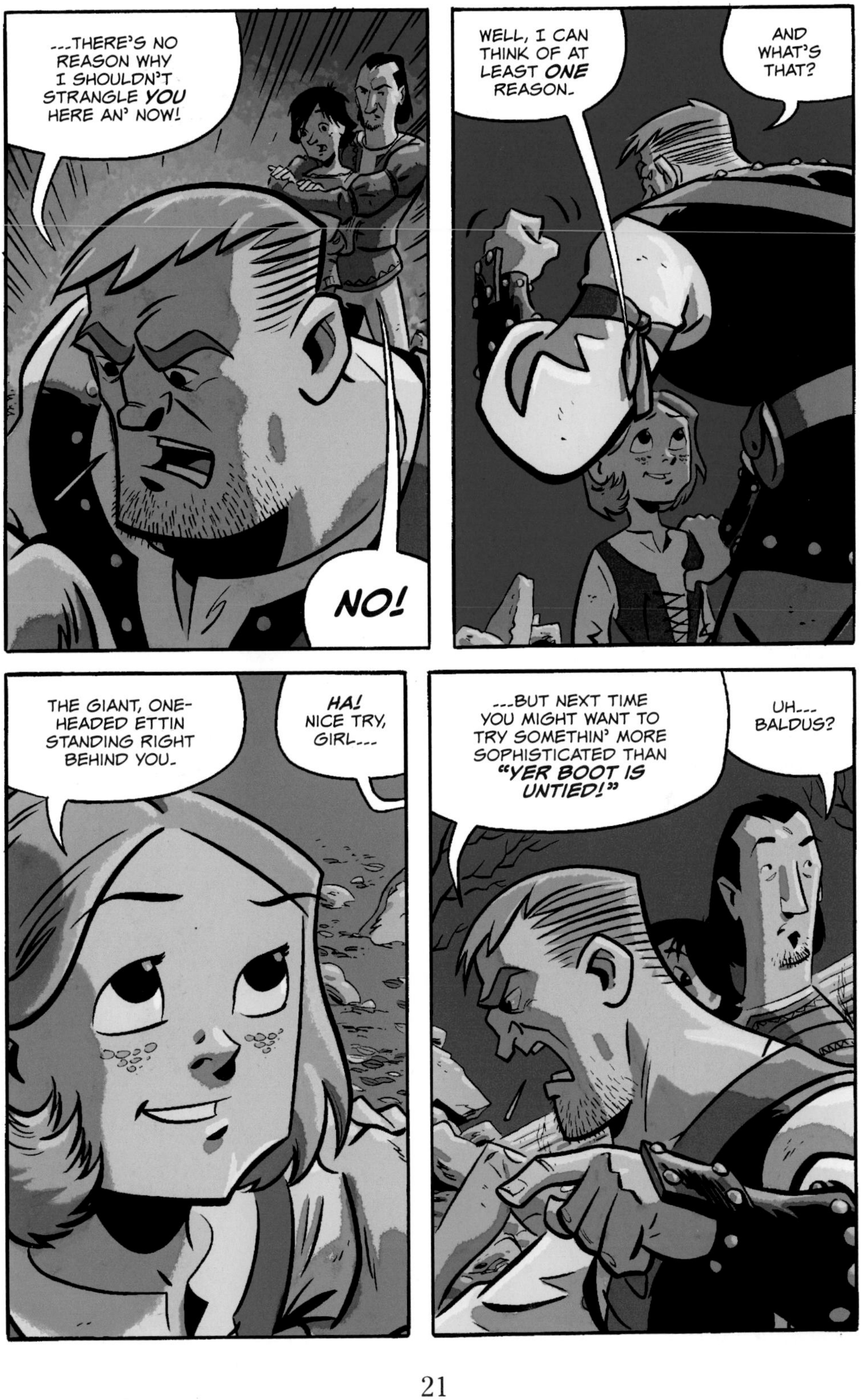

...THERE'S NO REASON WHY I SHOULDN'T STRANGLE YOU HERE AN' NOW!
NO!
WELL, I CAN THINK OF AT LEAST ONE REASON.
AND WHAT'S THAT?
THE GIANT, ONE-HEADED ETTIN STANDING RIGHT BEHIND YOU.
HA! NICE TRY, GIRL...
...BUT NEXT TIME YOU MIGHT WANT TO TRY SOMETHIN' MORE SOPHISTICATED THAN "YER BOOT IS UNTIED!"
UH... BALDUS?

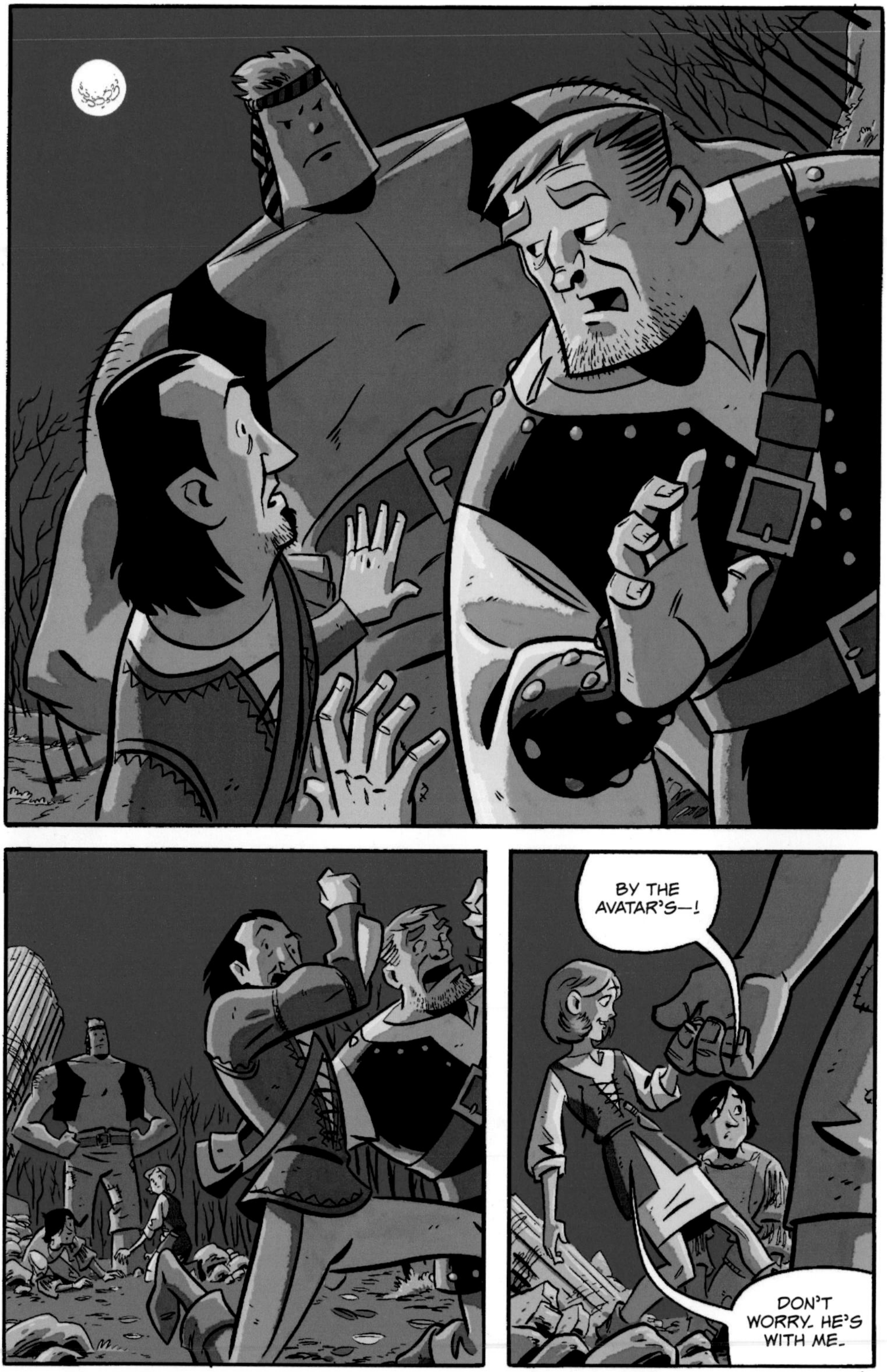
BY THE AVATAR'S—!
DON'T WORRY. HE'S WITH ME.

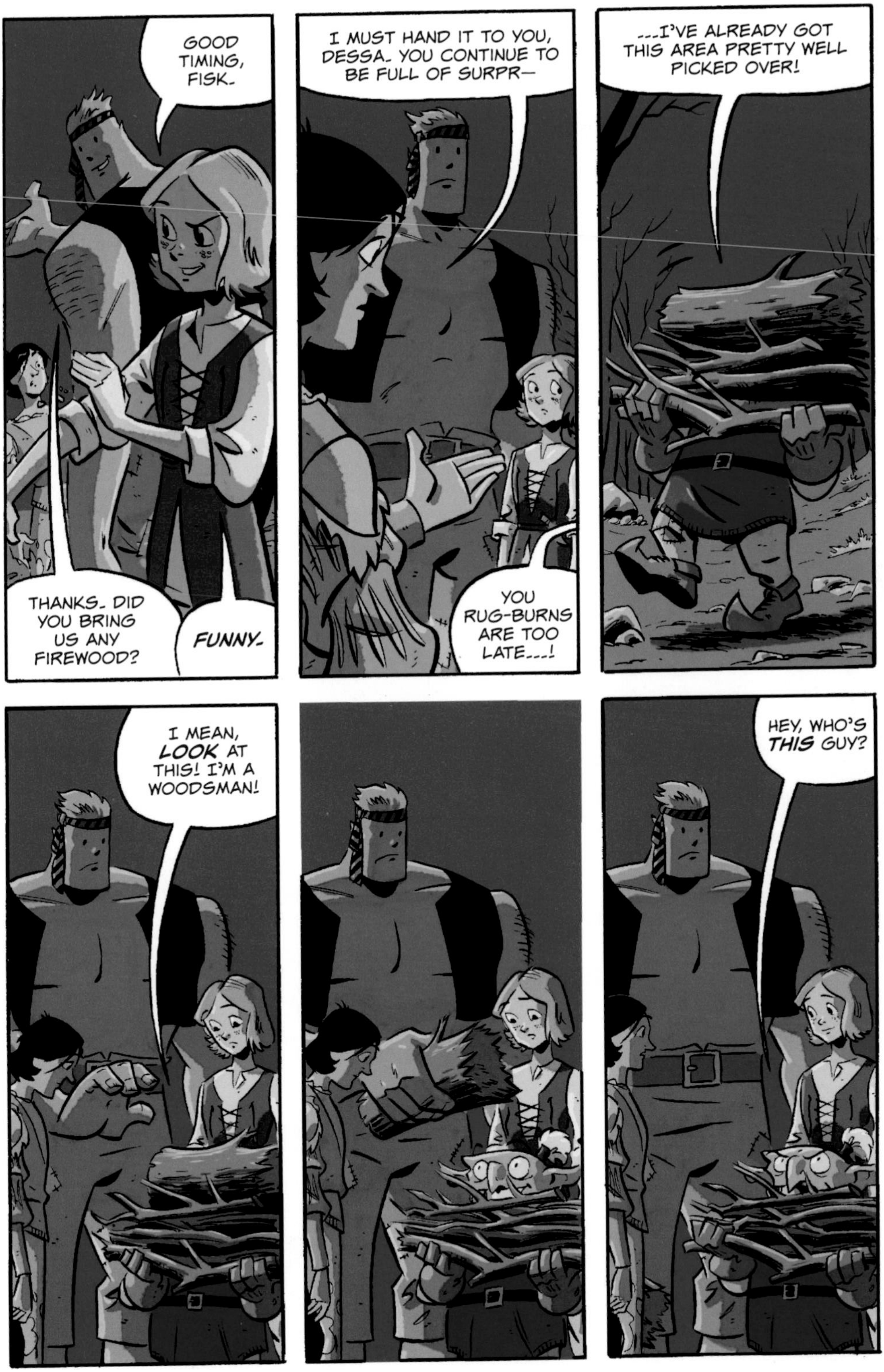
GOOD TIMING, FISK.
THANKS. DID YOU BRING US ANY FIREWOOD?
FUNNY.
I MUST HAND IT TO YOU, DESSA. YOU CONTINUE TO BE FULL OF SURPR—
YOU RUG-BURNS ARE TOO LATE...!
...I'VE ALREADY GOT THIS AREA PRETTY WELL PICKED OVER!
I MEAN, LOOK AT THIS! I'M A WOODSMAN!
HEY, WHO'S THIS GUY?

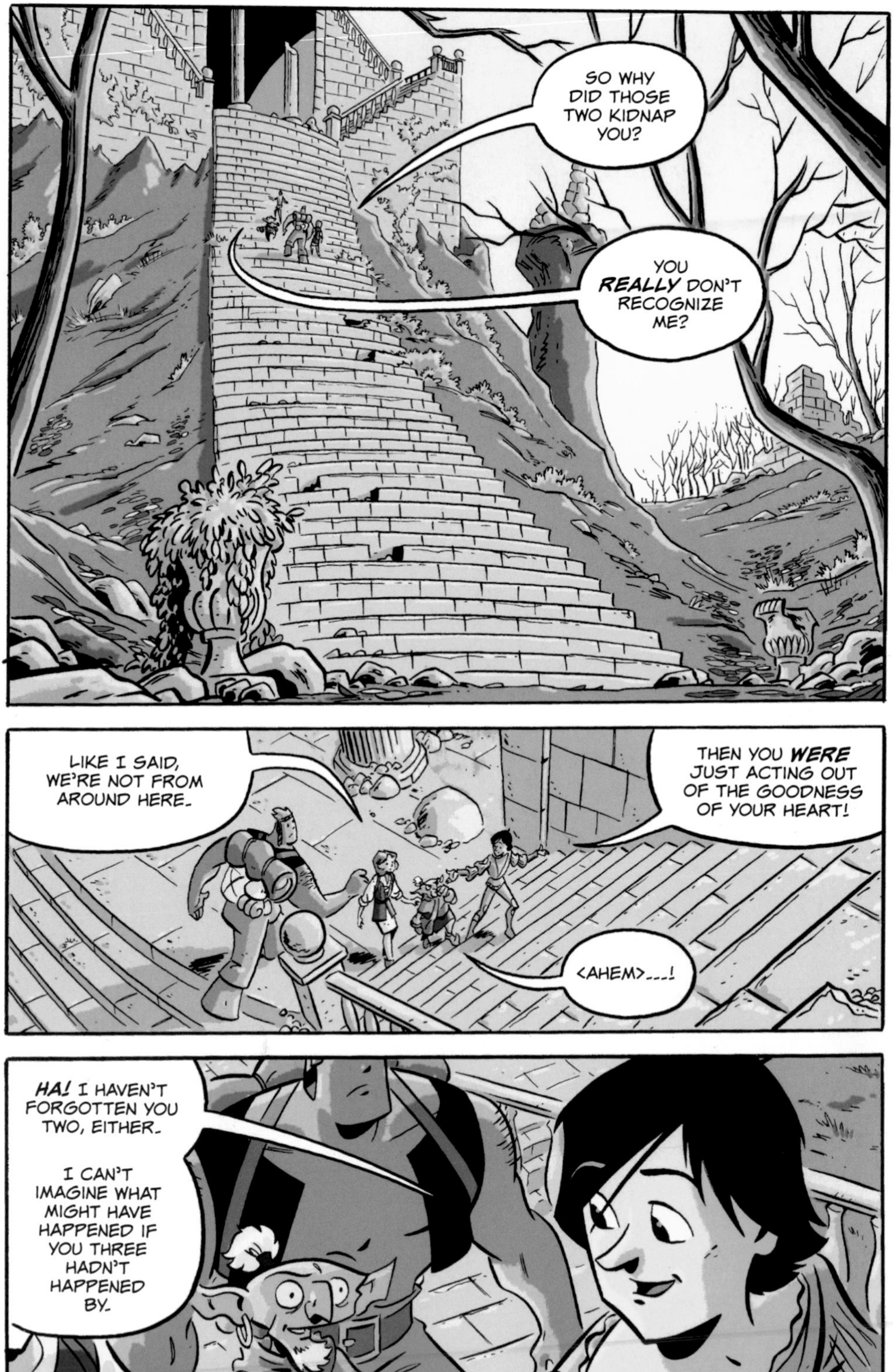
SO WHY DID THOSE TWO KIDNAP YOU?
YOU REALLY DON'T RECOGNIZE ME?
LIKE I SAID, WE'RE NOT FROM AROUND HERE.
THEN YOU WERE JUST ACTING OUT OF THE GOODNESS OF YOUR HEART!
<AHEM>...!
HA! I HAVEN'T FORGOTTEN YOU TWO, EITHER.
I CAN'T IMAGINE WHAT MIGHT HAVE HAPPENED IF YOU THREE HADN'T HAPPENED BY.

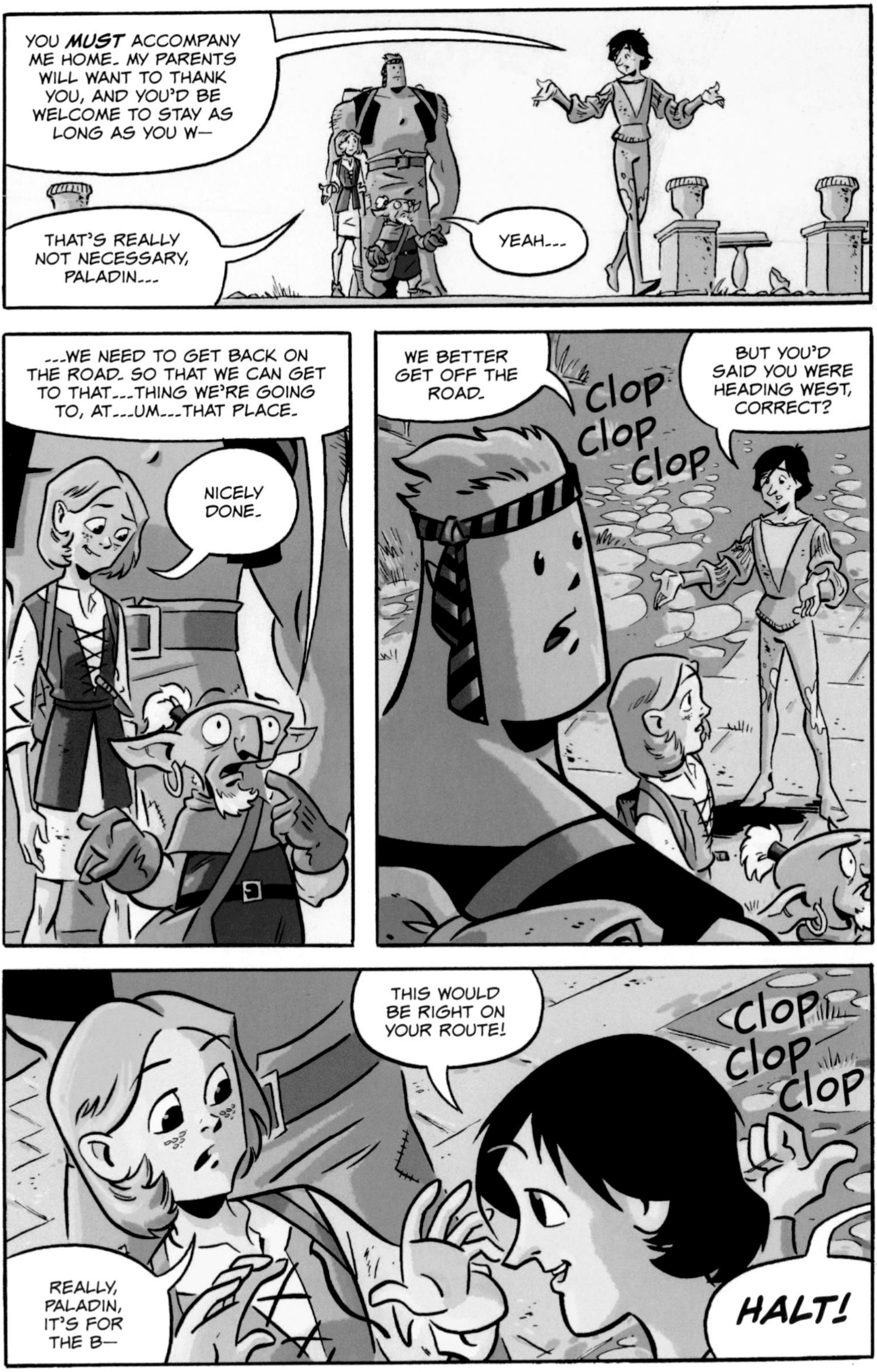

YOU *MUST* ACCOMPANY ME HOME. MY PARENTS WILL WANT TO THANK YOU, AND YOU'D BE WELCOME TO STAY AS LONG AS YOU W—
THAT'S REALLY NOT NECESSARY, PALADIN...
YEAH...
...WE NEED TO GET BACK ON THE ROAD. SO THAT WE CAN GET TO THAT...THING WE'RE GOING TO, AT...UM...THAT PLACE.
NICELY DONE.
WE BETTER GET OFF THE ROAD.
Clop Clop Clop
BUT YOU'D SAID YOU WERE HEADING WEST, CORRECT?
THIS WOULD BE RIGHT ON YOUR ROUTE!
Clop Clop Clop
REALLY, PALADIN, IT'S FOR THE B—
HALT!

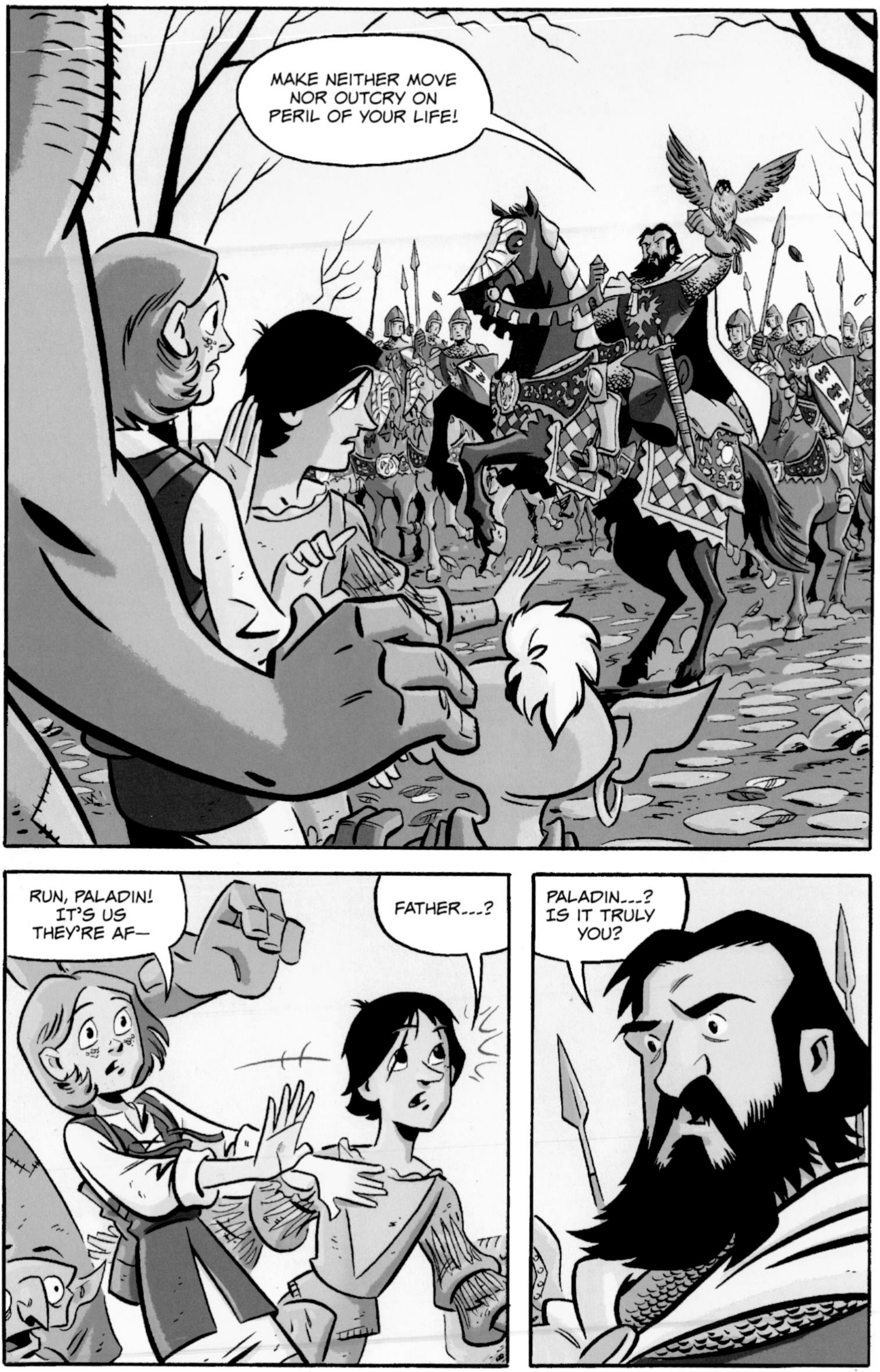
MAKE NEITHER MOVE NOR OUTCRY ON PERIL OF YOUR LIFE!
RUN, PALADIN! IT'S US THEY'RE AF—
FATHER...?
PALADIN...? IS IT TRULY YOU?

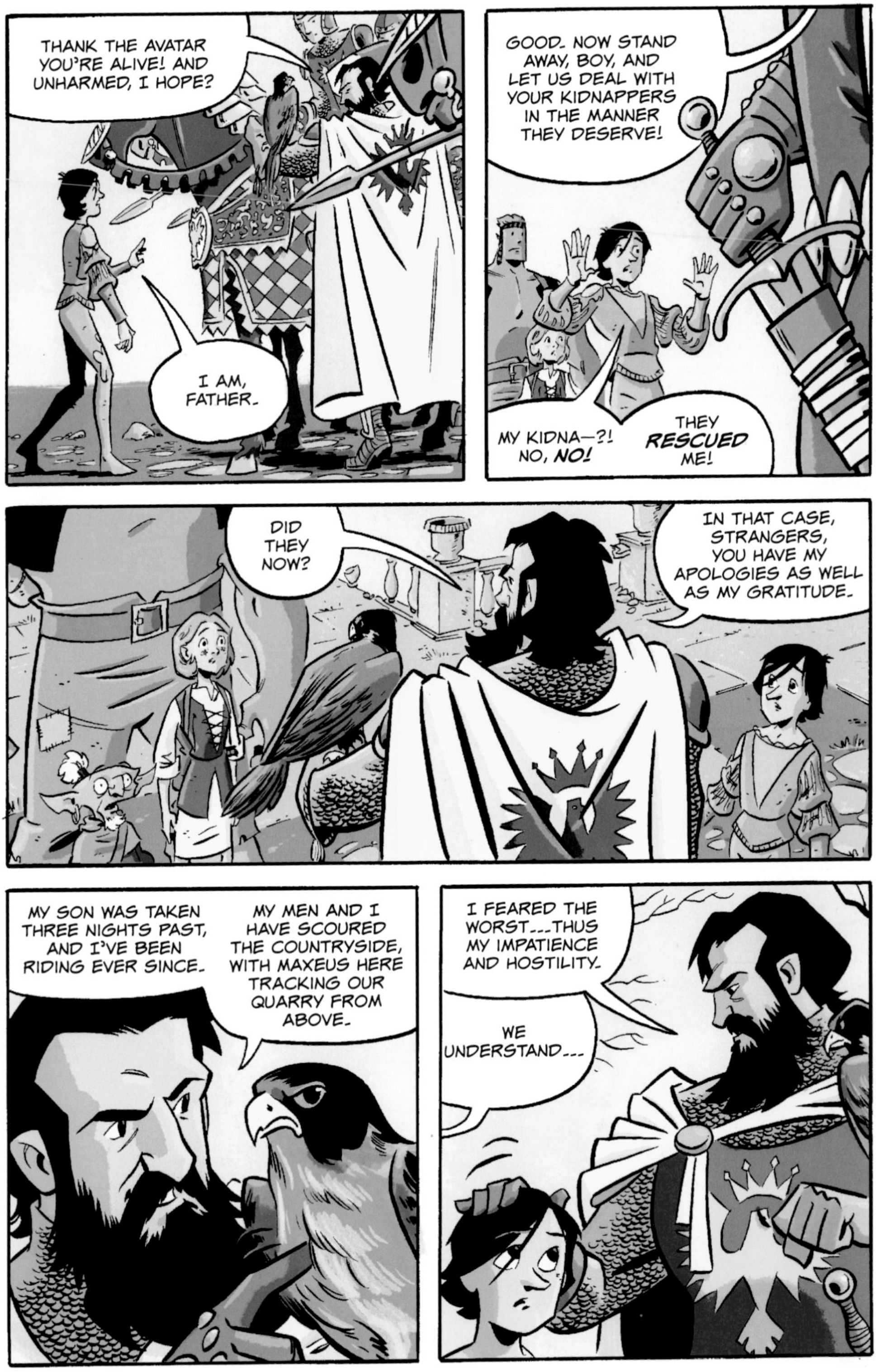
THANK THE AVATAR YOU'RE ALIVE! AND UNHARMED, I HOPE?
I AM, FATHER.
GOOD. NOW STAND AWAY, BOY, AND LET US DEAL WITH YOUR KIDNAPPERS IN THE MANNER THEY DESERVE!
MY KIDNA—?! NO, NO!
THEY RESCUED ME!
DID THEY NOW?
IN THAT CASE, STRANGERS, YOU HAVE MY APOLOGIES AS WELL AS MY GRATITUDE.
MY SON WAS TAKEN THREE NIGHTS PAST, AND I'VE BEEN RIDING EVER SINCE.
MY MEN AND I HAVE SCOURED THE COUNTRYSIDE, WITH MAXEUS HERE TRACKING OUR QUARRY FROM ABOVE.
I FEARED THE WORST...THUS MY IMPATIENCE AND HOSTILITY.
WE UNDERSTAND...

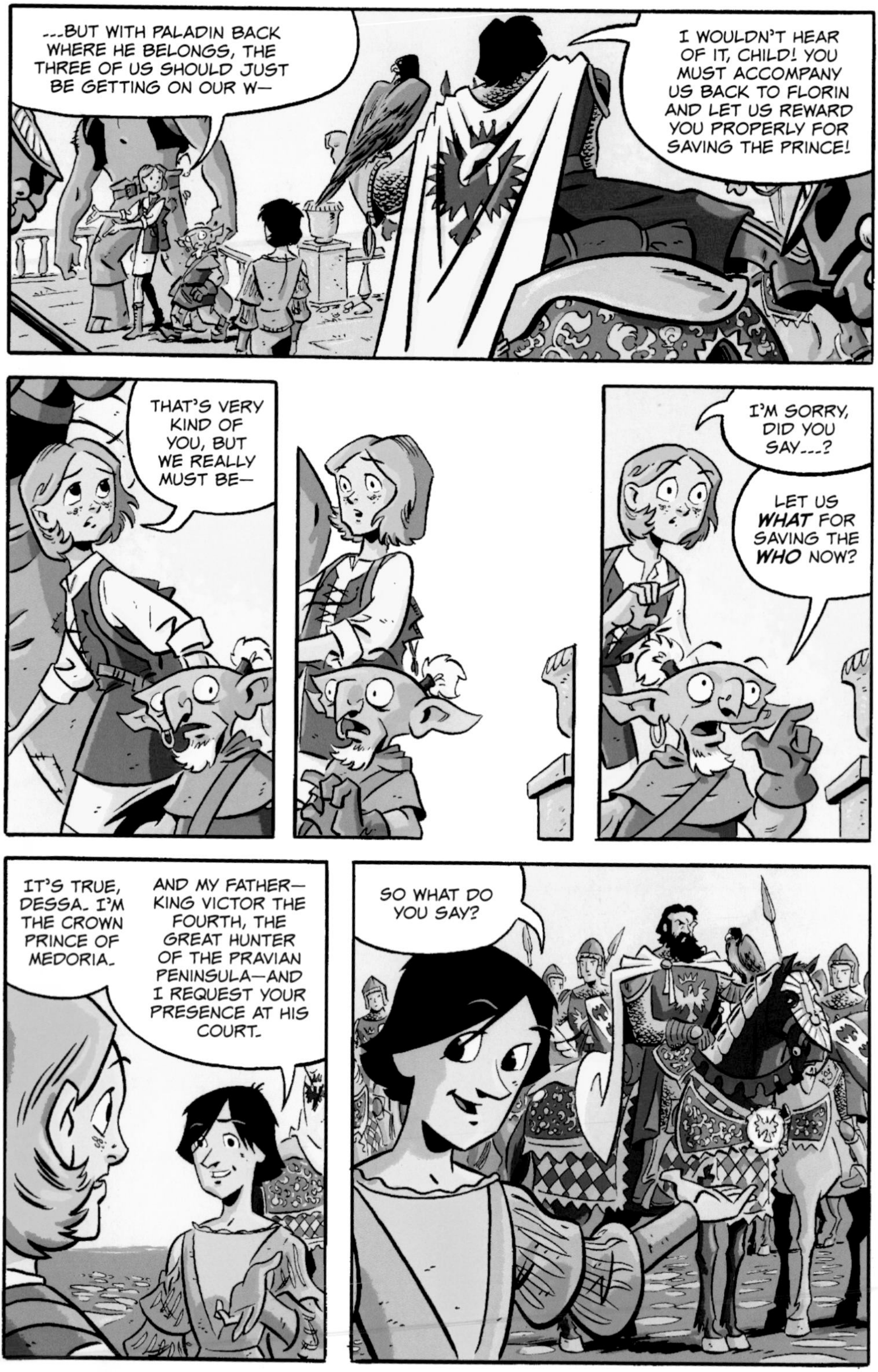

...BUT WITH PALADIN BACK WHERE HE BELONGS, THE THREE OF US SHOULD JUST BE GETTING ON OUR W—
I WOULDN'T HEAR OF IT, CHILD! YOU MUST ACCOMPANY US BACK TO FLORIN AND LET US REWARD YOU PROPERLY FOR SAVING THE PRINCE!
THAT'S VERY KIND OF YOU, BUT WE REALLY MUST BE—
I'M SORRY, DID YOU SAY...?
LET US *WHAT* FOR SAVING THE *WHO* NOW?
IT'S TRUE, DESSA. I'M THE CROWN PRINCE OF MEDORIA.
AND MY FATHER— KING VICTOR THE FOURTH, THE GREAT HUNTER OF THE PRAVIAN PENINSULA—AND I REQUEST YOUR PRESENCE AT HIS COURT.
SO WHAT DO YOU SAY?

ACT TWO
JOUST

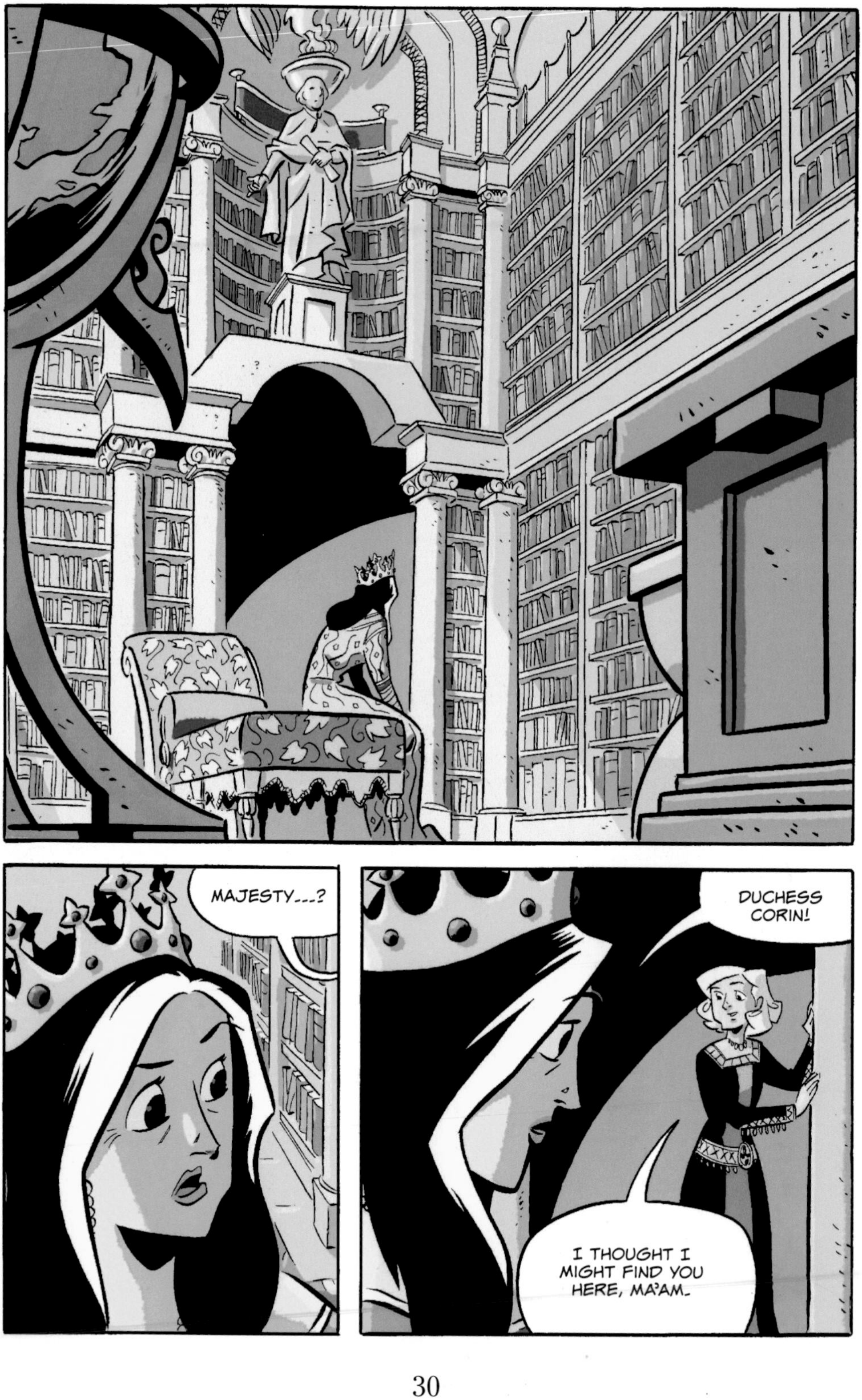
MAJESTY...?
DUCHESS CORIN!
I THOUGHT I MIGHT FIND YOU HERE, MA'AM.

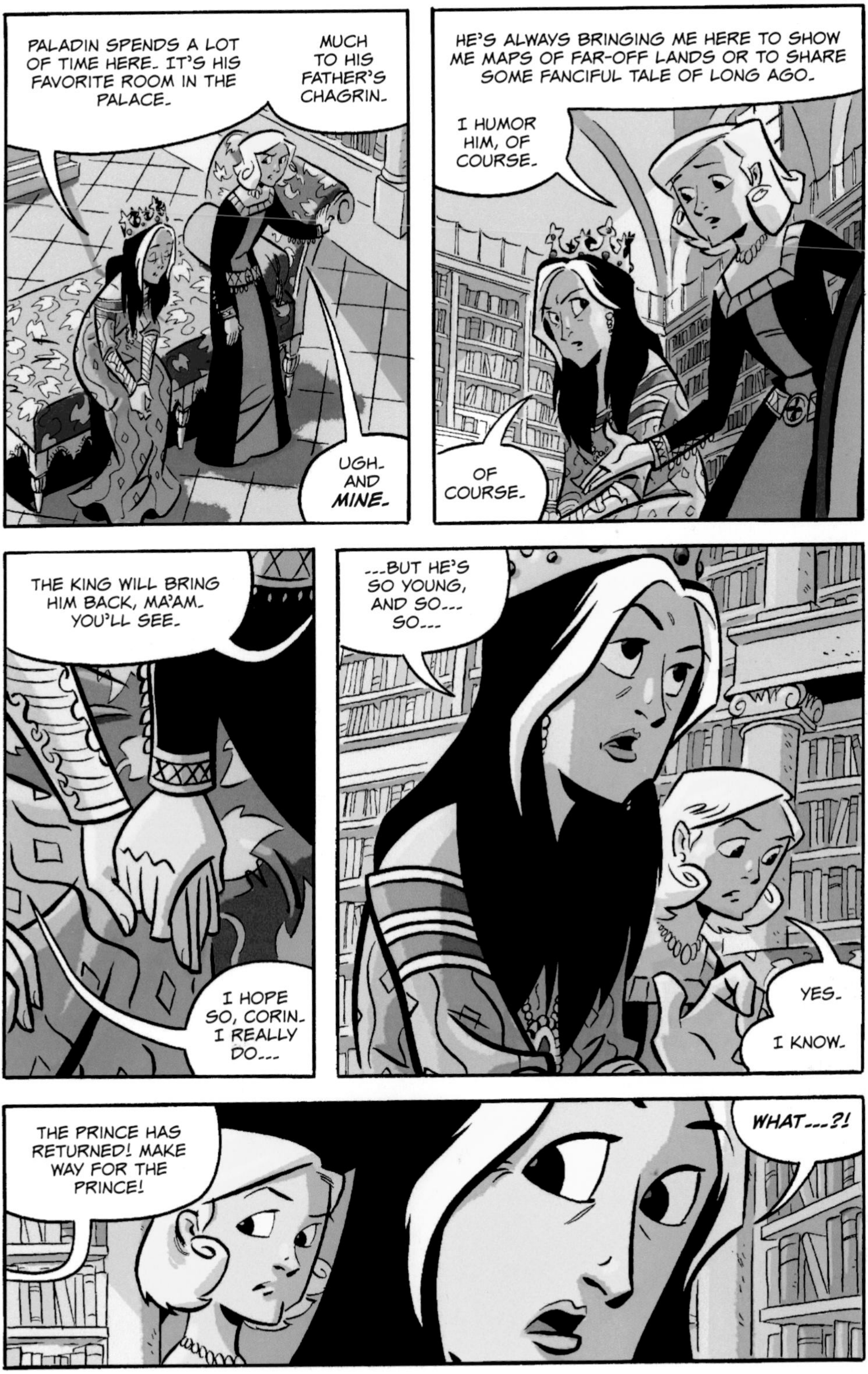
PALADIN SPENDS A LOT OF TIME HERE. IT'S HIS FAVORITE ROOM IN THE PALACE.
MUCH TO HIS FATHER'S CHAGRIN.
UGH. AND *MINE.*
HE'S ALWAYS BRINGING ME HERE TO SHOW ME MAPS OF FAR-OFF LANDS OR TO SHARE SOME FANCIFUL TALE OF LONG AGO.
I HUMOR HIM, OF COURSE.
OF COURSE.
THE KING WILL BRING HIM BACK, MA'AM. YOU'LL SEE.
I HOPE SO, CORIN. I REALLY DO...
...BUT HE'S SO YOUNG, AND SO... SO...
YES.
I KNOW.
THE PRINCE HAS RETURNED! MAKE WAY FOR THE PRINCE!
WHAT...?!

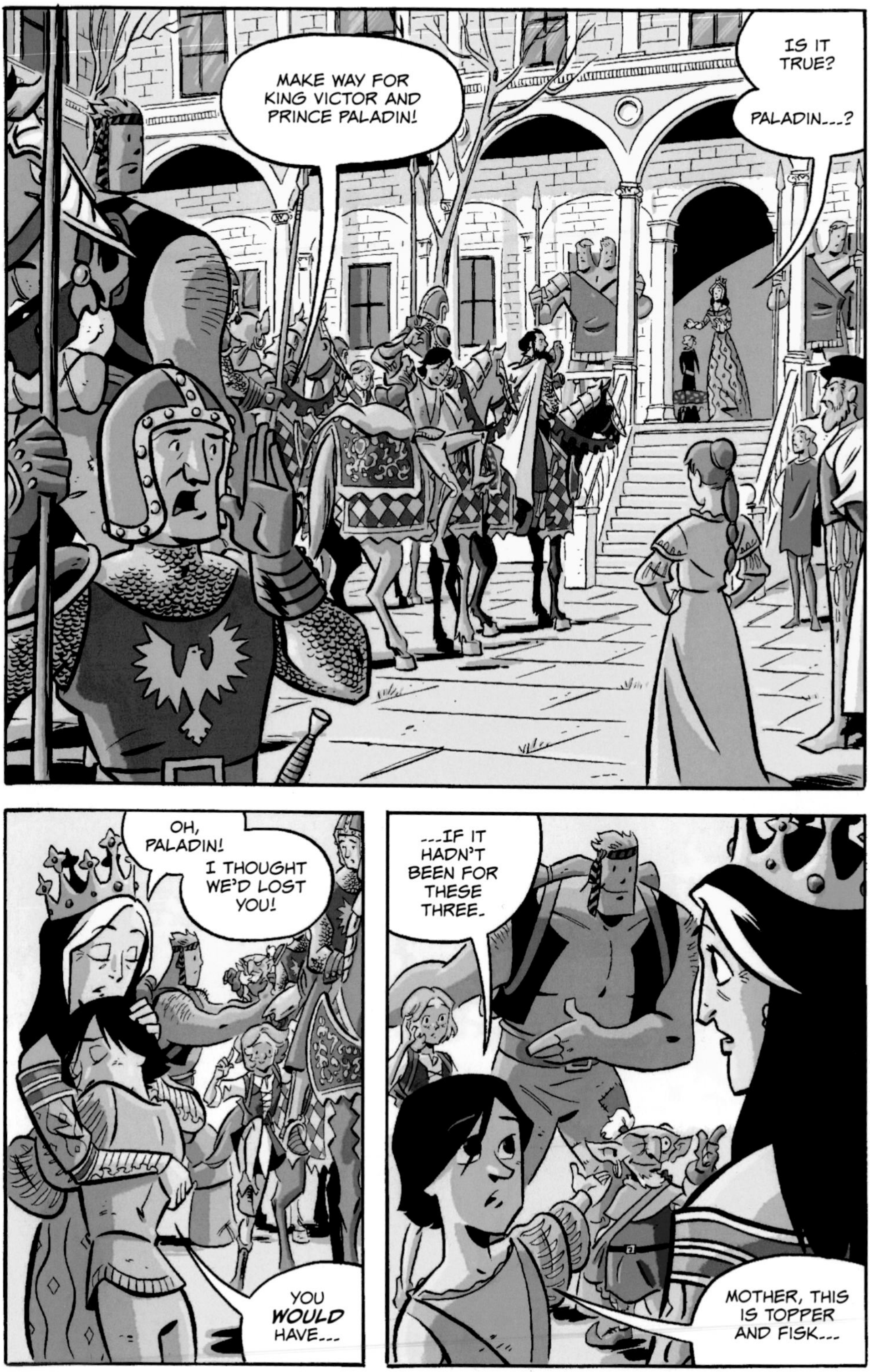
MAKE WAY FOR KING VICTOR AND PRINCE PALADIN!
IS IT TRUE?
PALADIN...?
OH, PALADIN!
I THOUGHT WE'D LOST YOU!
YOU *WOULD* HAVE...
...IF IT HADN'T BEEN FOR THESE THREE.
MOTHER, THIS IS TOPPER AND FISK...

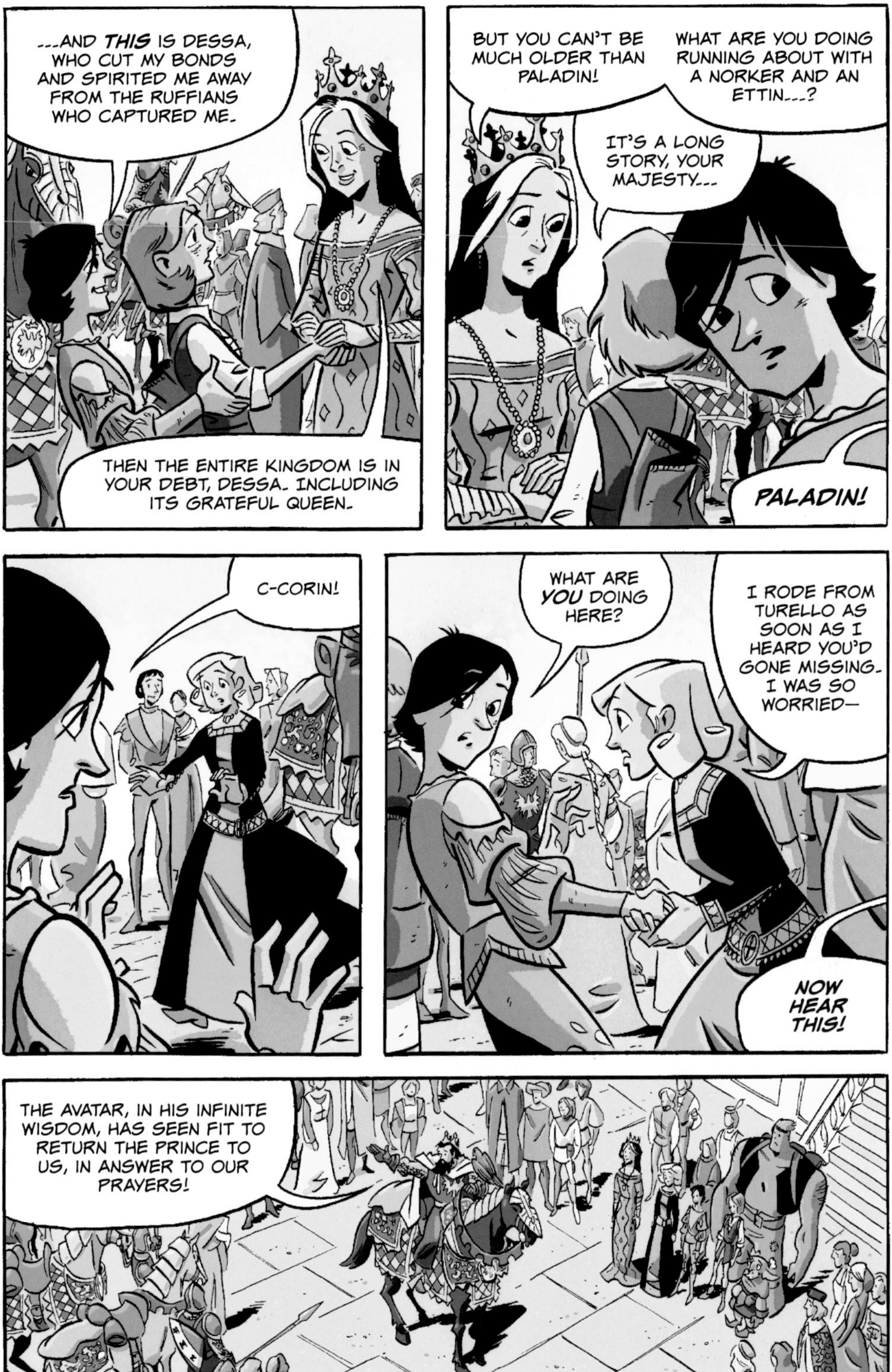
...AND THIS IS DESSA, WHO CUT MY BONDS AND SPIRITED ME AWAY FROM THE RUFFIANS WHO CAPTURED ME.
THEN THE ENTIRE KINGDOM IS IN YOUR DEBT, DESSA. INCLUDING ITS GRATEFUL QUEEN.
BUT YOU CAN'T BE MUCH OLDER THAN PALADIN!
WHAT ARE YOU DOING RUNNING ABOUT WITH A NORKER AND AN ETTIN...?
IT'S A LONG STORY, YOUR MAJESTY...
PALADIN!
C-CORIN!
WHAT ARE YOU DOING HERE?
I RODE FROM TURELLO AS SOON AS I HEARD YOU'D GONE MISSING. I WAS SO WORRIED—
NOW HEAR THIS!
THE AVATAR, IN HIS INFINITE WISDOM, HAS SEEN FIT TO RETURN THE PRINCE TO US, IN ANSWER TO OUR PRAYERS!

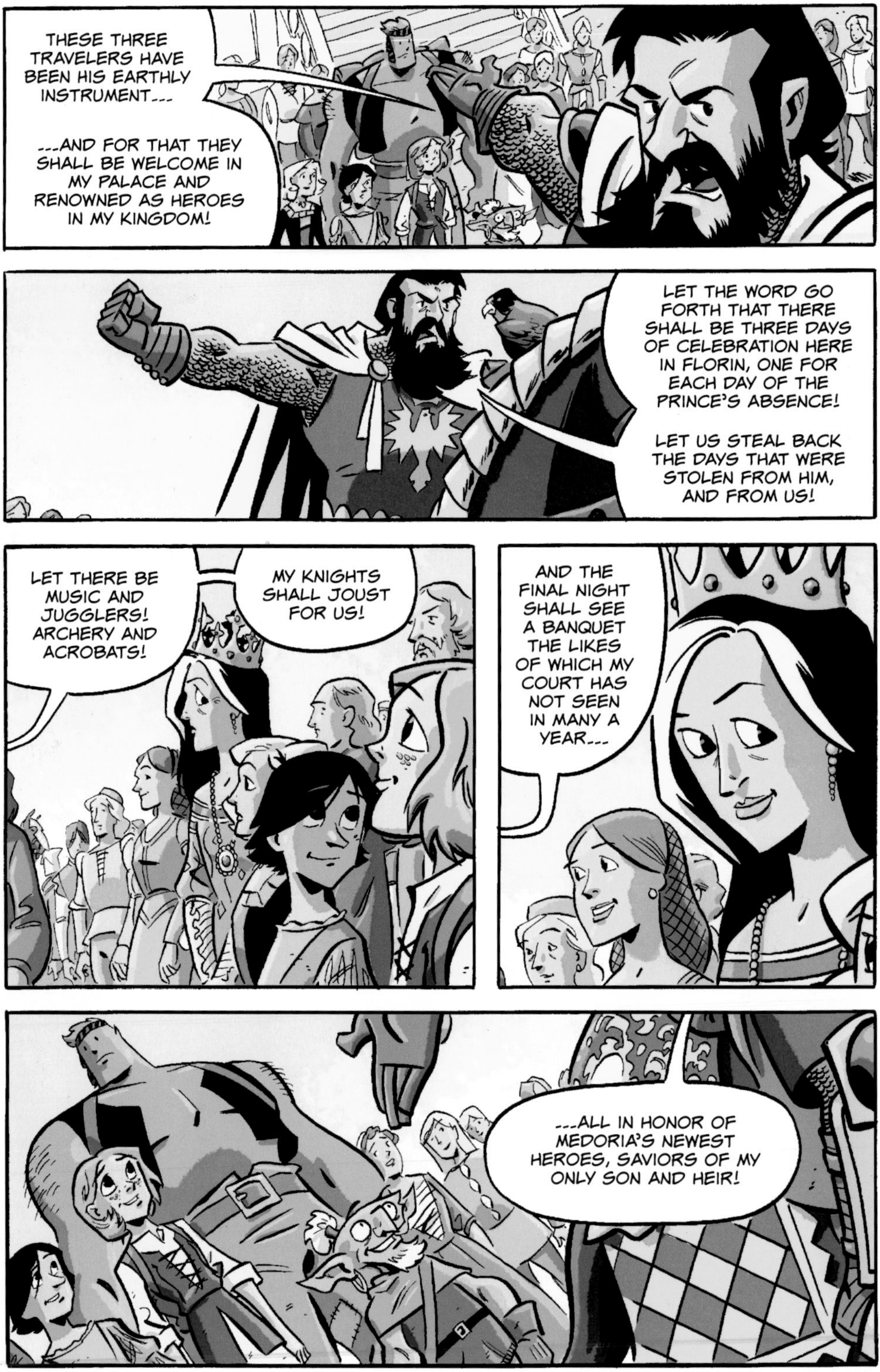
THESE THREE TRAVELERS HAVE BEEN HIS EARTHLY INSTRUMENT---
---AND FOR THAT THEY SHALL BE WELCOME IN MY PALACE AND RENOWNED AS HEROES IN MY KINGDOM!
LET THE WORD GO FORTH THAT THERE SHALL BE THREE DAYS OF CELEBRATION HERE IN FLORIN, ONE FOR EACH DAY OF THE PRINCE'S ABSENCE!
LET US STEAL BACK THE DAYS THAT WERE STOLEN FROM HIM, AND FROM US!
LET THERE BE MUSIC AND JUGGLERS! ARCHERY AND ACROBATS!
MY KNIGHTS SHALL JOUST FOR US!
AND THE FINAL NIGHT SHALL SEE A BANQUET THE LIKES OF WHICH MY COURT HAS NOT SEEN IN MANY A YEAR---
---ALL IN HONOR OF MEDORIA'S NEWEST HEROES, SAVIORS OF MY ONLY SON AND HEIR!

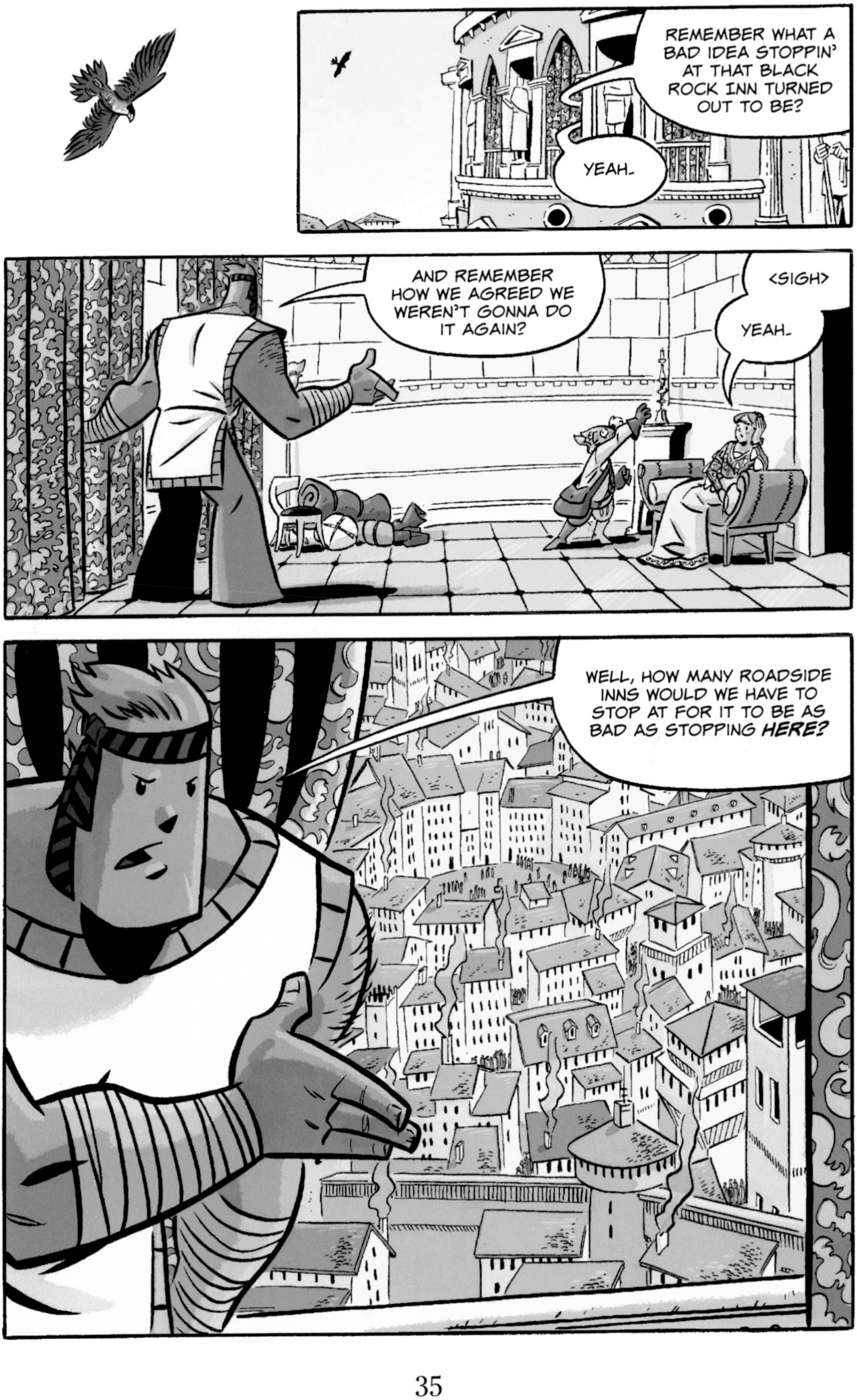
REMEMBER WHAT A BAD IDEA STOPPIN' AT THAT BLACK ROCK INN TURNED OUT TO BE?
YEAH…
AND REMEMBER HOW WE AGREED WE WEREN'T GONNA DO IT AGAIN?
<SIGH>
YEAH…
WELL, HOW MANY ROADSIDE INNS WOULD WE HAVE TO STOP AT FOR IT TO BE AS BAD AS STOPPING *HERE?*

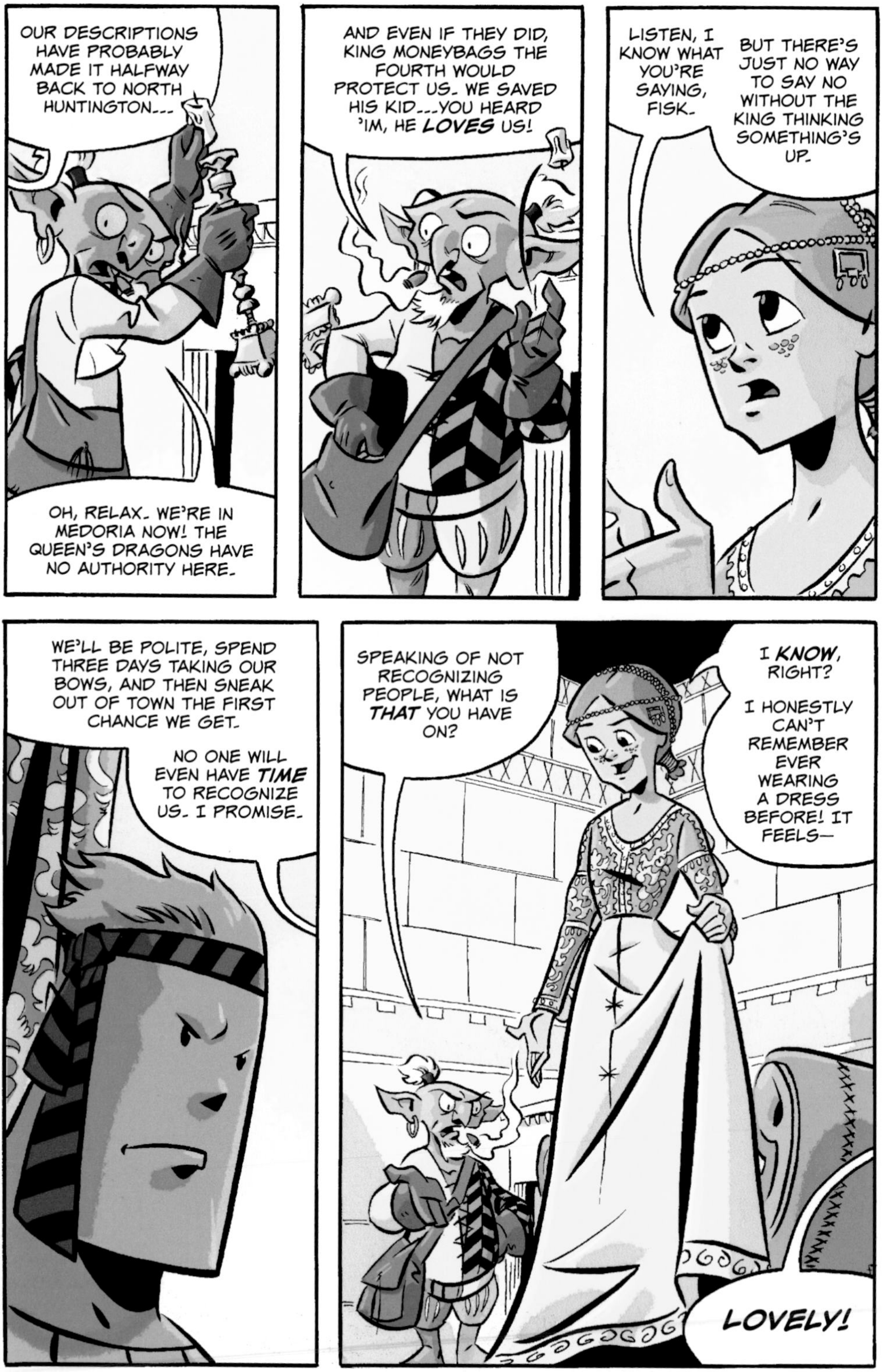
OUR DESCRIPTIONS HAVE PROBABLY MADE IT HALFWAY BACK TO NORTH HUNTINGTON...
OH, RELAX. WE'RE IN MEDORIA NOW! THE QUEEN'S DRAGONS HAVE NO AUTHORITY HERE.
AND EVEN IF THEY DID, KING MONEYBAGS THE FOURTH WOULD PROTECT US. WE SAVED HIS KID...YOU HEARD 'IM, HE LOVES US!
LISTEN, I KNOW WHAT YOU'RE SAYING, FISK.
BUT THERE'S JUST NO WAY TO SAY NO WITHOUT THE KING THINKING SOMETHING'S UP.
WE'LL BE POLITE, SPEND THREE DAYS TAKING OUR BOWS, AND THEN SNEAK OUT OF TOWN THE FIRST CHANCE WE GET.
NO ONE WILL EVEN HAVE TIME TO RECOGNIZE US. I PROMISE.
SPEAKING OF NOT RECOGNIZING PEOPLE, WHAT IS THAT YOU HAVE ON?
I KNOW, RIGHT?
I HONESTLY CAN'T REMEMBER EVER WEARING A DRESS BEFORE! IT FEELS—
LOVELY!

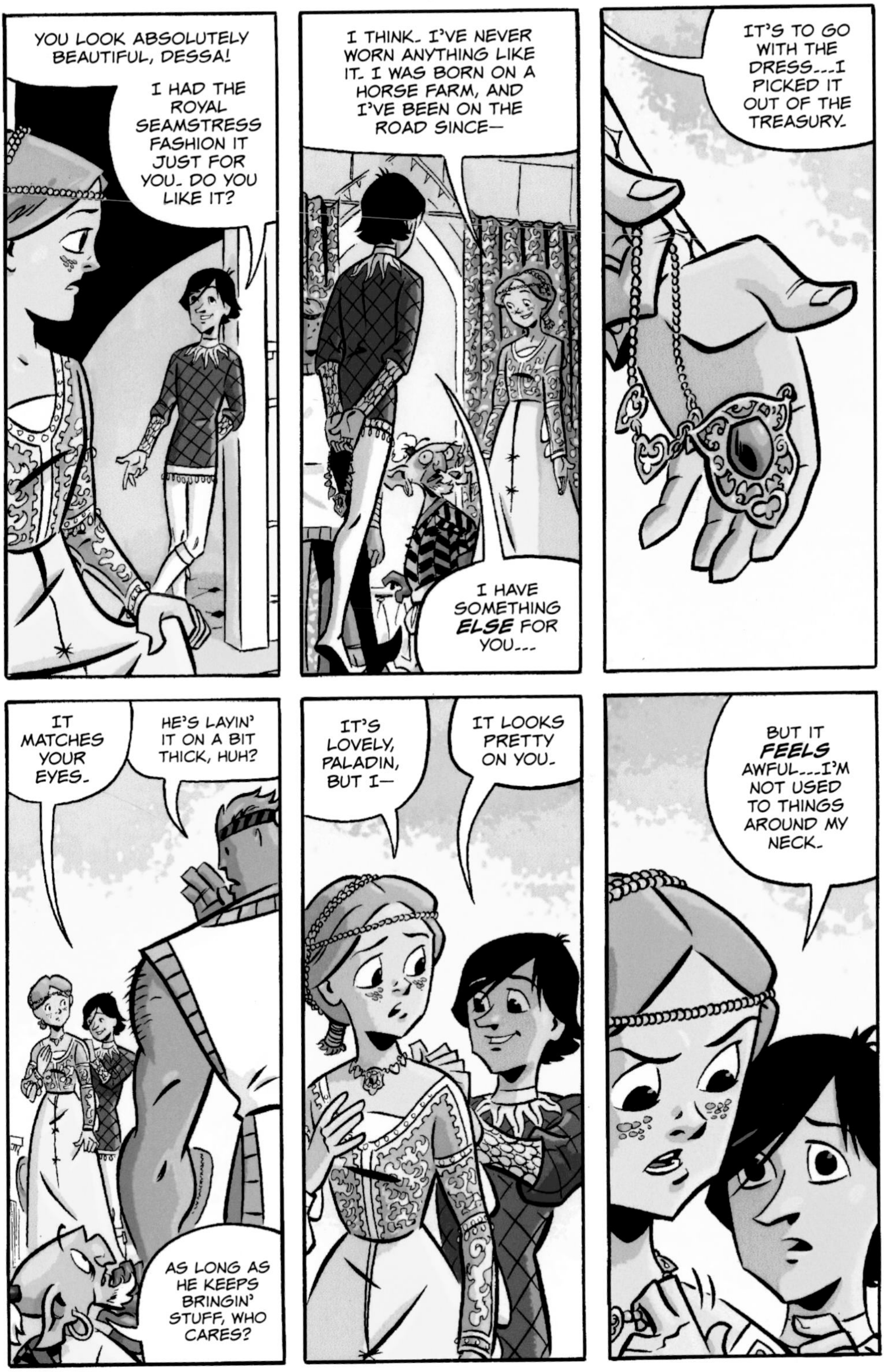
YOU LOOK ABSOLUTELY BEAUTIFUL, DESSA!
I HAD THE ROYAL SEAMSTRESS FASHION IT JUST FOR YOU. DO YOU LIKE IT?
I THINK. I'VE NEVER WORN ANYTHING LIKE IT. I WAS BORN ON A HORSE FARM, AND I'VE BEEN ON THE ROAD SINCE—
I HAVE SOMETHING *ELSE* FOR YOU...
IT'S TO GO WITH THE DRESS...I PICKED IT OUT OF THE TREASURY.
IT MATCHES YOUR EYES.
HE'S LAYIN' IT ON A BIT THICK, HUH?
AS LONG AS HE KEEPS BRINGIN' STUFF, WHO CARES?
IT'S LOVELY, PALADIN, BUT I—
IT LOOKS PRETTY ON YOU.
BUT IT *FEELS* AWFUL...I'M NOT USED TO THINGS AROUND MY NECK.

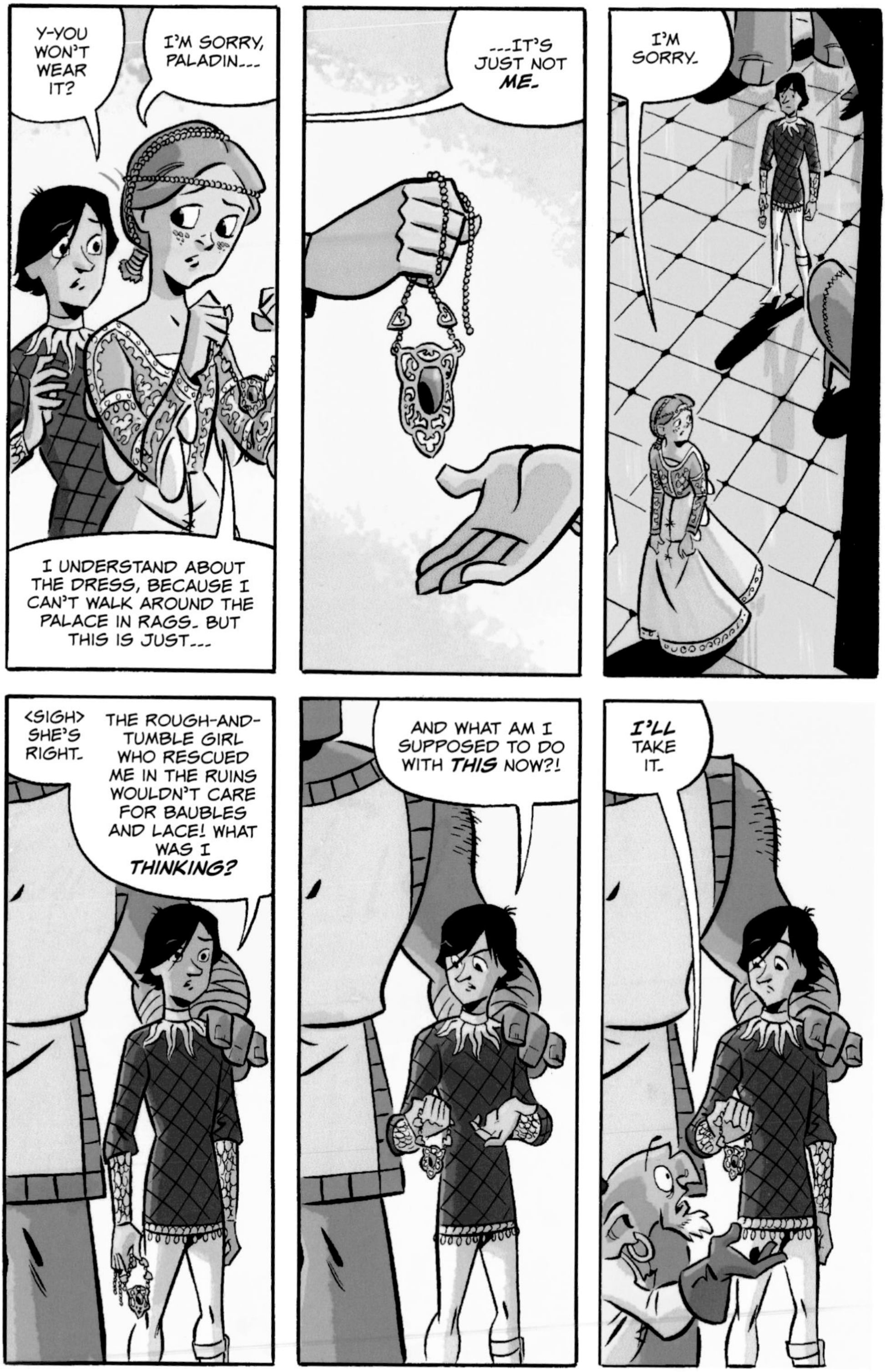
Y-YOU WON'T WEAR IT?
I'M SORRY, PALADIN...
I UNDERSTAND ABOUT THE DRESS, BECAUSE I CAN'T WALK AROUND THE PALACE IN RAGS. BUT THIS IS JUST...
...IT'S JUST NOT *ME.*
I'M SORRY.
<SIGH> SHE'S RIGHT.
THE ROUGH-AND-TUMBLE GIRL WHO RESCUED ME IN THE RUINS WOULDN'T CARE FOR BAUBLES AND LACE! WHAT WAS I *THINKING?*
AND WHAT AM I SUPPOSED TO DO WITH *THIS* NOW?!
I'LL TAKE IT.

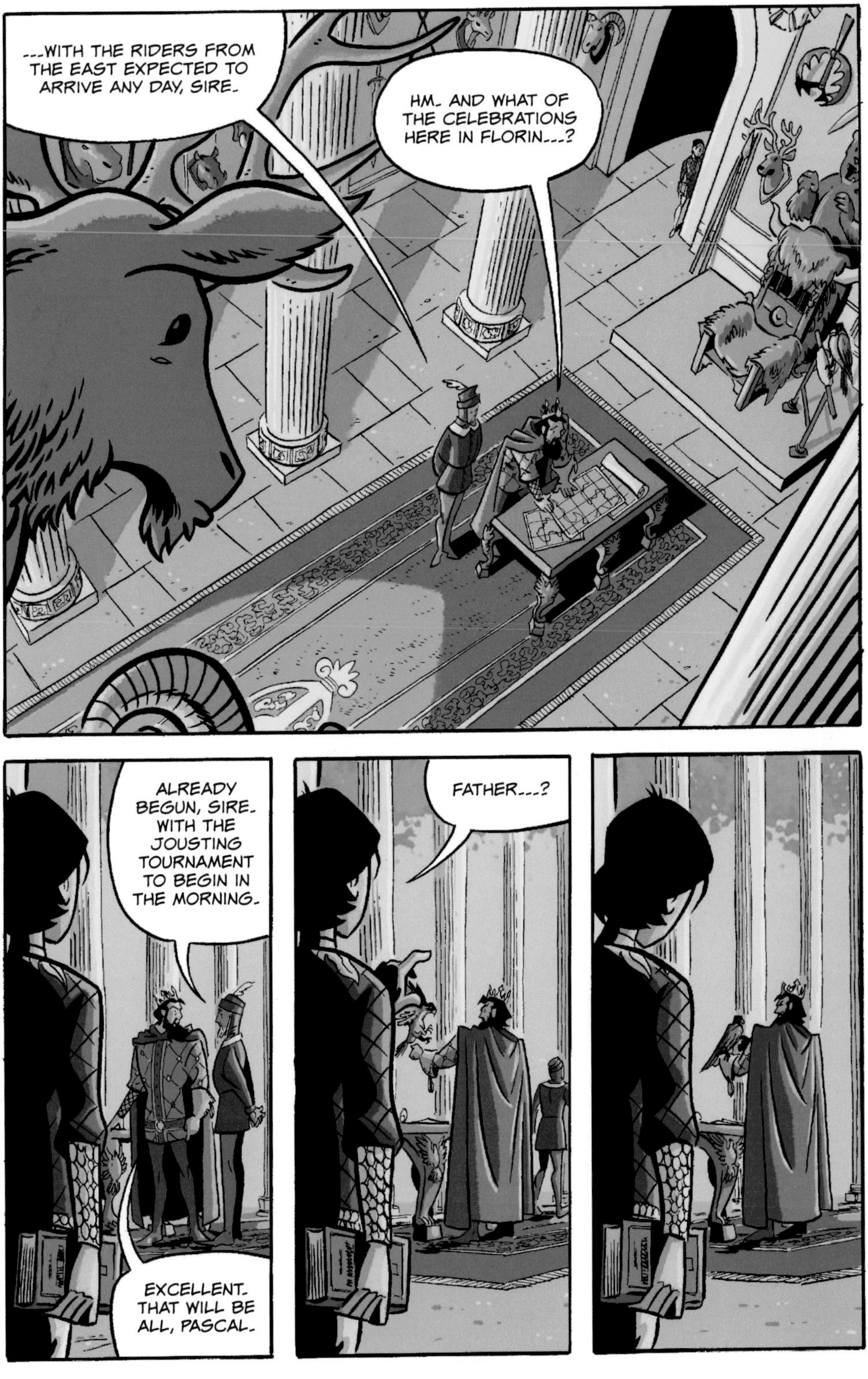

...WITH THE RIDERS FROM THE EAST EXPECTED TO ARRIVE ANY DAY, SIRE.
HM. AND WHAT OF THE CELEBRATIONS HERE IN FLORIN...?
ALREADY BEGUN, SIRE. WITH THE JOUSTING TOURNAMENT TO BEGIN IN THE MORNING.
EXCELLENT. THAT WILL BE ALL, PASCAL.
FATHER...?

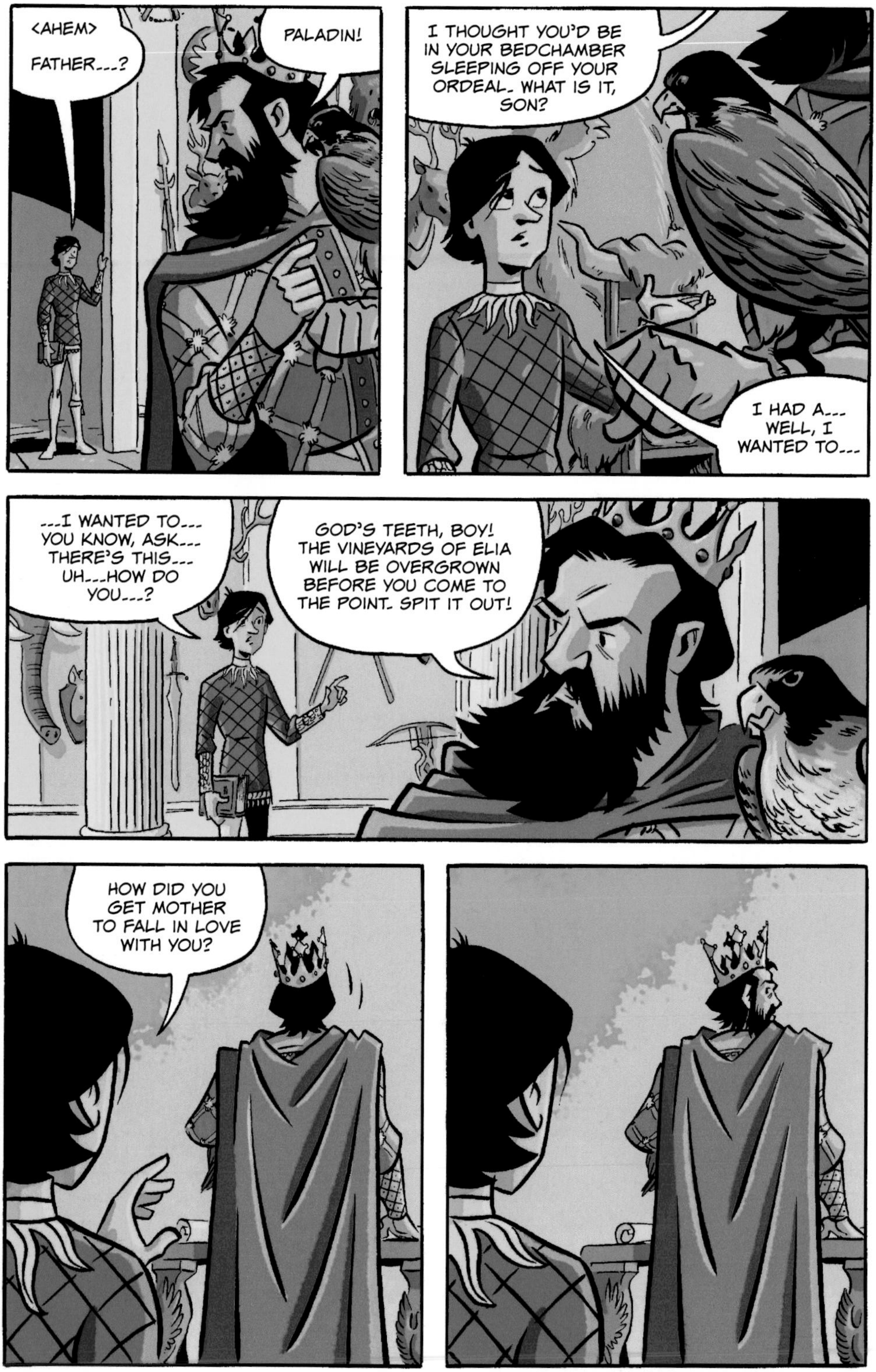
<AHEM>
FATHER...?
PALADIN!
I THOUGHT YOU'D BE IN YOUR BEDCHAMBER SLEEPING OFF YOUR ORDEAL. WHAT IS IT, SON?
I HAD A... WELL, I WANTED TO...
...I WANTED TO... YOU KNOW, ASK... THERE'S THIS... UH...HOW DO YOU...?
GOD'S TEETH, BOY! THE VINEYARDS OF ELIA WILL BE OVERGROWN BEFORE YOU COME TO THE POINT. SPIT IT OUT!
HOW DID YOU GET MOTHER TO FALL IN LOVE WITH YOU?

I BEG YOUR PARDON?

I'M SORRY, I-I SHOULDN'T HAVE ASKED...I'LL—

NO, NO...

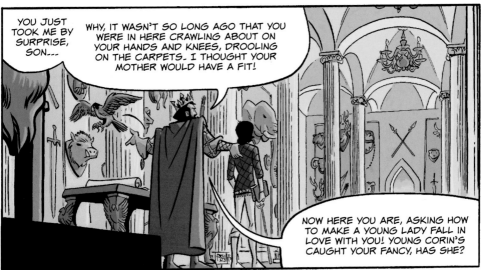

YOU JUST TOOK ME BY SURPRISE, SON...

WHY, IT WASN'T SO LONG AGO THAT YOU WERE IN HERE CRAWLING ABOUT ON YOUR HANDS AND KNEES, DROOLING ON THE CARPETS. I THOUGHT YOUR MOTHER WOULD HAVE A FIT!

NOW HERE YOU ARE, ASKING HOW TO MAKE A YOUNG LADY FALL IN LOVE WITH YOU! YOUNG CORIN'S CAUGHT YOUR FANCY, HAS SHE?

WELL, ACTUALLY, IT'S—

SPLENDID! SHE'S A PRETTY YOUNG THING, FOR CERTAIN, WELL CULTURED AND TITLED...

...AND HER FATHER, THE DUKE OF TURELLO, IS SOMEONE I'D VERY MUCH LIKE TO HAVE CLOSER TIES TO MY COURT.

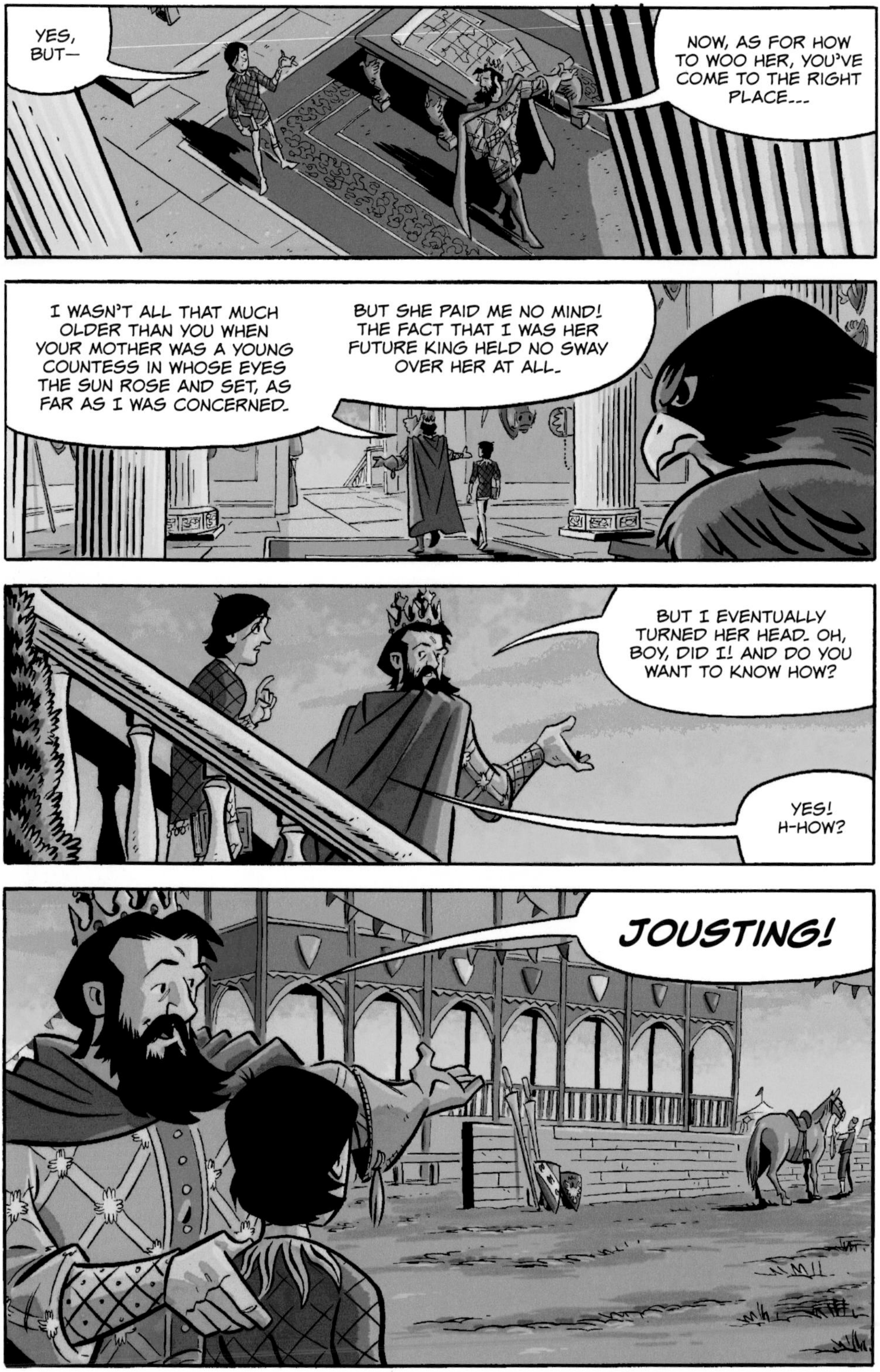

YES, BUT—
NOW, AS FOR HOW TO WOO HER, YOU'VE COME TO THE RIGHT PLACE...
I WASN'T ALL THAT MUCH OLDER THAN YOU WHEN YOUR MOTHER WAS A YOUNG COUNTESS IN WHOSE EYES THE SUN ROSE AND SET, AS FAR AS I WAS CONCERNED.
BUT SHE PAID ME NO MIND! THE FACT THAT I WAS HER FUTURE KING HELD NO SWAY OVER HER AT ALL.
BUT I EVENTUALLY TURNED HER HEAD. OH, BOY, DID I! AND DO YOU WANT TO KNOW HOW?
YES! H-HOW?
JOUSTING!

"JOUSTING"...?

IT'S THE SPORT OF KINGS, BOY!

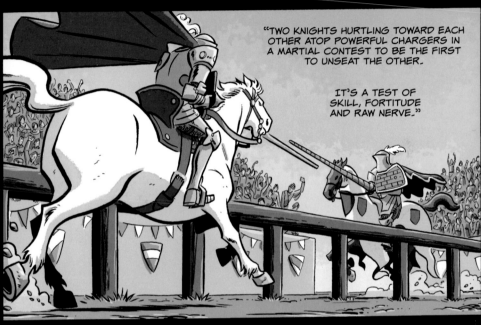

"TWO KNIGHTS HURTLING TOWARD EACH OTHER ATOP POWERFUL CHARGERS IN A MARTIAL CONTEST TO BE THE FIRST TO UNSEAT THE OTHER.

IT'S A TEST OF SKILL, FORTITUDE AND RAW NERVE."

I'VE ALWAYS HOPED YOU'D START SHOWING AN INTEREST IN THE MANLY ARTS, PALADIN...

BUT I WAS ASKING ABOUT—

ALL OF YOUR BOOKS AND SUCH ARE FINE, AND HAVE THEIR PLACE...

...BUT WHAT *REALLY* MAKES A MAN IS THE KIND OF PHYSICAL METTLE THAT CAN ONLY BE PROPERLY DEMONSTRATED ON THE TOURNAMENT FIELD!

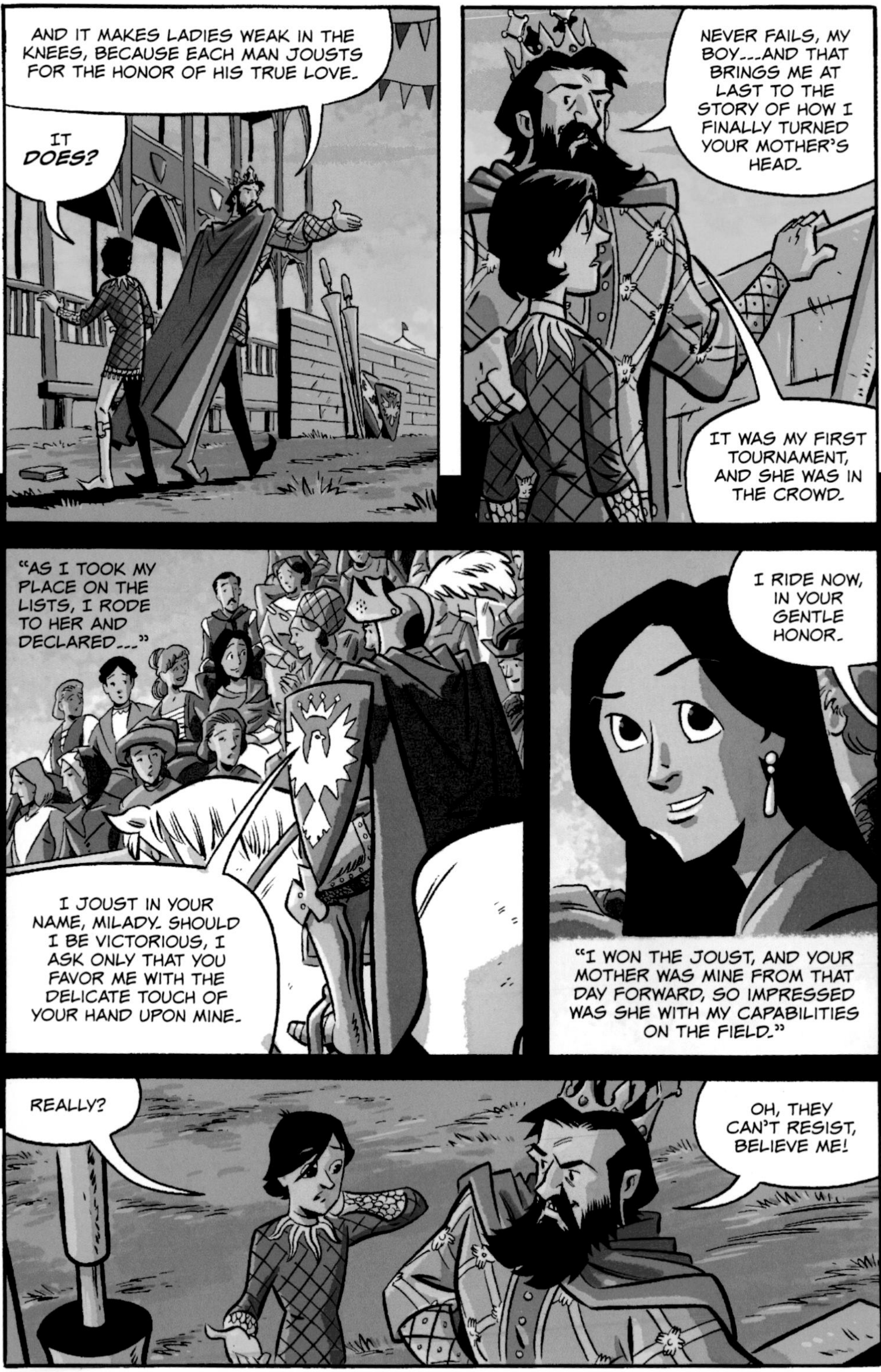
AND IT MAKES LADIES WEAK IN THE KNEES, BECAUSE EACH MAN JOUSTS FOR THE HONOR OF HIS TRUE LOVE.
IT *DOES?*
NEVER FAILS, MY BOY... AND THAT BRINGS ME AT LAST TO THE STORY OF HOW I FINALLY TURNED YOUR MOTHER'S HEAD.
IT WAS MY FIRST TOURNAMENT, AND SHE WAS IN THE CROWD.
"AS I TOOK MY PLACE ON THE LISTS, I RODE TO HER AND DECLARED..."
I JOUST IN YOUR NAME, MILADY. SHOULD I BE VICTORIOUS, I ASK ONLY THAT YOU FAVOR ME WITH THE DELICATE TOUCH OF YOUR HAND UPON MINE.
I RIDE NOW, IN YOUR GENTLE HONOR.
"I WON THE JOUST, AND YOUR MOTHER WAS MINE FROM THAT DAY FORWARD, SO IMPRESSED WAS SHE WITH MY CAPABILITIES ON THE FIELD."
REALLY?
OH, THEY CAN'T RESIST, BELIEVE ME!

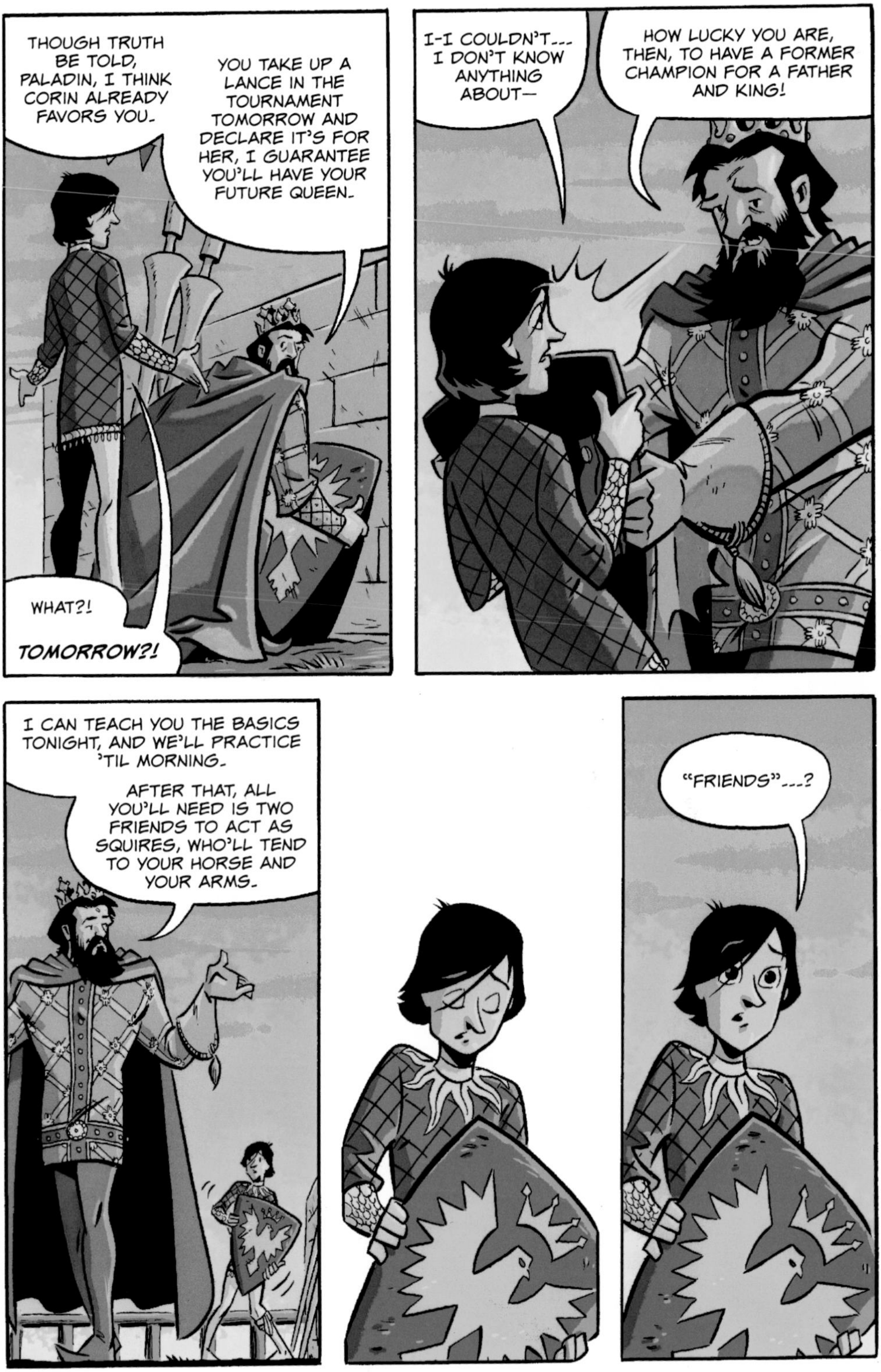
THOUGH TRUTH BE TOLD, PALADIN, I THINK CORIN ALREADY FAVORS YOU.
YOU TAKE UP A LANCE IN THE TOURNAMENT TOMORROW AND DECLARE IT'S FOR HER, I GUARANTEE YOU'LL HAVE YOUR FUTURE QUEEN.
WHAT?!
TOMORROW?!
I-I COULDN'T... I DON'T KNOW ANYTHING ABOUT—
HOW LUCKY YOU ARE, THEN, TO HAVE A FORMER CHAMPION FOR A FATHER AND KING!
I CAN TEACH YOU THE BASICS TONIGHT, AND WE'LL PRACTICE 'TIL MORNING.
AFTER THAT, ALL YOU'LL NEED IS TWO FRIENDS TO ACT AS SQUIRES, WHO'LL TEND TO YOUR HORSE AND YOUR ARMS.
"FRIENDS"...?

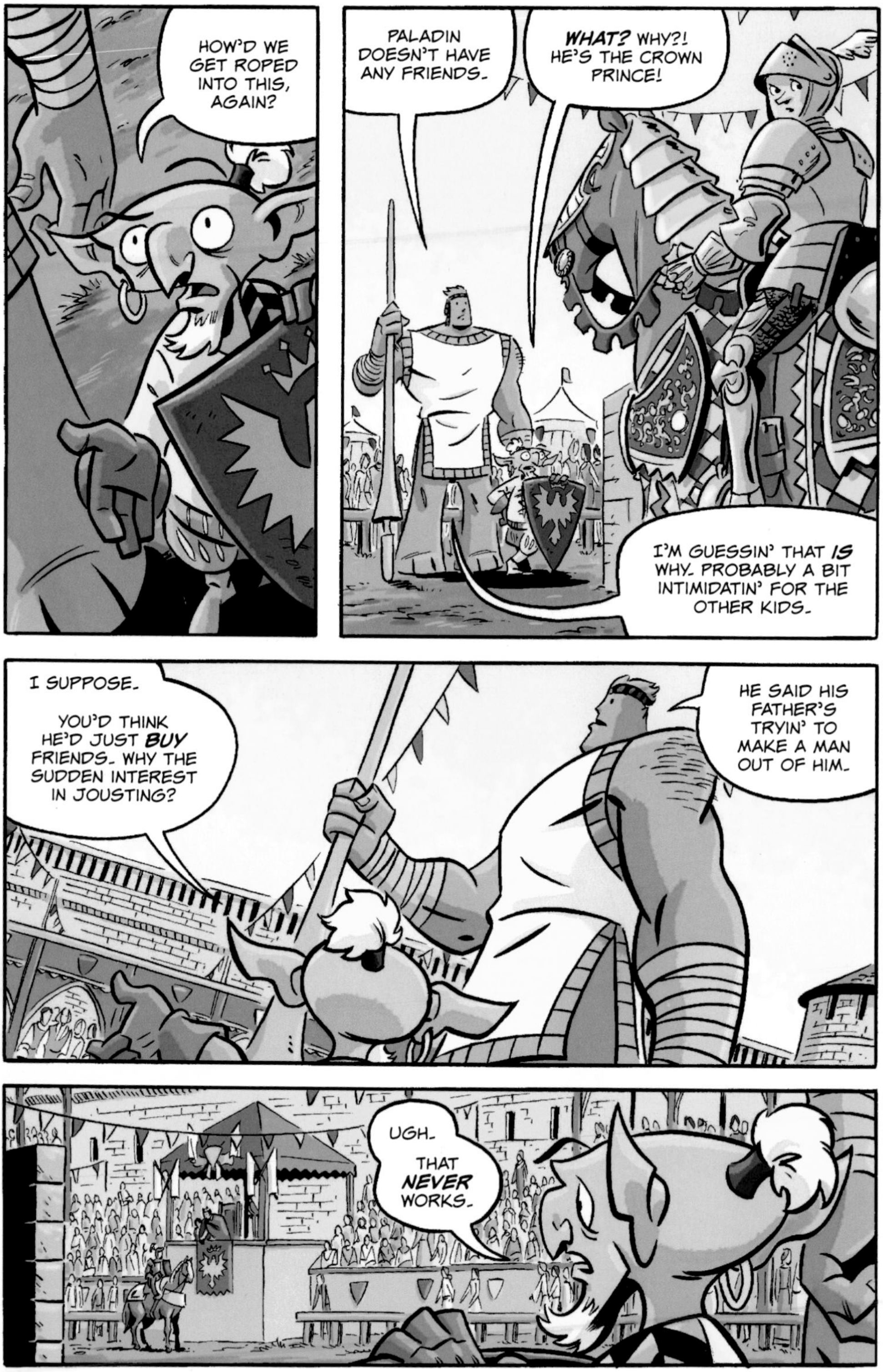
HOW'D WE GET ROPED INTO THIS, AGAIN?
PALADIN DOESN'T HAVE ANY FRIENDS.
WHAT? WHY?! HE'S THE CROWN PRINCE!
I'M GUESSIN' THAT *IS* WHY. PROBABLY A BIT INTIMIDATIN' FOR THE OTHER KIDS.
I SUPPOSE.
YOU'D THINK HE'D JUST *BUY* FRIENDS. WHY THE SUDDEN INTEREST IN JOUSTING?
HE SAID HIS FATHER'S TRYIN' TO MAKE A MAN OUT OF HIM.
UGH.
THAT *NEVER* WORKS.

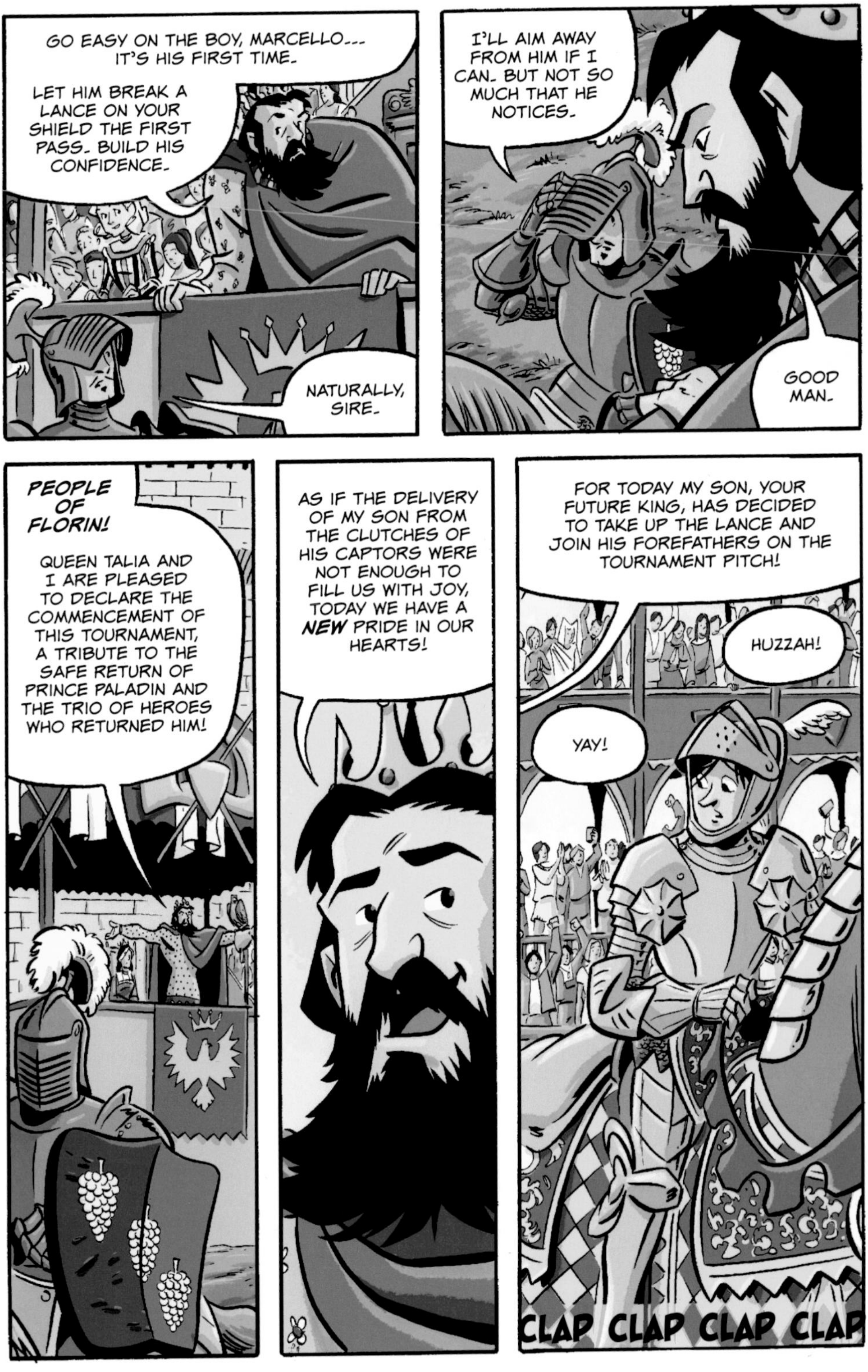
GO EASY ON THE BOY, MARCELLO... IT'S HIS FIRST TIME.
LET HIM BREAK A LANCE ON YOUR SHIELD THE FIRST PASS. BUILD HIS CONFIDENCE.
NATURALLY, SIRE.
I'LL AIM AWAY FROM HIM IF I CAN. BUT NOT SO MUCH THAT HE NOTICES.
GOOD MAN.
PEOPLE OF FLORIN!
QUEEN TALIA AND I ARE PLEASED TO DECLARE THE COMMENCEMENT OF THIS TOURNAMENT, A TRIBUTE TO THE SAFE RETURN OF PRINCE PALADIN AND THE TRIO OF HEROES WHO RETURNED HIM!
AS IF THE DELIVERY OF MY SON FROM THE CLUTCHES OF HIS CAPTORS WERE NOT ENOUGH TO FILL US WITH JOY, TODAY WE HAVE A NEW PRIDE IN OUR HEARTS!
FOR TODAY MY SON, YOUR FUTURE KING, HAS DECIDED TO TAKE UP THE LANCE AND JOIN HIS FOREFATHERS ON THE TOURNAMENT PITCH!
HUZZAH!
YAY!
CLAP CLAP CLAP CLAP

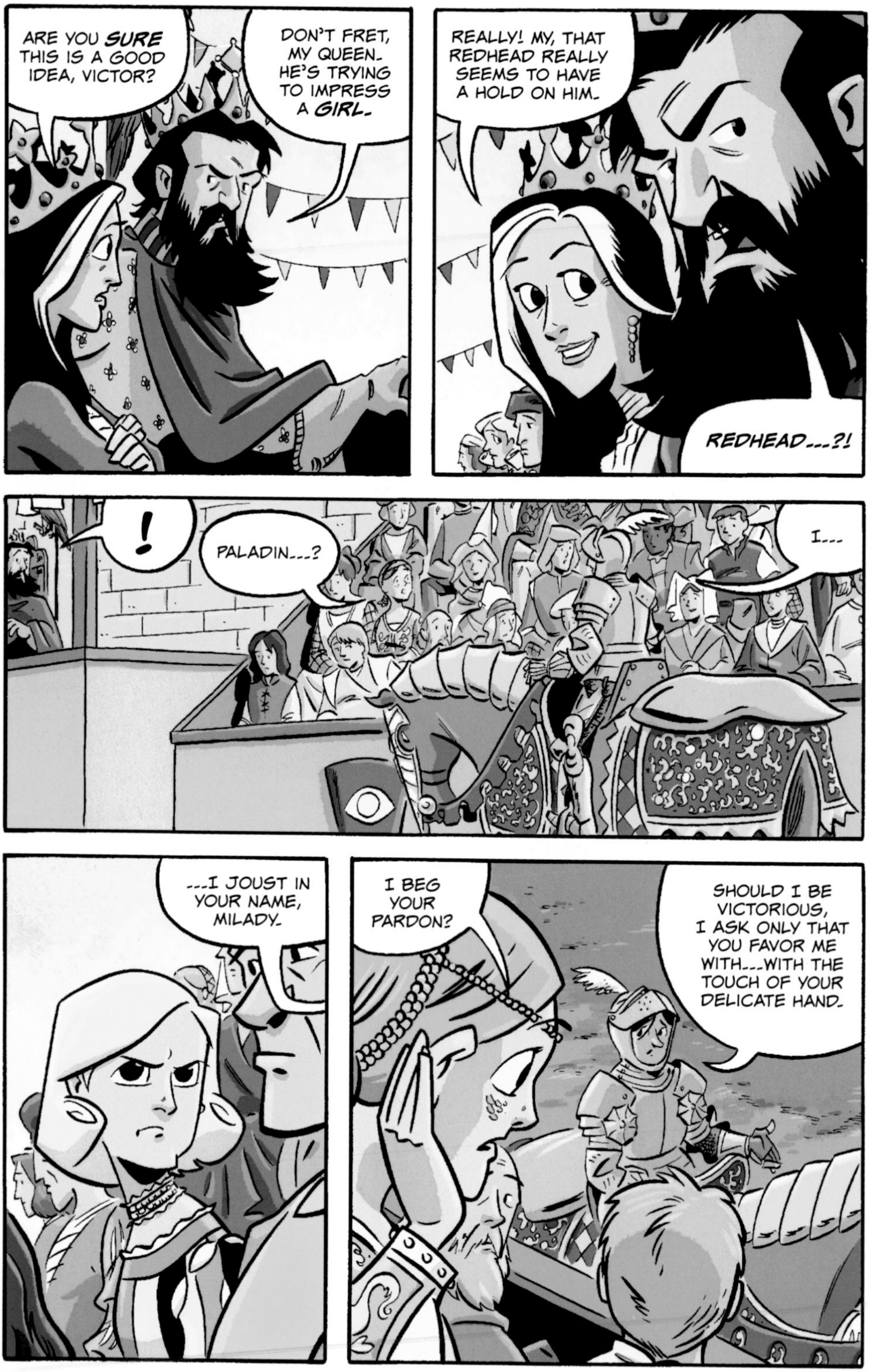
ARE YOU SURE THIS IS A GOOD IDEA, VICTOR?
DON'T FRET, MY QUEEN. HE'S TRYING TO IMPRESS A GIRL.
REALLY! MY, THAT REDHEAD REALLY SEEMS TO HAVE A HOLD ON HIM.
REDHEAD...?!
!
PALADIN...?
I...
...I JOUST IN YOUR NAME, MILADY.
I BEG YOUR PARDON?
SHOULD I BE VICTORIOUS, I ASK ONLY THAT YOU FAVOR ME WITH...WITH THE TOUCH OF YOUR DELICATE HAND.

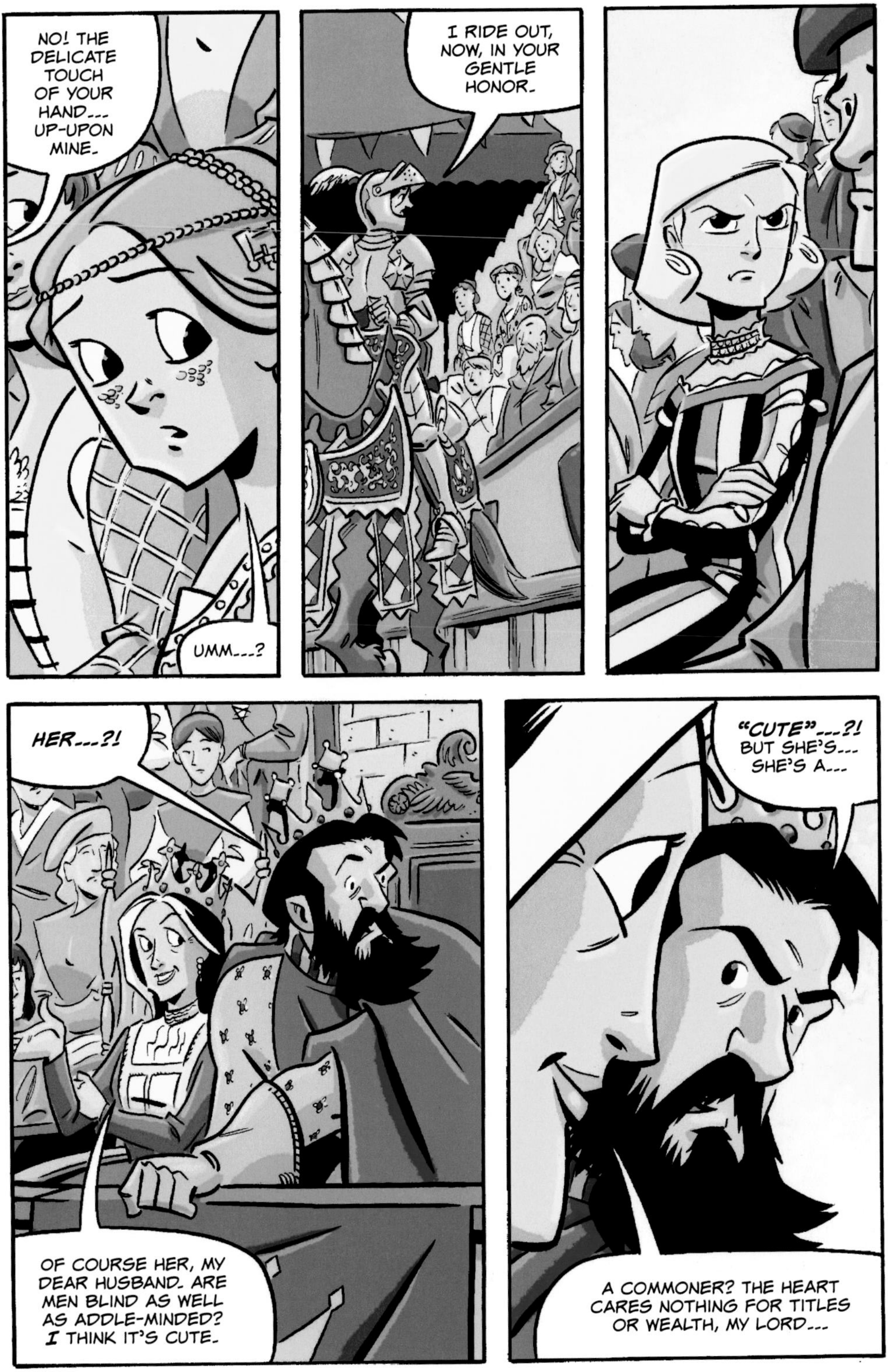
NO! THE DELICATE TOUCH OF YOUR HAND... UP-UPON MINE.
UMM...?
I RIDE OUT, NOW, IN YOUR GENTLE HONOR.
HER...?!
OF COURSE HER, MY DEAR HUSBAND. ARE MEN BLIND AS WELL AS ADDLE-MINDED? *I* THINK IT'S CUTE.
"CUTE"...?! BUT SHE'S... SHE'S A...
A COMMONER? THE HEART CARES NOTHING FOR TITLES OR WEALTH, MY LORD...

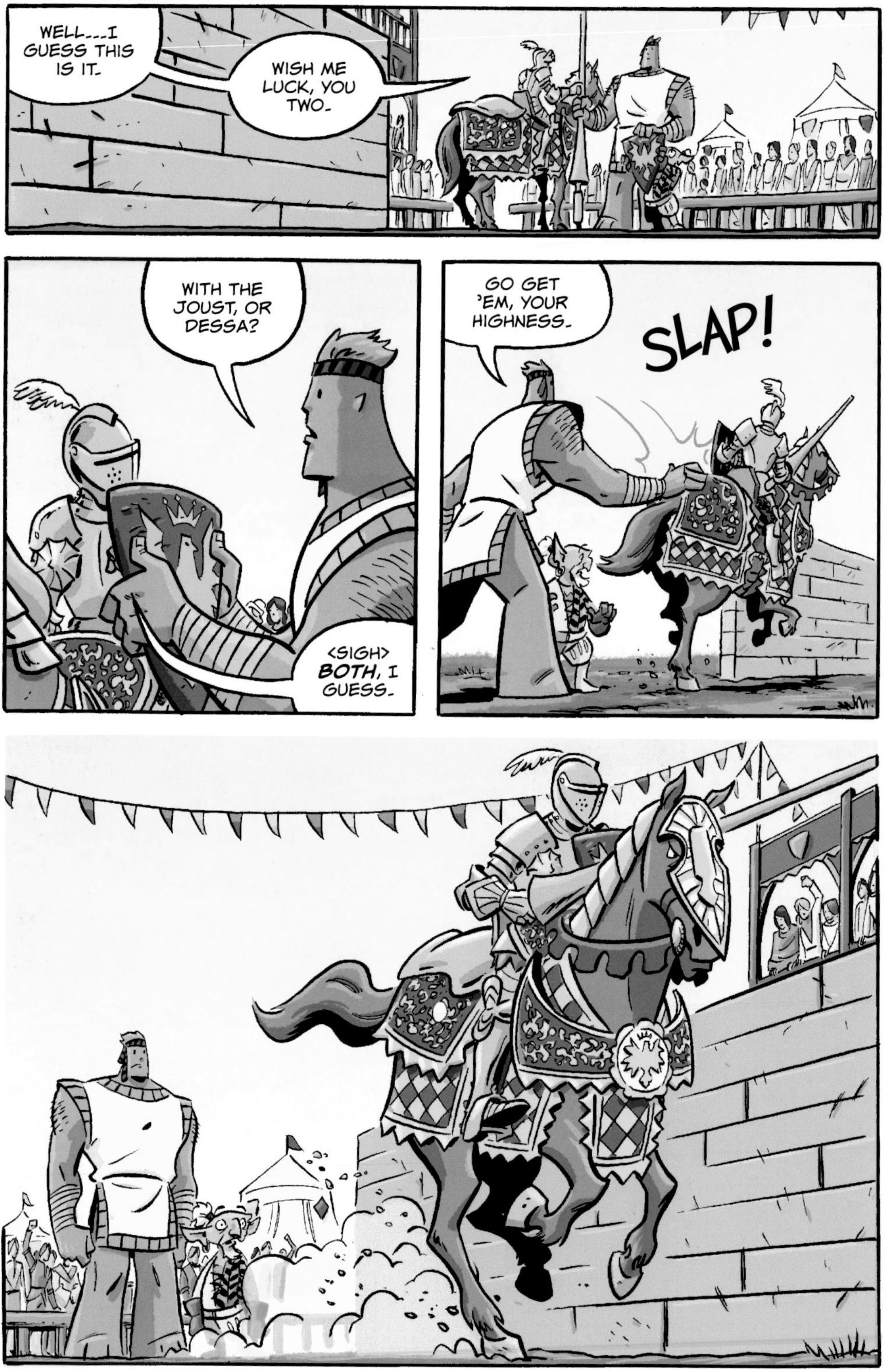
WELL...I GUESS THIS IS IT.
WISH ME LUCK, YOU TWO.
WITH THE JOUST, OR DESSA?
<SIGH> BOTH, I GUESS.
GO GET 'EM, YOUR HIGHNESS.
SLAP!

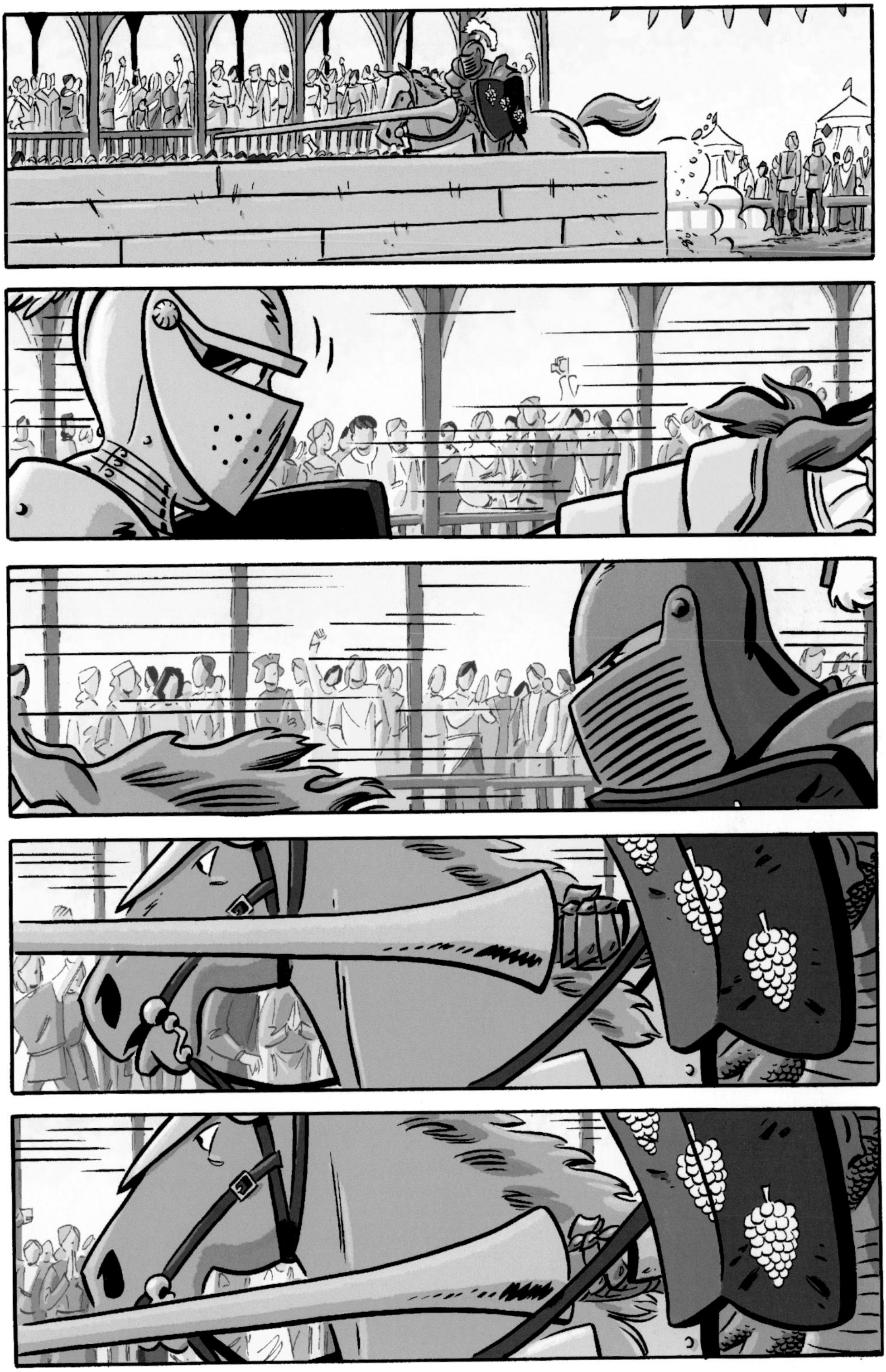

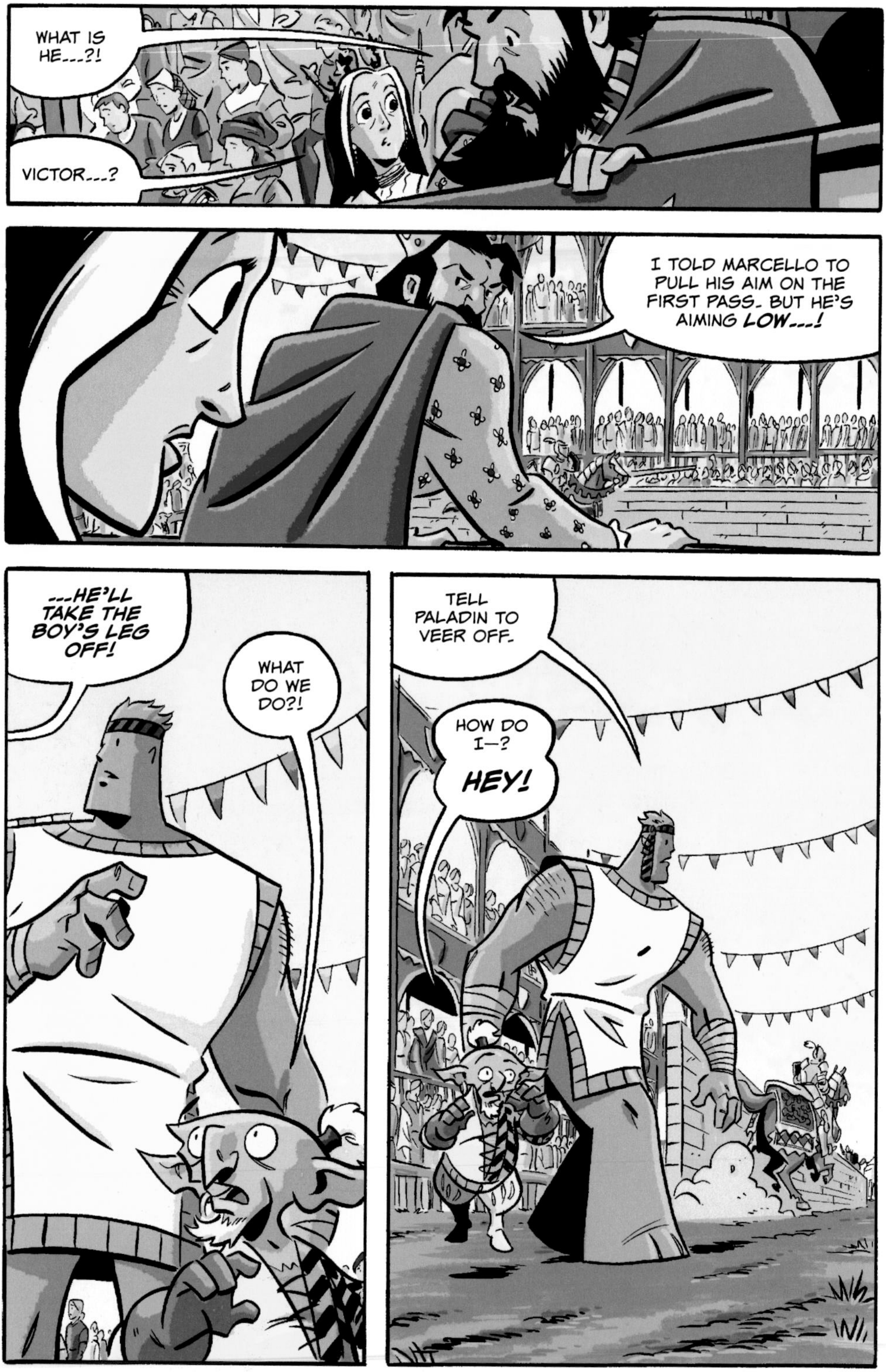
WHAT IS HE...?!
VICTOR...?
I TOLD MARCELLO TO PULL HIS AIM ON THE FIRST PASS. BUT HE'S AIMING **LOW...!**
...HE'LL TAKE THE BOY'S LEG OFF!
WHAT DO WE DO?!
TELL PALADIN TO VEER OFF.
HOW DO I—?
HEY!

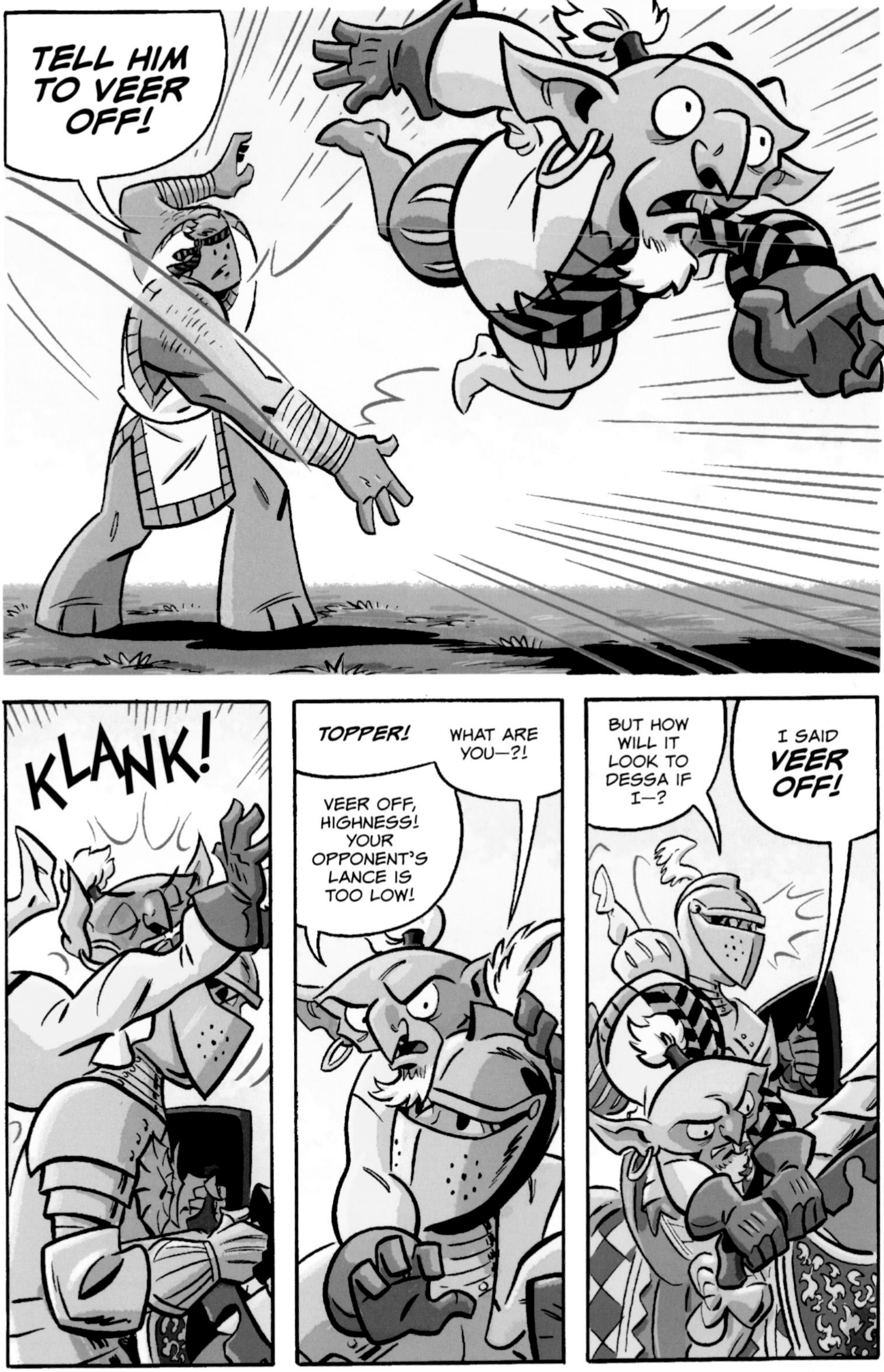
TELL HIM TO VEER OFF!
KLANK!
TOPPER!
WHAT ARE YOU—?!
VEER OFF, HIGHNESS! YOUR OPPONENT'S LANCE IS TOO LOW!
BUT HOW WILL IT LOOK TO DESSA IF I—?
I SAID VEER OFF!

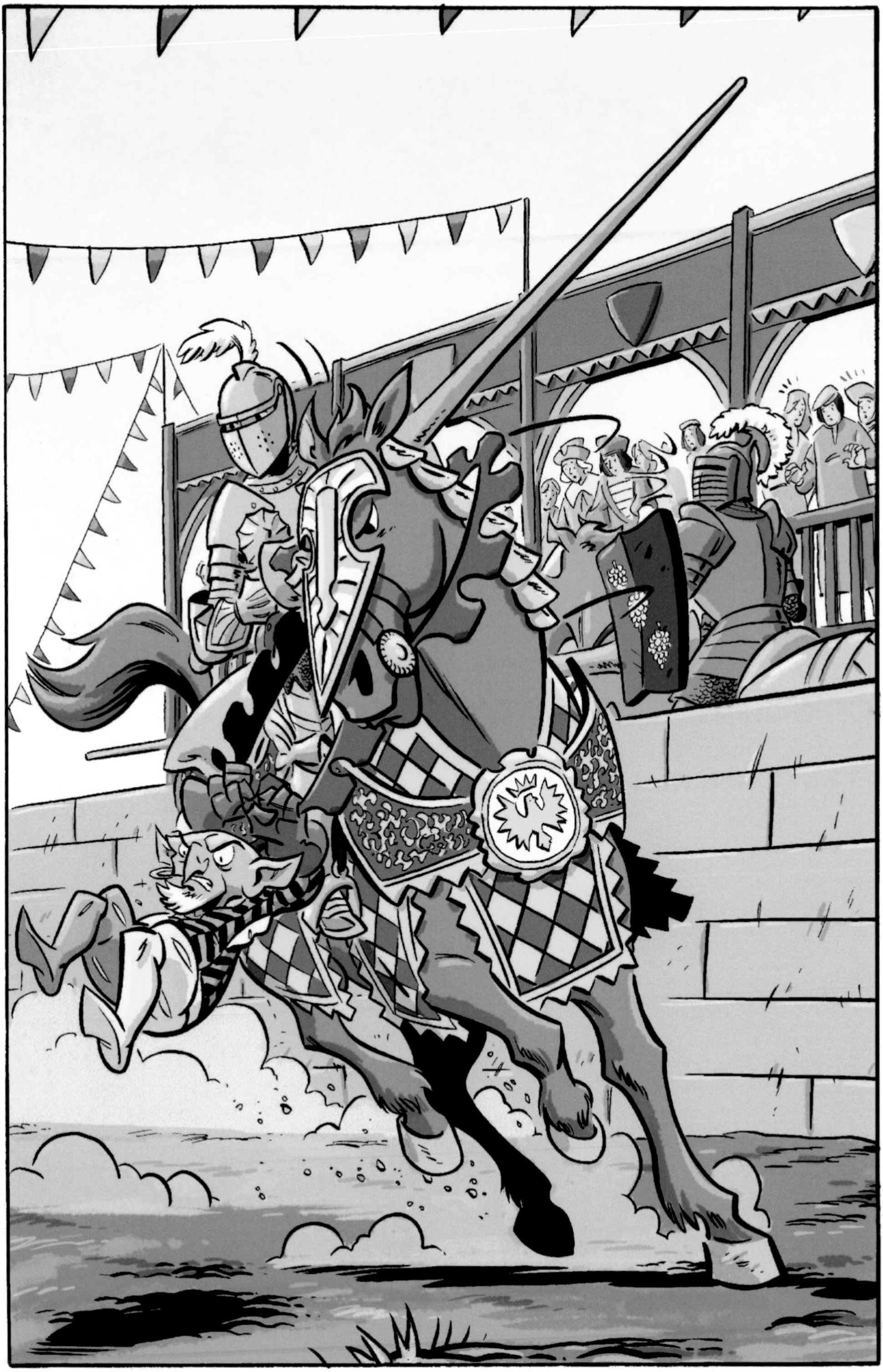

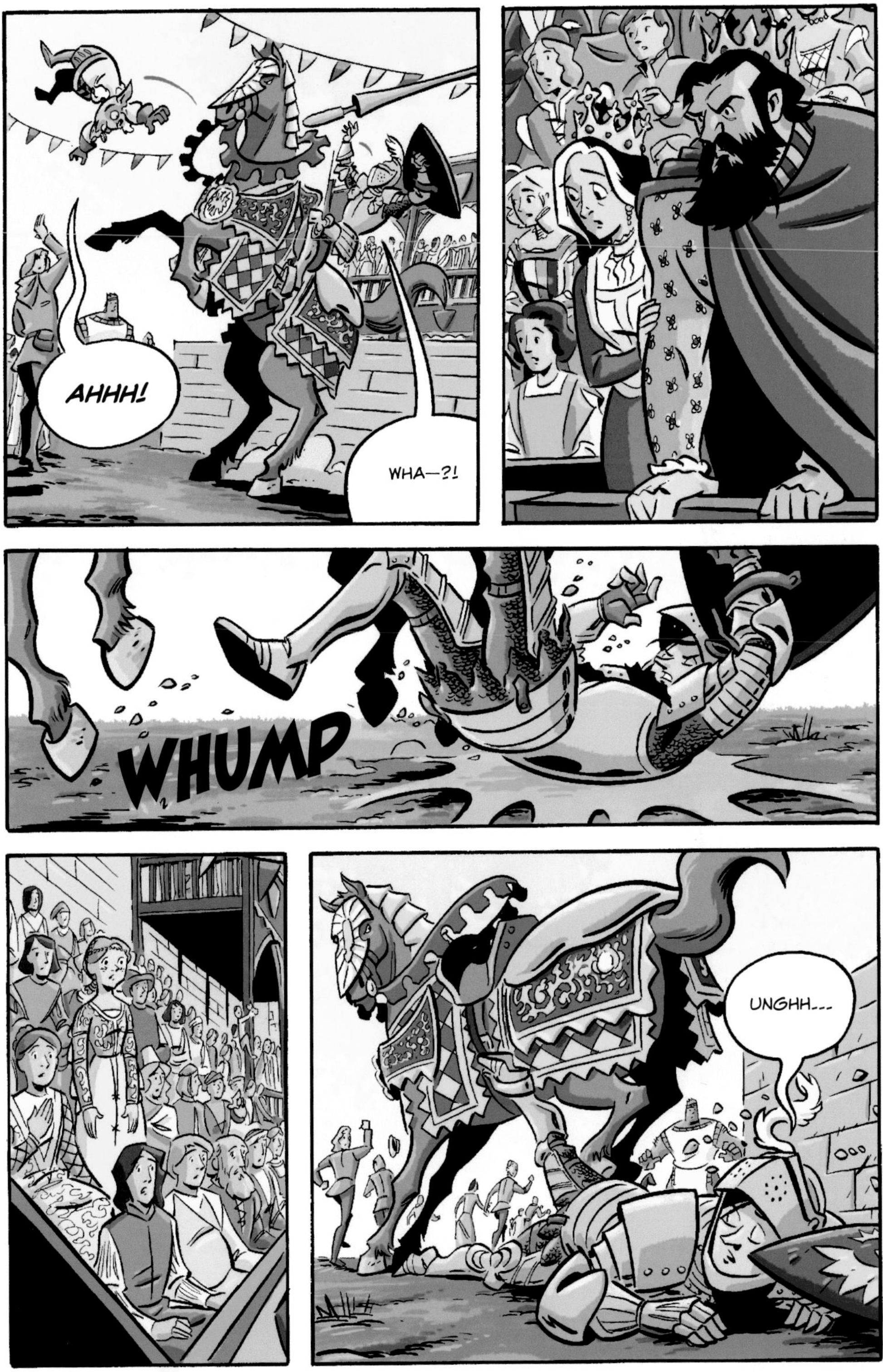
AHHH!
WHA—?!
WHUMP
UNGHH...

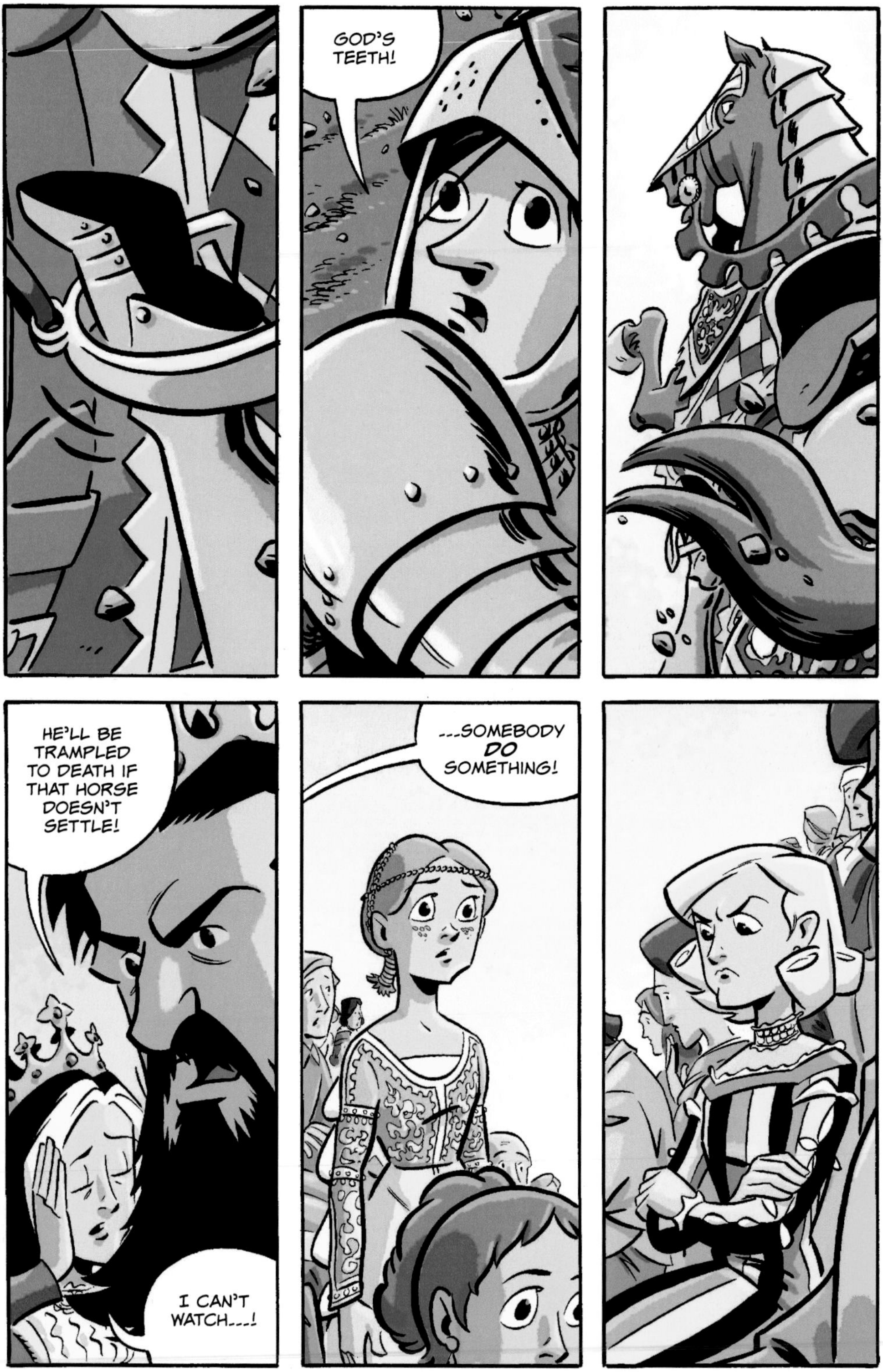
GOD'S TEETH!
HE'LL BE TRAMPLED TO DEATH IF THAT HORSE DOESN'T SETTLE!
I CAN'T WATCH...!
...SOMEBODY *DO* SOMETHING!

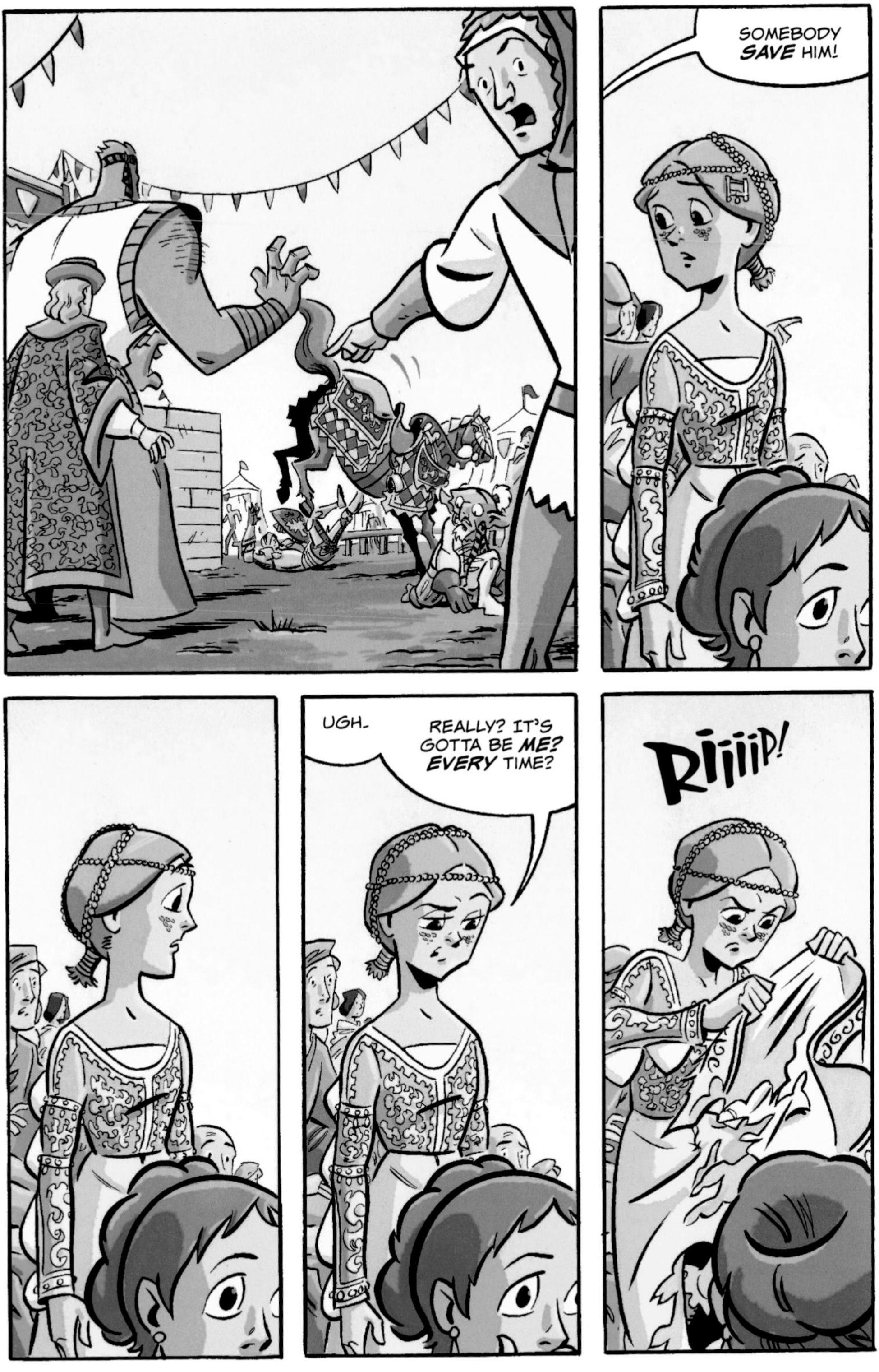

SOMEBODY SAVE HIM!
UGH.
REALLY? IT'S GOTTA BE ME? EVERY TIME?
RIIIIP!

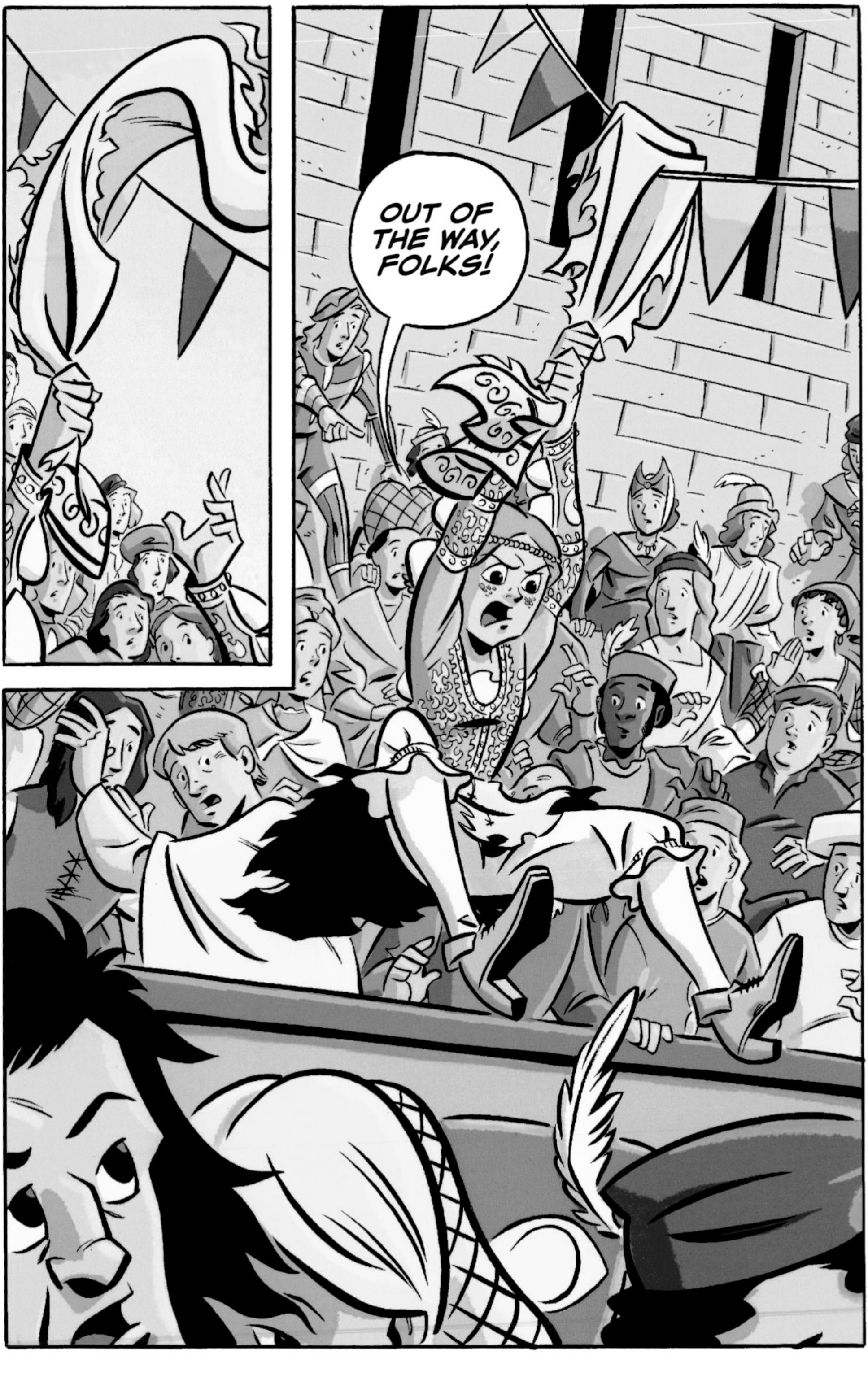
OUT OF THE WAY, FOLKS!

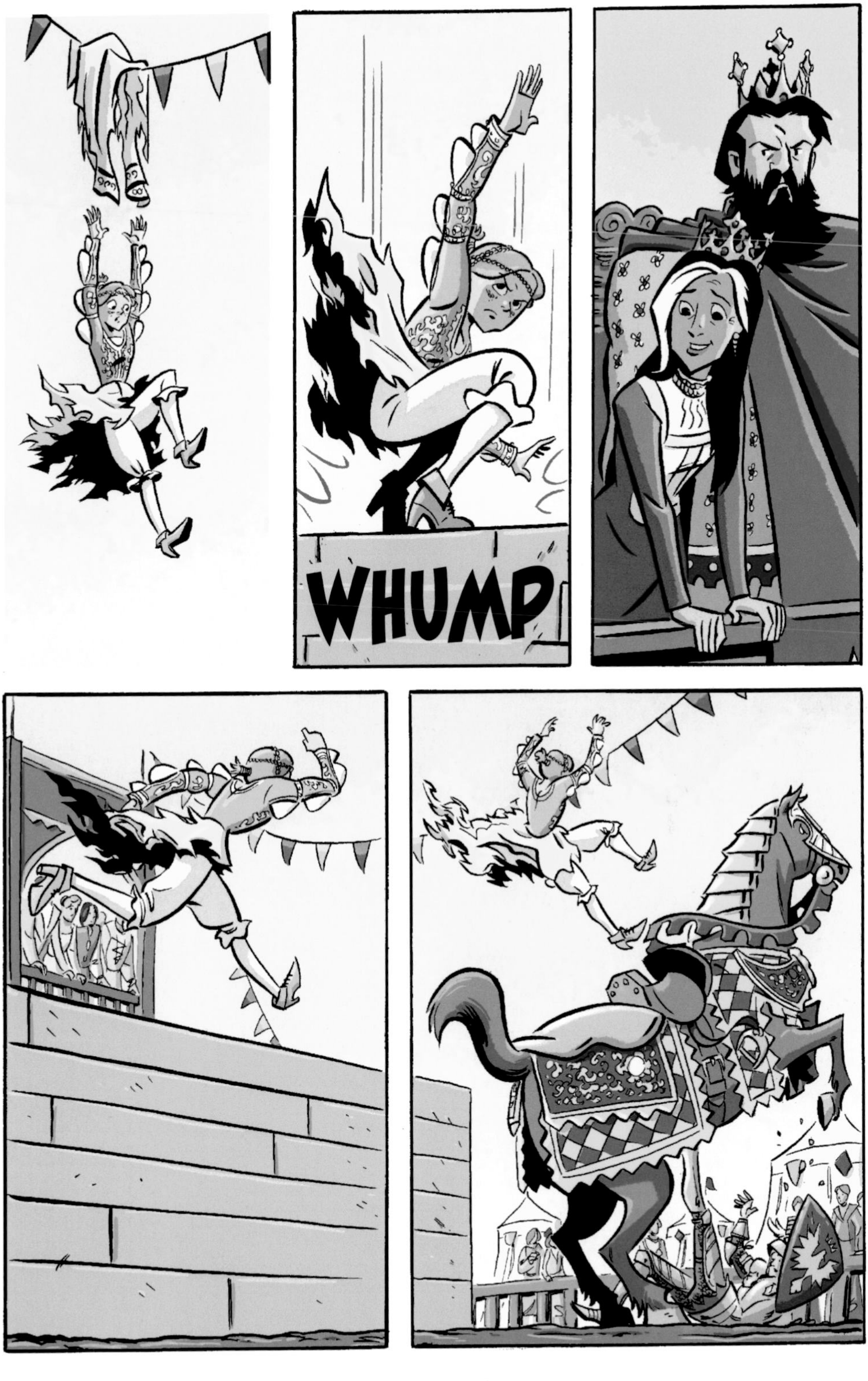
WHUMP

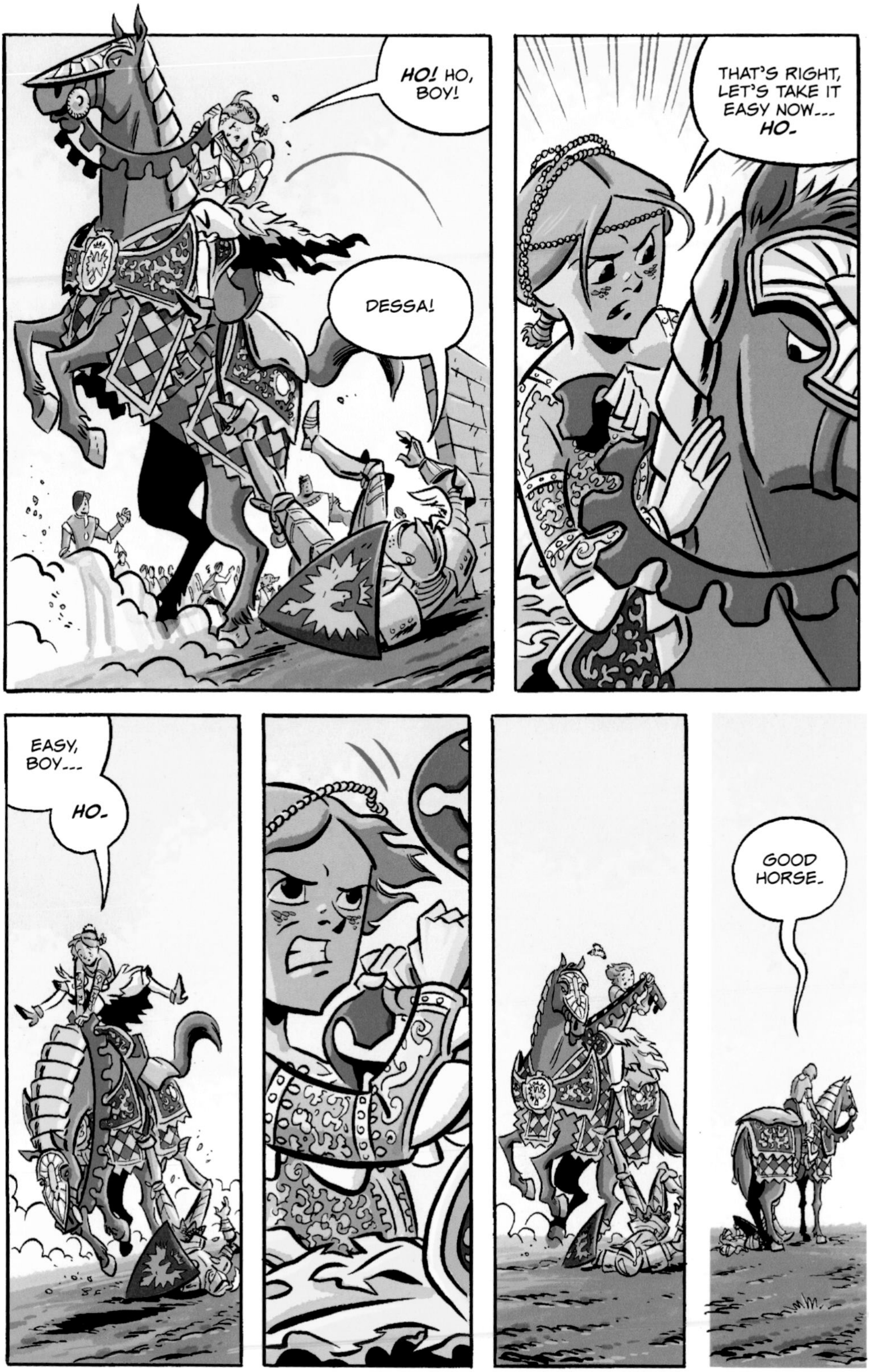
HO! HO, BOY!
DESSA!
THAT'S RIGHT, LET'S TAKE IT EASY NOW... HO.
EASY, BOY...
HO.
GOOD HORSE.

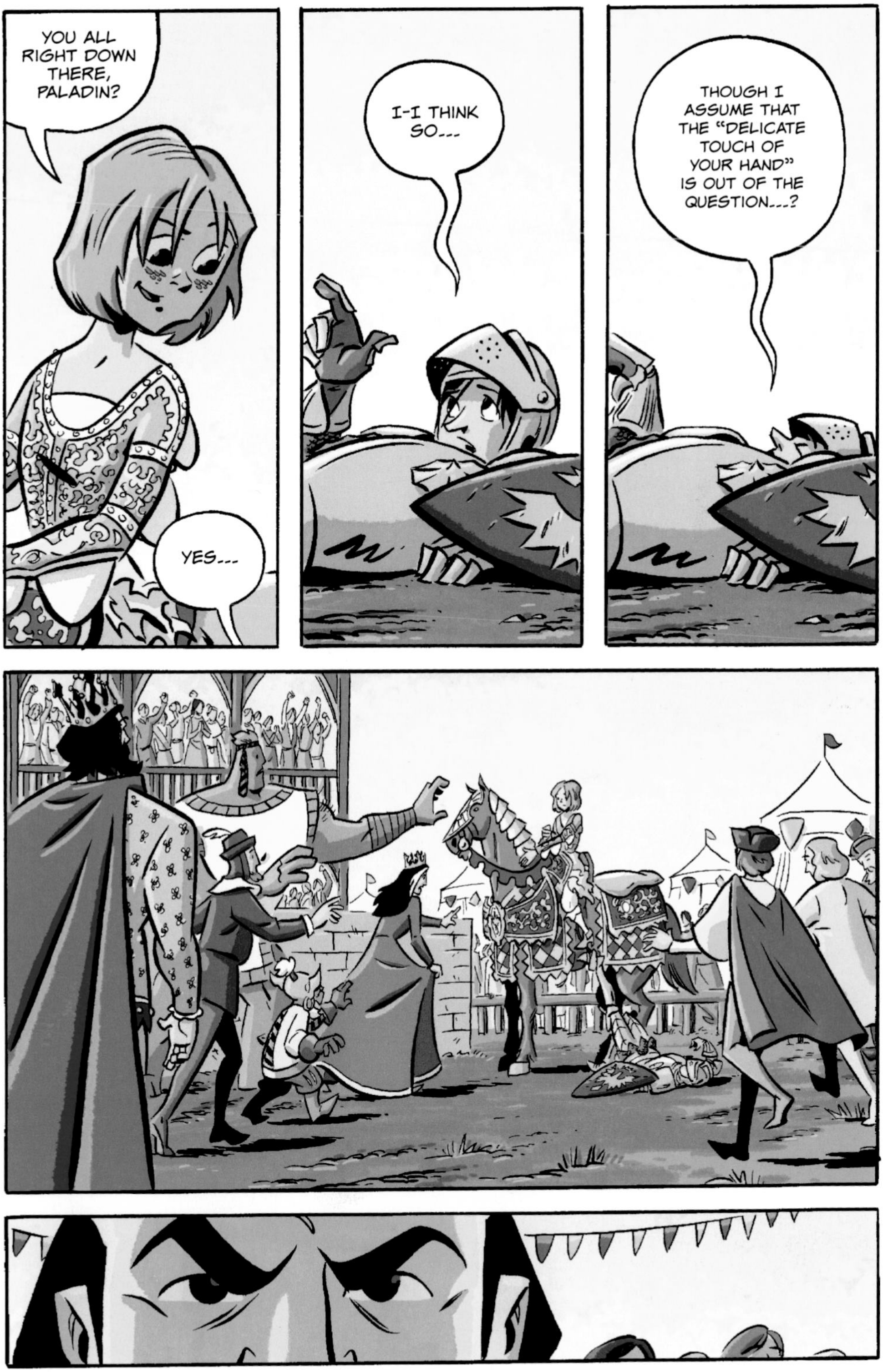
YOU ALL RIGHT DOWN THERE, PALADIN?
YES...
I-I THINK SO...
THOUGH I ASSUME THAT THE "DELICATE TOUCH OF YOUR HAND" IS OUT OF THE QUESTION...?

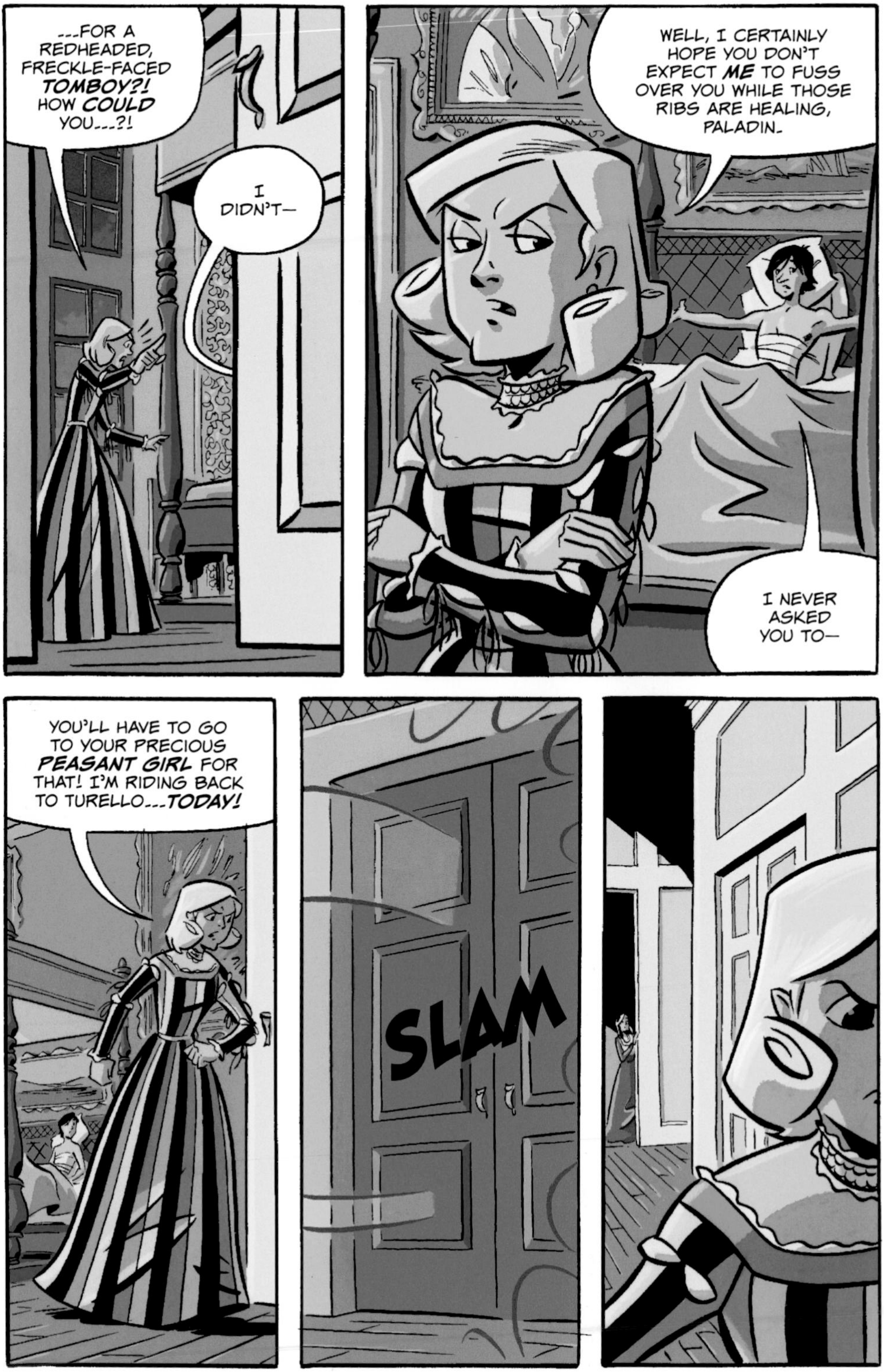

---FOR A REDHEADED, FRECKLE-FACED TOMBOY?! HOW COULD YOU---?!
I DIDN'T—
WELL, I CERTAINLY HOPE YOU DON'T EXPECT ME TO FUSS OVER YOU WHILE THOSE RIBS ARE HEALING, PALADIN.
I NEVER ASKED YOU TO—
YOU'LL HAVE TO GO TO YOUR PRECIOUS PEASANT GIRL FOR THAT! I'M RIDING BACK TO TURELLO---TODAY!
SLAM

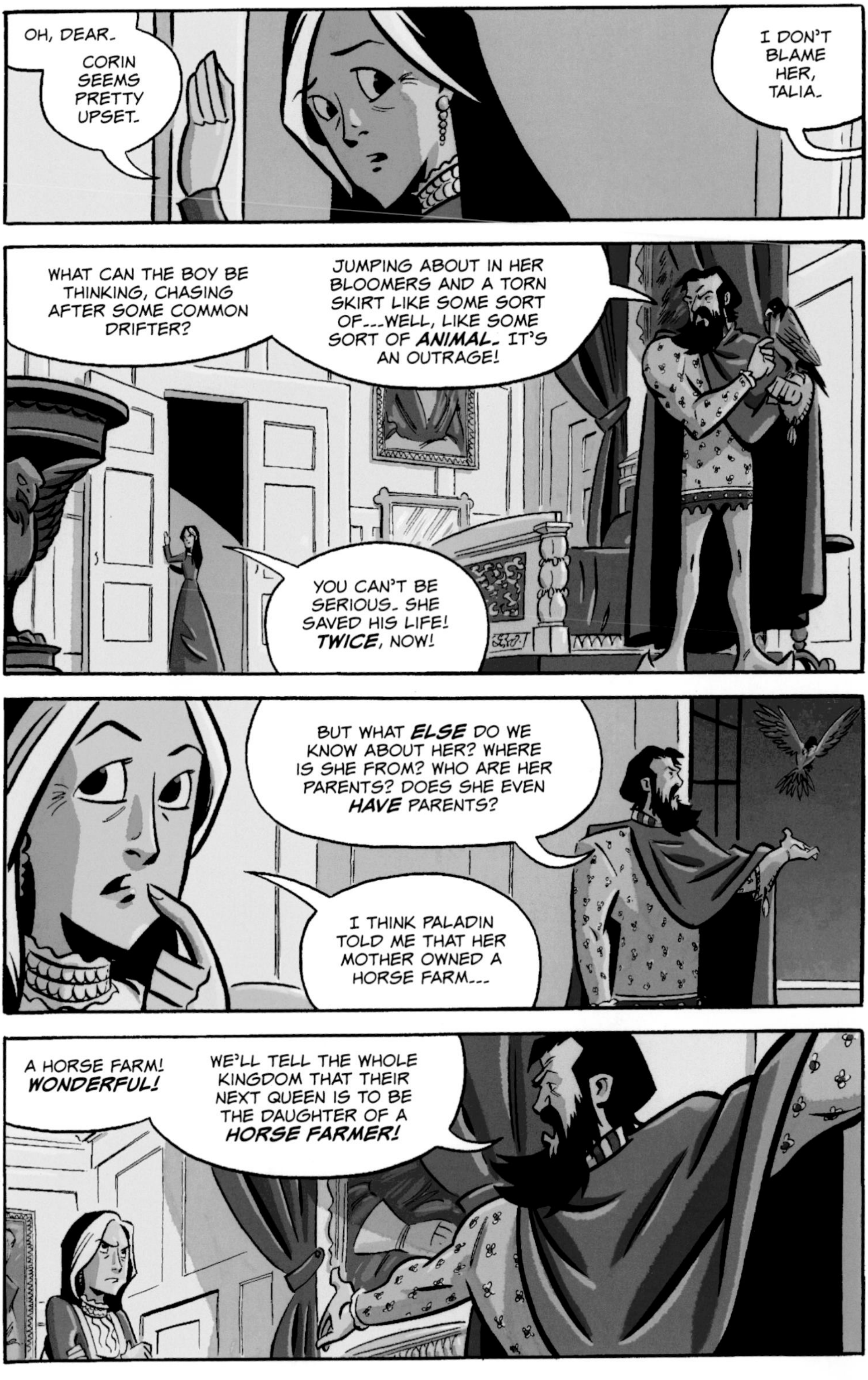
OH, DEAR.
CORIN SEEMS PRETTY UPSET.
I DON'T BLAME HER, TALIA.
WHAT CAN THE BOY BE THINKING, CHASING AFTER SOME COMMON DRIFTER?
JUMPING ABOUT IN HER BLOOMERS AND A TORN SKIRT LIKE SOME SORT OF...WELL, LIKE SOME SORT OF ANIMAL. IT'S AN OUTRAGE!
YOU CAN'T BE SERIOUS. SHE SAVED HIS LIFE! TWICE, NOW!
BUT WHAT ELSE DO WE KNOW ABOUT HER? WHERE IS SHE FROM? WHO ARE HER PARENTS? DOES SHE EVEN HAVE PARENTS?
I THINK PALADIN TOLD ME THAT HER MOTHER OWNED A HORSE FARM...
A HORSE FARM! WONDERFUL!
WE'LL TELL THE WHOLE KINGDOM THAT THEIR NEXT QUEEN IS TO BE THE DAUGHTER OF A HORSE FARMER!

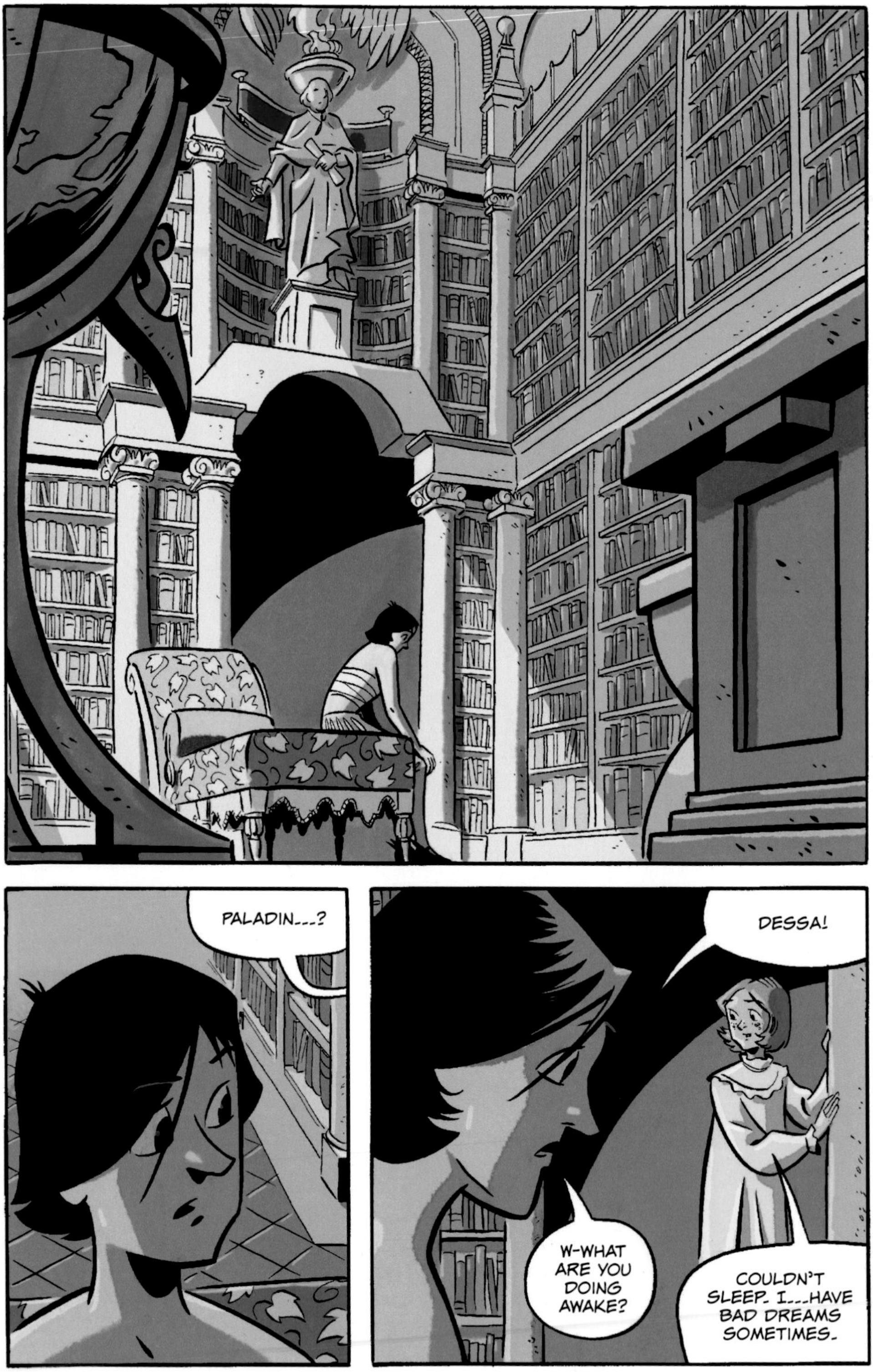
PALADIN...?
DESSA!
W-WHAT ARE YOU DOING AWAKE?
COULDN'T SLEEP. I...HAVE BAD DREAMS SOMETIMES.

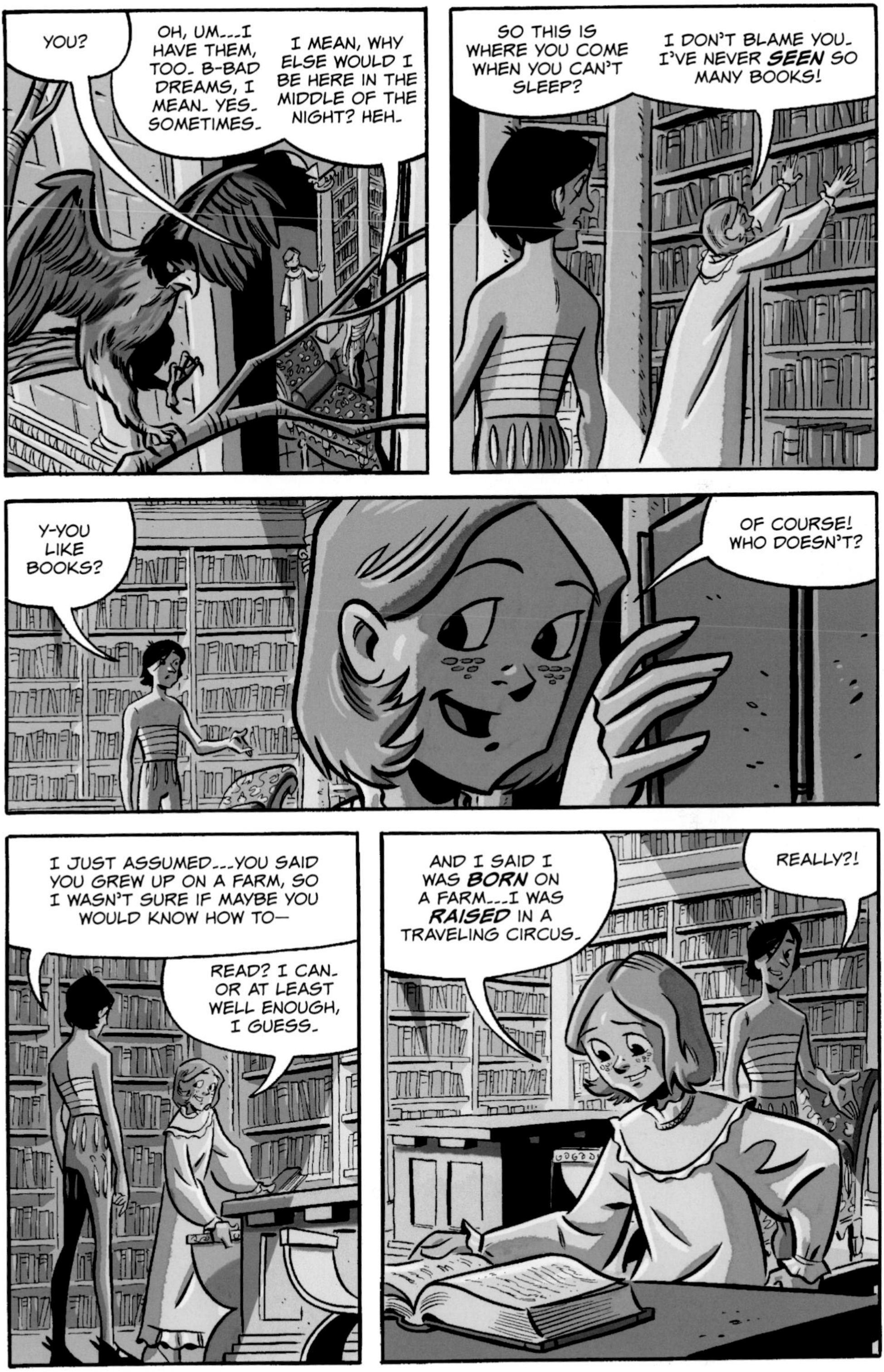
YOU?
OH, UM...I HAVE THEM, TOO. B-BAD DREAMS, I MEAN. YES. SOMETIMES.
I MEAN, WHY ELSE WOULD I BE HERE IN THE MIDDLE OF THE NIGHT? HEH.
SO THIS IS WHERE YOU COME WHEN YOU CAN'T SLEEP?
I DON'T BLAME YOU. I'VE NEVER SEEN SO MANY BOOKS!
Y-YOU LIKE BOOKS?
OF COURSE! WHO DOESN'T?
I JUST ASSUMED...YOU SAID YOU GREW UP ON A FARM, SO I WASN'T SURE IF MAYBE YOU WOULD KNOW HOW TO—
READ? I CAN. OR AT LEAST WELL ENOUGH, I GUESS.
AND I SAID I WAS BORN ON A FARM...I WAS RAISED IN A TRAVELING CIRCUS.
REALLY?!

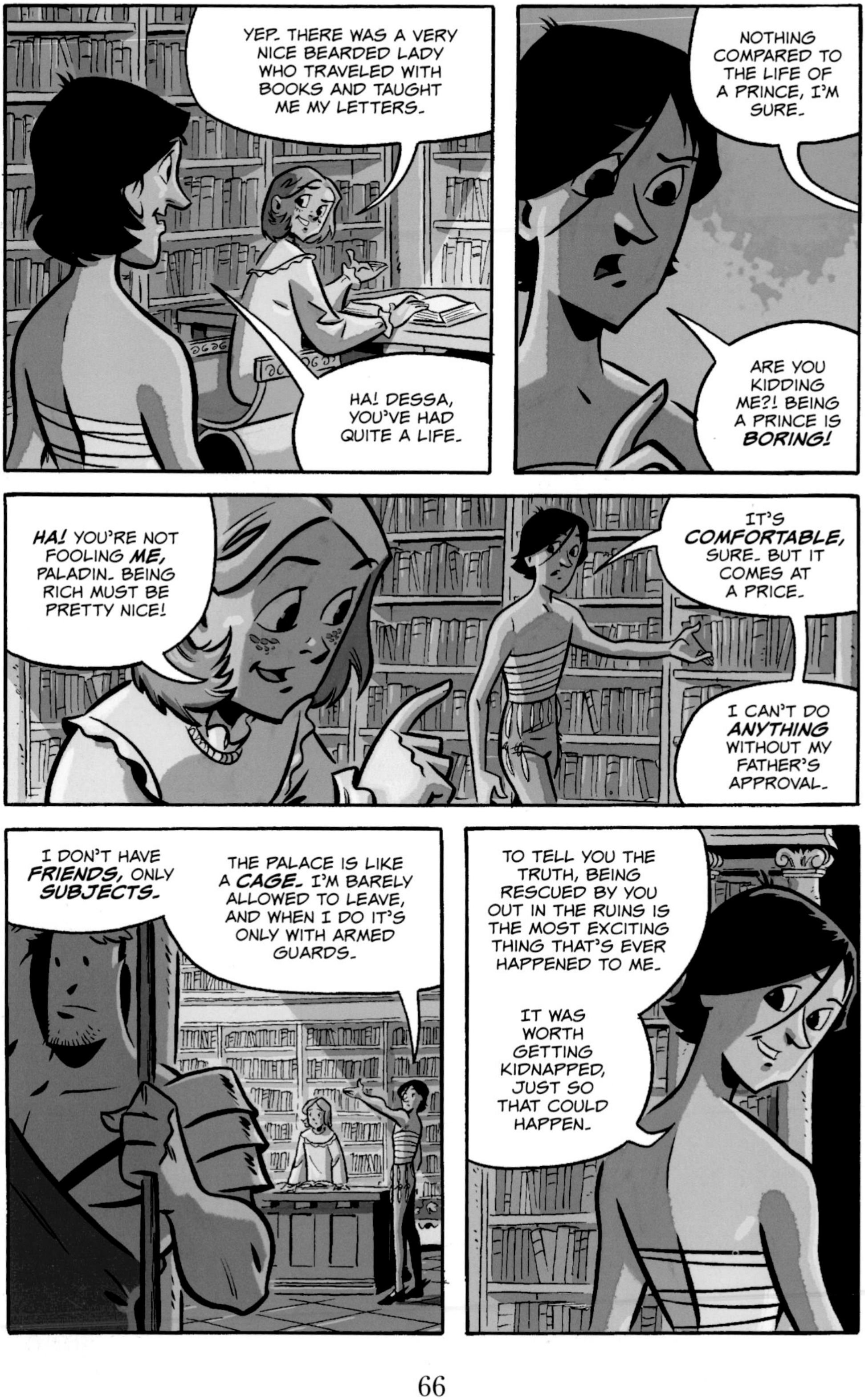
YEP. THERE WAS A VERY NICE BEARDED LADY WHO TRAVELED WITH BOOKS AND TAUGHT ME MY LETTERS.
HA! DESSA, YOU'VE HAD QUITE A LIFE.
NOTHING COMPARED TO THE LIFE OF A PRINCE, I'M SURE.
ARE YOU KIDDING ME?! BEING A PRINCE IS **BORING!**
HA! YOU'RE NOT FOOLING **ME,** PALADIN. BEING RICH MUST BE PRETTY NICE!
IT'S **COMFORTABLE,** SURE. BUT IT COMES AT A PRICE.
I CAN'T DO **ANYTHING** WITHOUT MY FATHER'S APPROVAL.
I DON'T HAVE **FRIENDS,** ONLY **SUBJECTS.**
THE PALACE IS LIKE A **CAGE.** I'M BARELY ALLOWED TO LEAVE, AND WHEN I DO IT'S ONLY WITH ARMED GUARDS.
TO TELL YOU THE TRUTH, BEING RESCUED BY YOU OUT IN THE RUINS IS THE MOST EXCITING THING THAT'S EVER HAPPENED TO ME.
IT WAS WORTH GETTING KIDNAPPED, JUST SO THAT COULD HAPPEN.

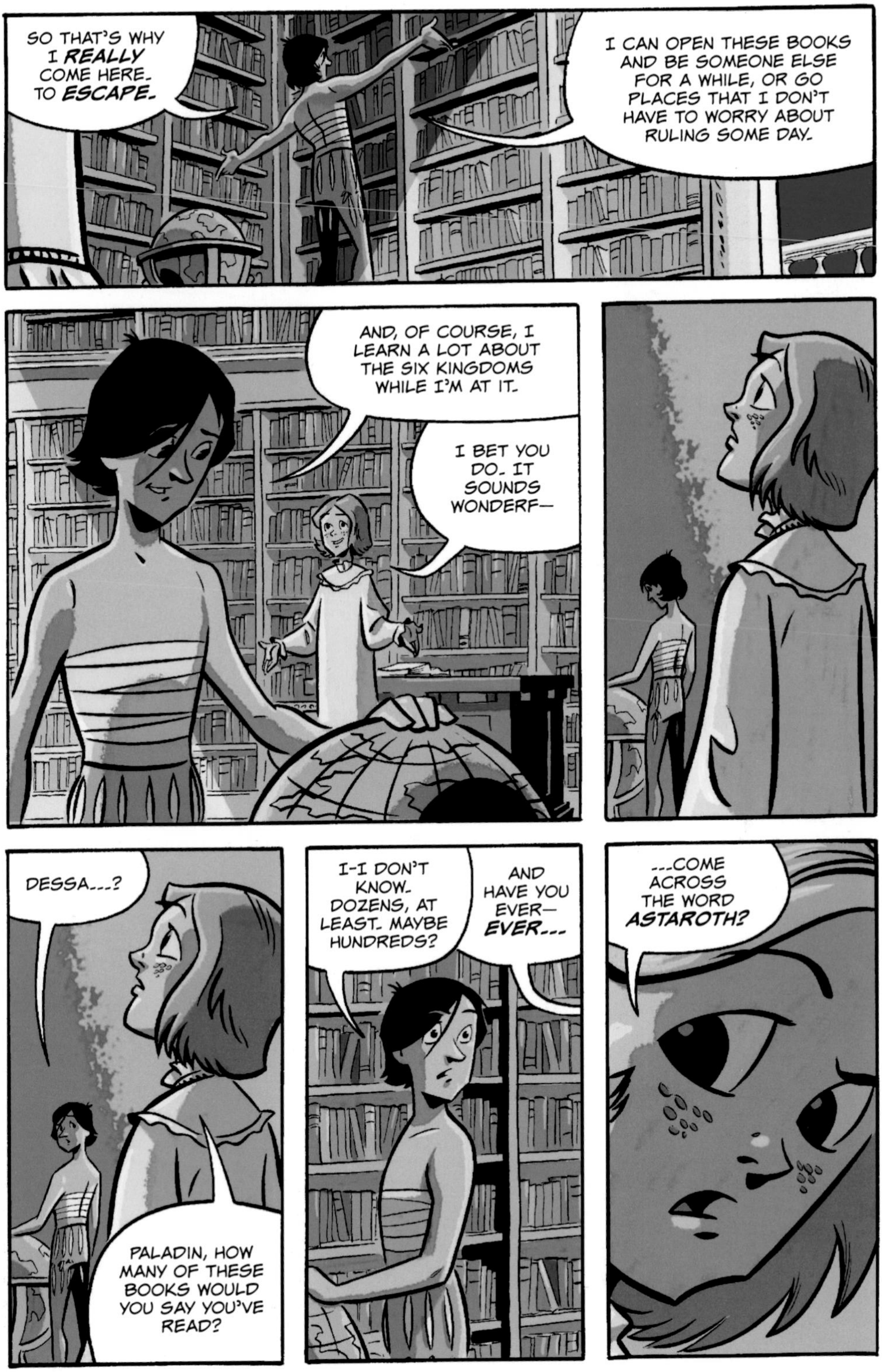
SO THAT'S WHY I *REALLY* COME HERE. TO *ESCAPE.*
I CAN OPEN THESE BOOKS AND BE SOMEONE ELSE FOR A WHILE, OR GO PLACES THAT I DON'T HAVE TO WORRY ABOUT RULING SOME DAY.
AND, OF COURSE, I LEARN A LOT ABOUT THE SIX KINGDOMS WHILE I'M AT IT.
I BET YOU DO. IT SOUNDS WONDERF—
DESSA...?
PALADIN, HOW MANY OF THESE BOOKS WOULD YOU SAY YOU'VE READ?
I-I DON'T KNOW. DOZENS, AT LEAST. MAYBE HUNDREDS?
AND HAVE YOU EVER— *EVER...*
...COME ACROSS THE WORD *ASTAROTH?*

I CAN'T *BELIEVE* YOU, VICTOR! DID YOU FALL IN LOVE WITH *ME* FOR MY *TITLE...?!*

THAT'S DIFFERENT.

AND JUST HOW IS IT DI—?

IT JUST *IS.* AND I DON'T WANT TO HEAR ANOTHER WORD ABOUT PALADIN AND THIS...THIS *VAGABOND!*

IF I'D KNOWN SOMETHING LIKE *THIS* WOULD HAPPEN, I'D HAVE JUST SENT HER ON HER WAY.

AND I'M CANCELING THE BANQUET TOMORROW NIGHT. THAT GIRL HAS ALREADY ENJOYED MORE OF OUR HOSPITALITY THAN I'M COMFORTABLE WITH.

OH, YOU'LL DO NO SUCH THING. DESSA AND HER FRIENDS CAN STAY AS LONG AS THEY LIKE.

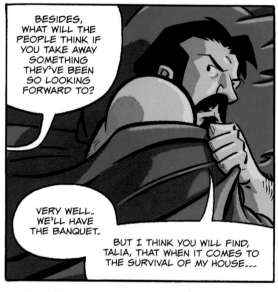

BESIDES, WHAT WILL THE PEOPLE THINK IF YOU TAKE AWAY SOMETHING THEY'VE BEEN SO LOOKING FORWARD TO?

VERY WELL. WE'LL HAVE THE BANQUET.

BUT I THINK YOU WILL FIND, TALIA, THAT WHEN IT COMES TO THE SURVIVAL OF MY HOUSE...

...THERE'S VERY *LITTLE* I WON'T DO.

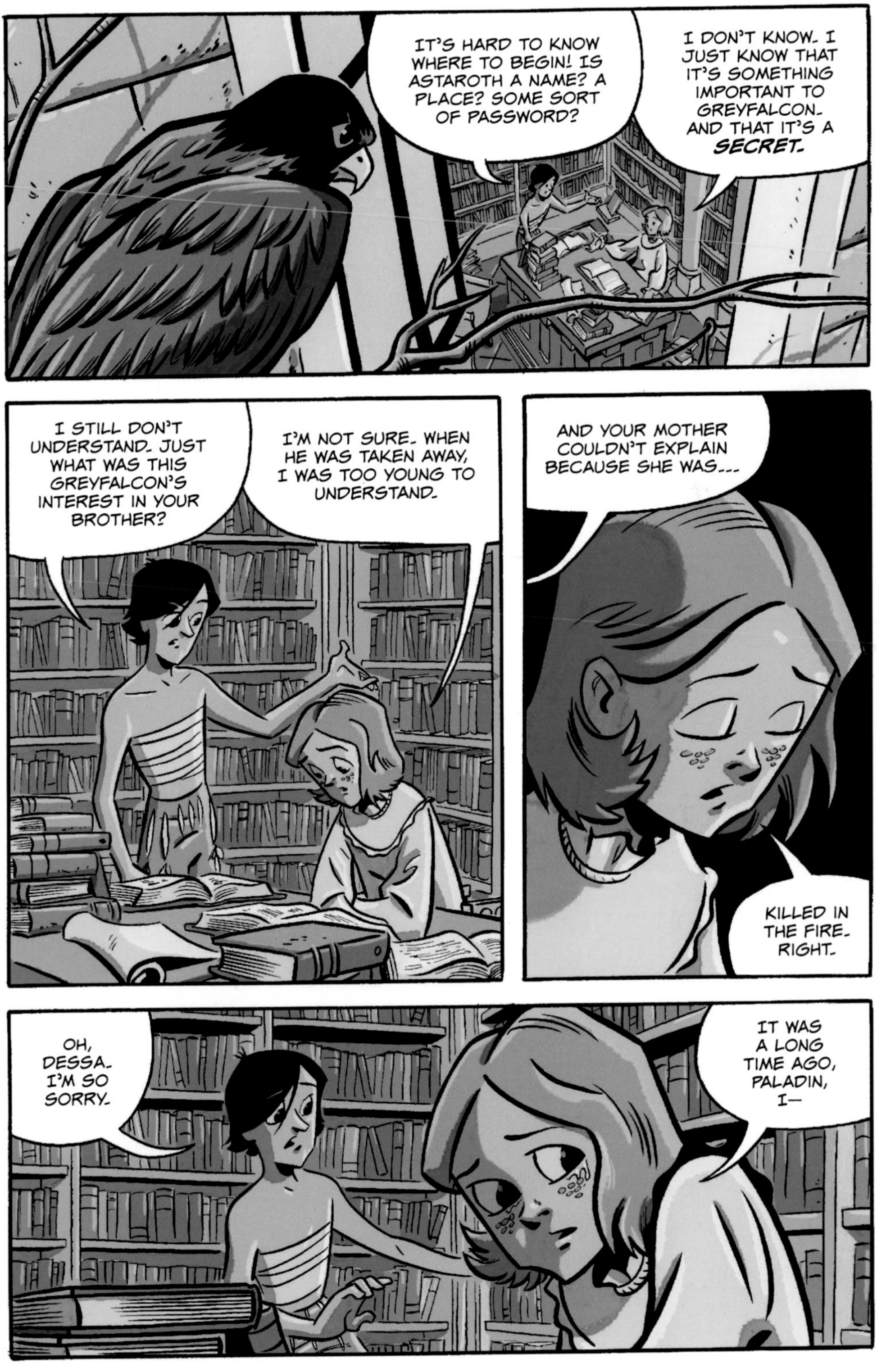
IT'S HARD TO KNOW WHERE TO BEGIN! IS ASTAROTH A NAME? A PLACE? SOME SORT OF PASSWORD?
I DON'T KNOW. I JUST KNOW THAT IT'S SOMETHING IMPORTANT TO GREYFALCON. AND THAT IT'S A SECRET.
I STILL DON'T UNDERSTAND. JUST WHAT WAS THIS GREYFALCON'S INTEREST IN YOUR BROTHER?
I'M NOT SURE. WHEN HE WAS TAKEN AWAY, I WAS TOO YOUNG TO UNDERSTAND.
AND YOUR MOTHER COULDN'T EXPLAIN BECAUSE SHE WAS...
KILLED IN THE FIRE. RIGHT.
OH, DESSA. I'M SO SORRY.
IT WAS A LONG TIME AGO, PALADIN, I—

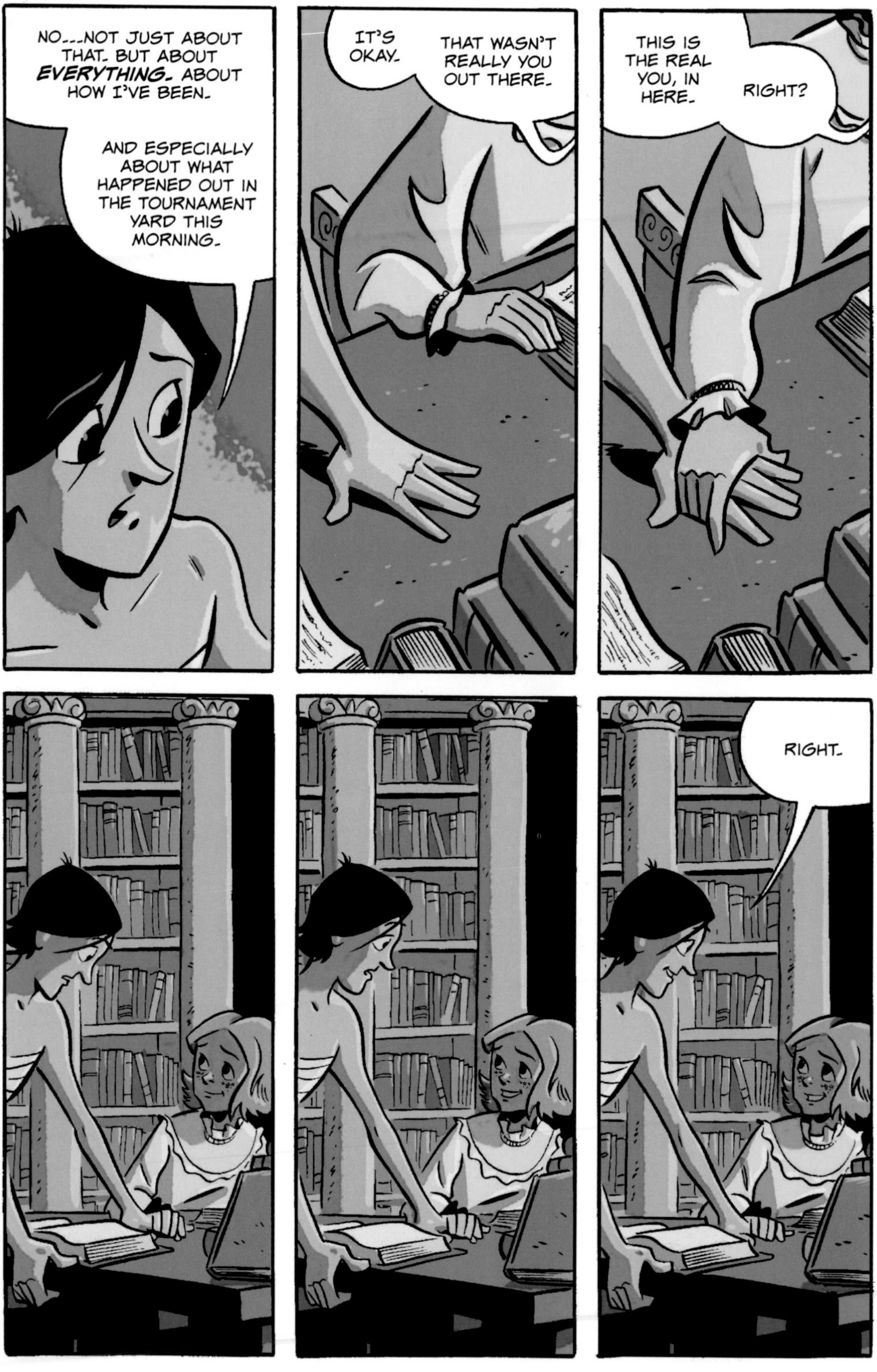
NO...NOT JUST ABOUT THAT. BUT ABOUT EVERYTHING. ABOUT HOW I'VE BEEN.
AND ESPECIALLY ABOUT WHAT HAPPENED OUT IN THE TOURNAMENT YARD THIS MORNING.
IT'S OKAY.
THAT WASN'T REALLY YOU OUT THERE.
THIS IS THE REAL YOU, IN HERE.
RIGHT?
RIGHT.

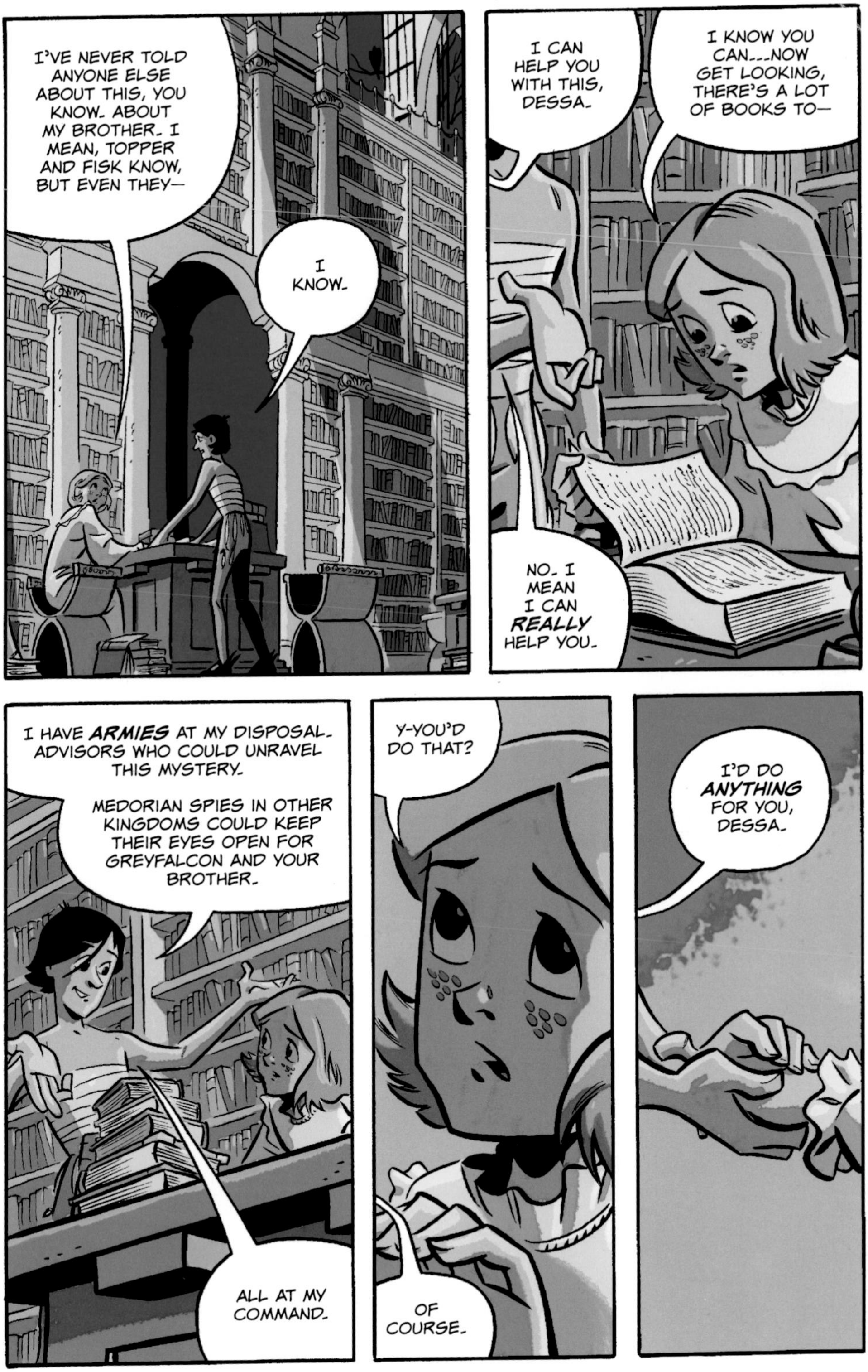
I'VE NEVER TOLD ANYONE ELSE ABOUT THIS, YOU KNOW. ABOUT MY BROTHER. I MEAN, TOPPER AND FISK KNOW, BUT EVEN THEY—
I KNOW.
I CAN HELP YOU WITH THIS, DESSA.
I KNOW YOU CAN...NOW GET LOOKING, THERE'S A LOT OF BOOKS TO—
NO. I MEAN I CAN ***REALLY*** HELP YOU.
I HAVE ***ARMIES*** AT MY DISPOSAL. ADVISORS WHO COULD UNRAVEL THIS MYSTERY.
MEDORIAN SPIES IN OTHER KINGDOMS COULD KEEP THEIR EYES OPEN FOR GREYFALCON AND YOUR BROTHER.
ALL AT MY COMMAND.
Y-YOU'D DO THAT?
OF COURSE.
I'D DO ***ANYTHING*** FOR YOU, DESSA.

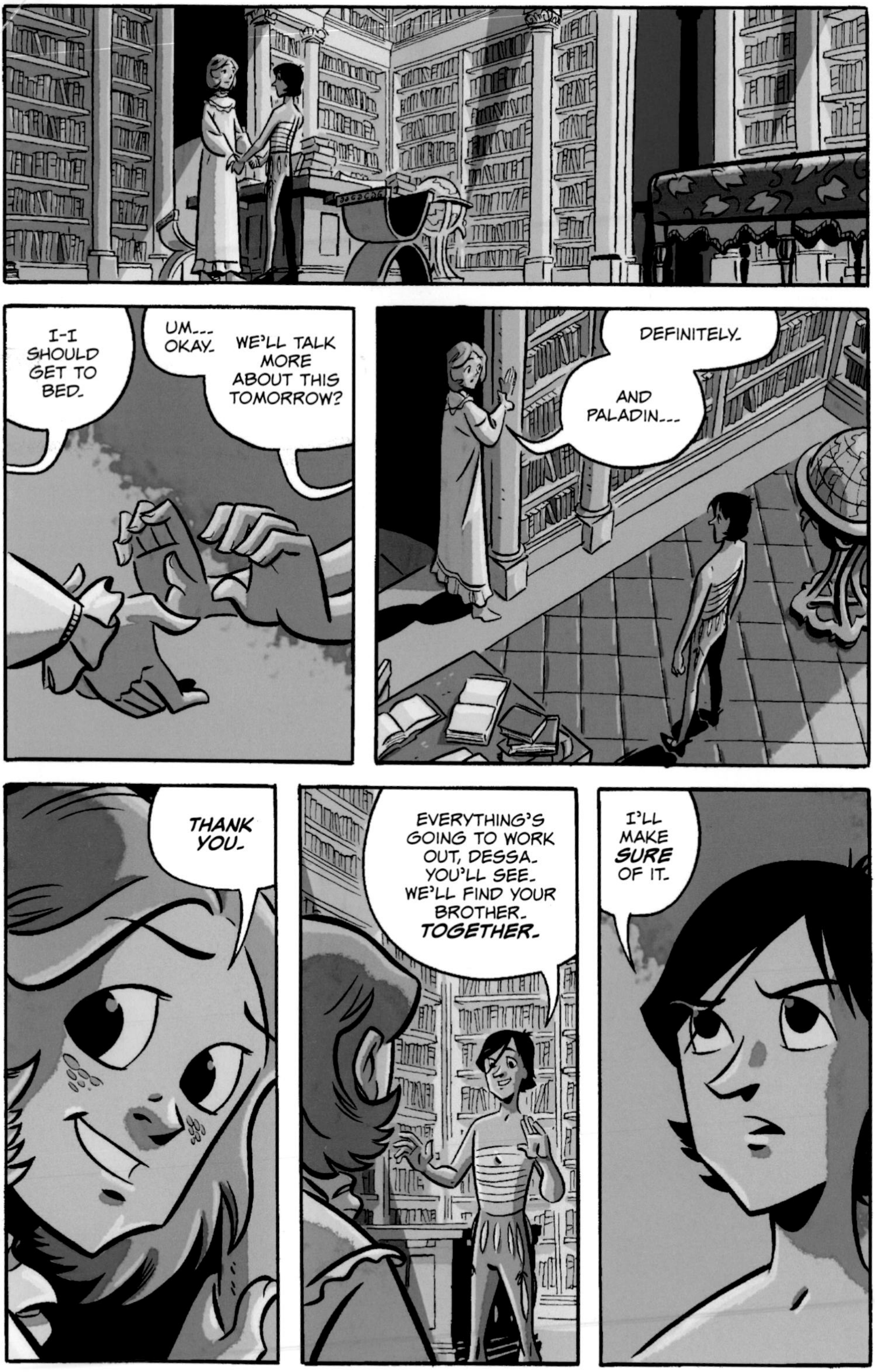
I-I SHOULD GET TO BED.
UM... OKAY.
WE'LL TALK MORE ABOUT THIS TOMORROW?
DEFINITELY.
AND PALADIN...
THANK YOU.
EVERYTHING'S GOING TO WORK OUT, DESSA. YOU'LL SEE. WE'LL FIND YOUR BROTHER. TOGETHER.
I'LL MAKE SURE OF IT.

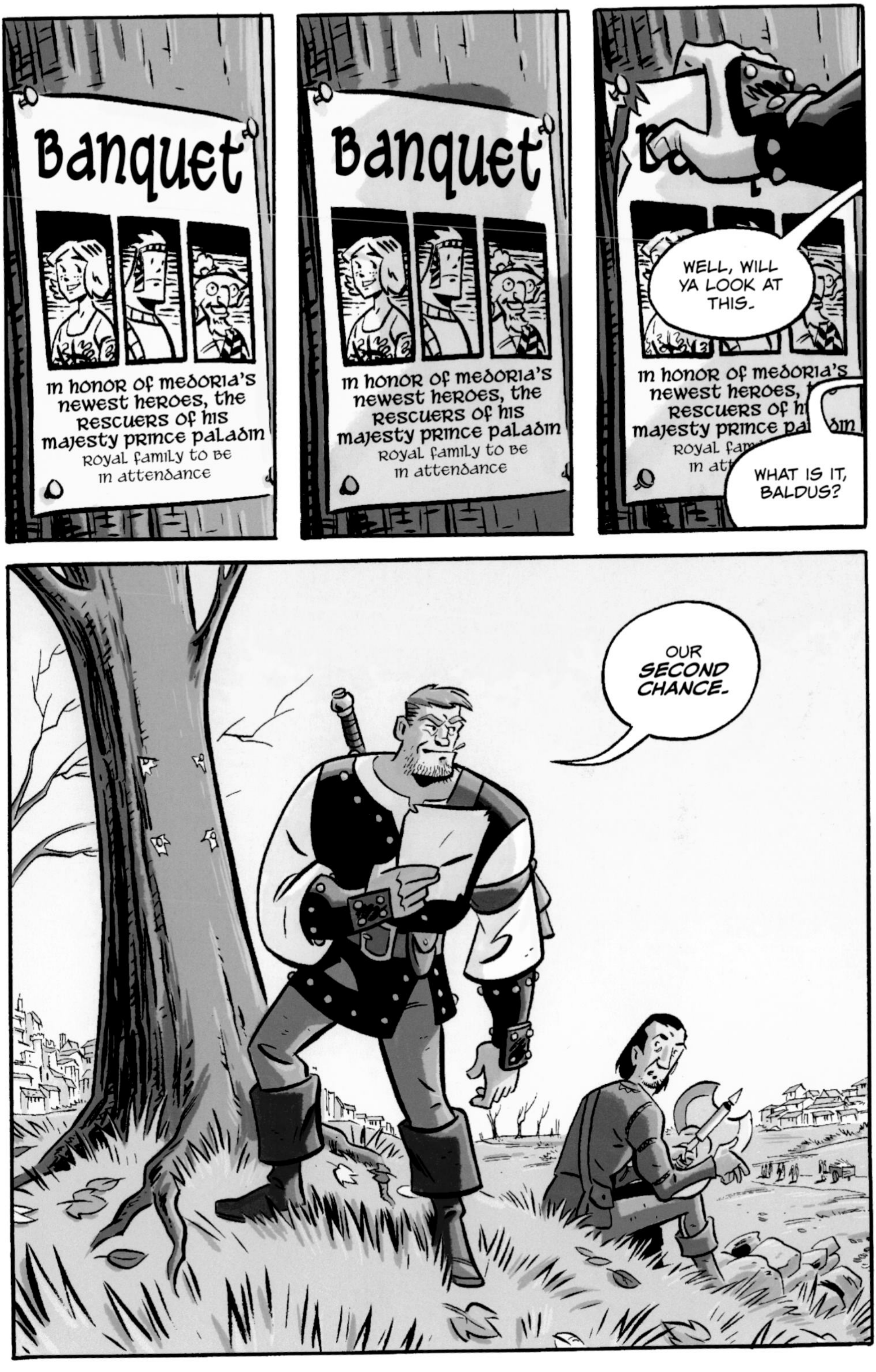
Banquet
in honor of medoria's newest heroes, the rescuers of his majesty prince paladin
Royal family to be in attendance
Banquet
in honor of medoria's newest heroes, the rescuers of his majesty prince paladin
Royal family to be in attendance
WELL, WILL YA LOOK AT THIS.
WHAT IS IT, BALDUS?
OUR *SECOND CHANCE*.

ACT THREE
BANQUET

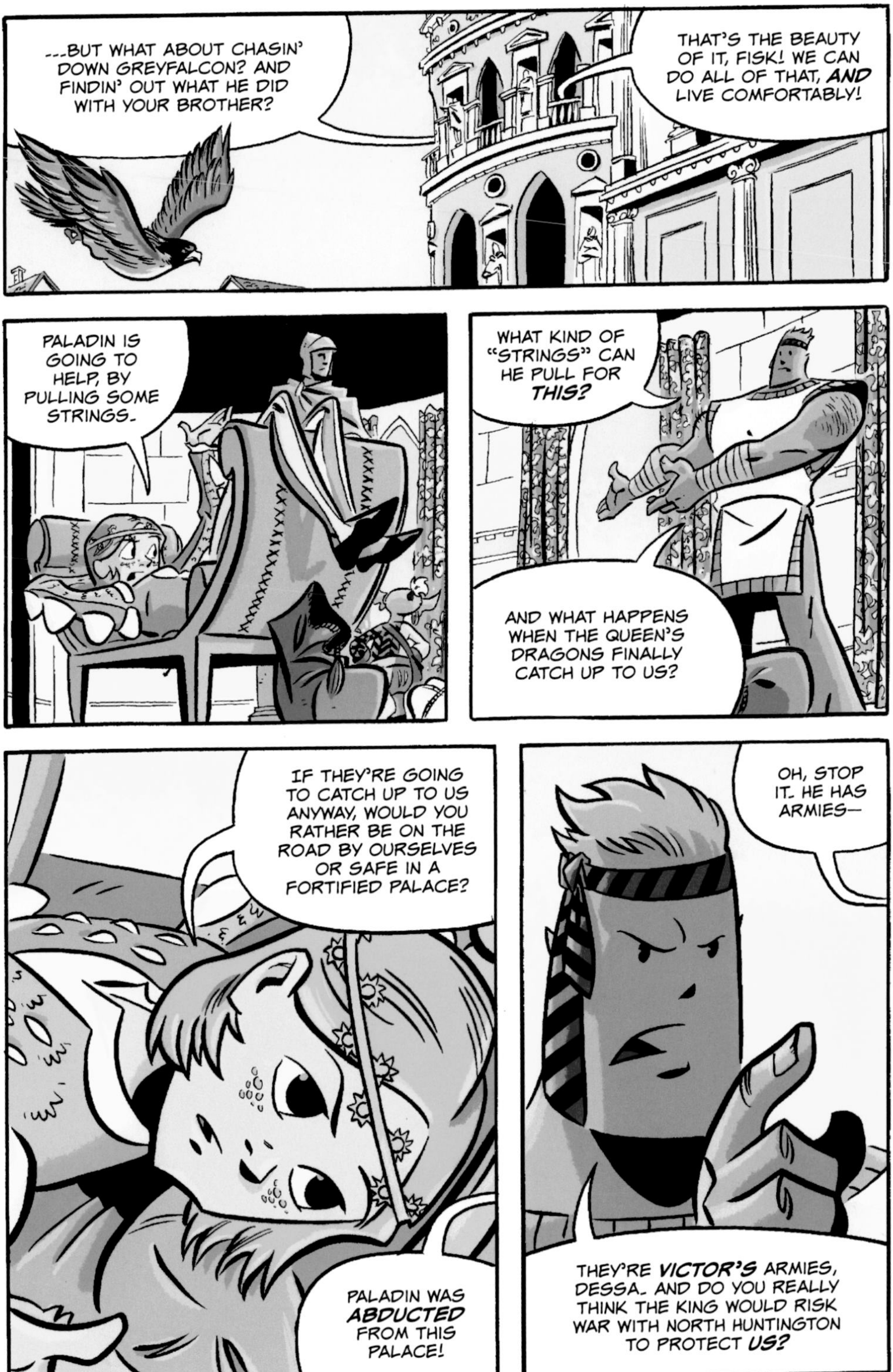

...BUT WHAT ABOUT CHASIN' DOWN GREYFALCON? AND FINDIN' OUT WHAT HE DID WITH YOUR BROTHER?
THAT'S THE BEAUTY OF IT, FISK! WE CAN DO ALL OF THAT, AND LIVE COMFORTABLY!
PALADIN IS GOING TO HELP, BY PULLING SOME STRINGS.
WHAT KIND OF "STRINGS" CAN HE PULL FOR THIS?
AND WHAT HAPPENS WHEN THE QUEEN'S DRAGONS FINALLY CATCH UP TO US?
IF THEY'RE GOING TO CATCH UP TO US ANYWAY, WOULD YOU RATHER BE ON THE ROAD BY OURSELVES OR SAFE IN A FORTIFIED PALACE?
PALADIN WAS ABDUCTED FROM THIS PALACE!
OH, STOP IT. HE HAS ARMIES—
THEY'RE VICTOR'S ARMIES, DESSA. AND DO YOU REALLY THINK THE KING WOULD RISK WAR WITH NORTH HUNTINGTON TO PROTECT US?

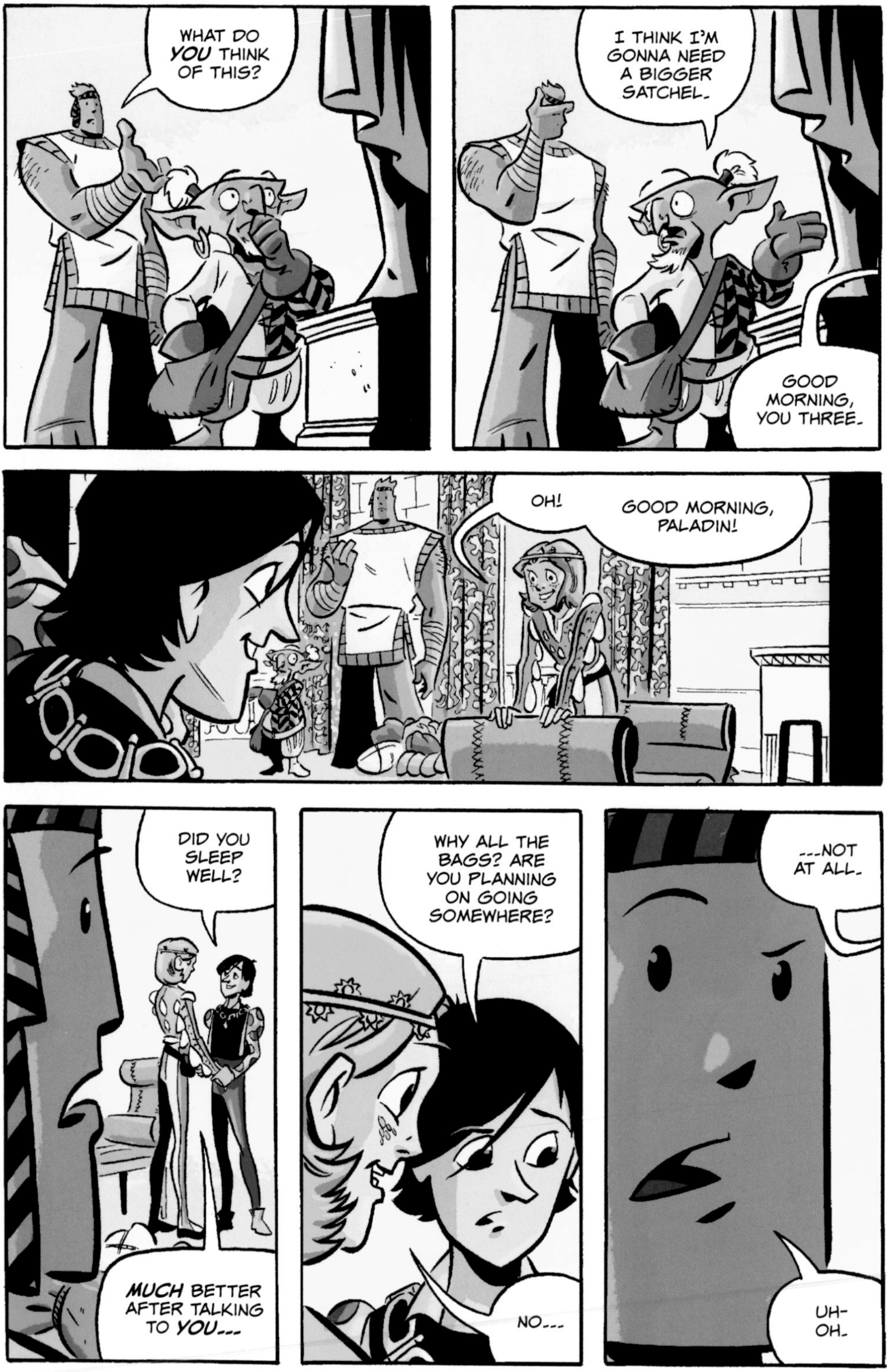
WHAT DO YOU THINK OF THIS?
I THINK I'M GONNA NEED A BIGGER SATCHEL.
GOOD MORNING, YOU THREE.
OH!
GOOD MORNING, PALADIN!
DID YOU SLEEP WELL?
MUCH BETTER AFTER TALKING TO YOU...
WHY ALL THE BAGS? ARE YOU PLANNING ON GOING SOMEWHERE?
NO...
...NOT AT ALL.
UH-OH.

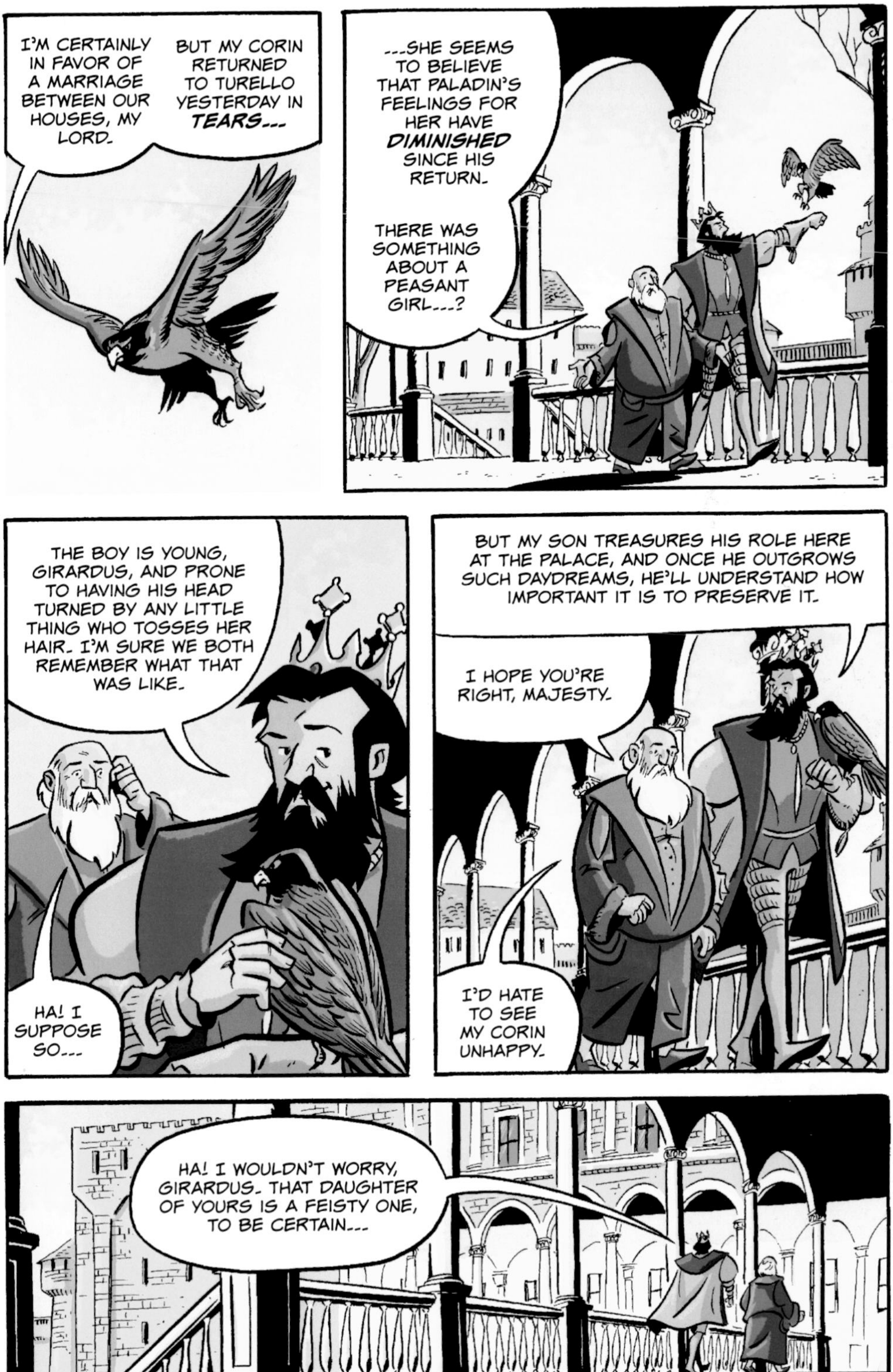
I'M CERTAINLY IN FAVOR OF A MARRIAGE BETWEEN OUR HOUSES, MY LORD.
BUT MY CORIN RETURNED TO TURELLO YESTERDAY IN TEARS...
...SHE SEEMS TO BELIEVE THAT PALADIN'S FEELINGS FOR HER HAVE DIMINISHED SINCE HIS RETURN.
THERE WAS SOMETHING ABOUT A PEASANT GIRL...?
THE BOY IS YOUNG, GIRARDUS, AND PRONE TO HAVING HIS HEAD TURNED BY ANY LITTLE THING WHO TOSSES HER HAIR. I'M SURE WE BOTH REMEMBER WHAT THAT WAS LIKE.
HA! I SUPPOSE SO...
BUT MY SON TREASURES HIS ROLE HERE AT THE PALACE, AND ONCE HE OUTGROWS SUCH DAYDREAMS, HE'LL UNDERSTAND HOW IMPORTANT IT IS TO PRESERVE IT.
I HOPE YOU'RE RIGHT, MAJESTY.
I'D HATE TO SEE MY CORIN UNHAPPY.
HA! I WOULDN'T WORRY, GIRARDUS. THAT DAUGHTER OF YOURS IS A FEISTY ONE, TO BE CERTAIN...

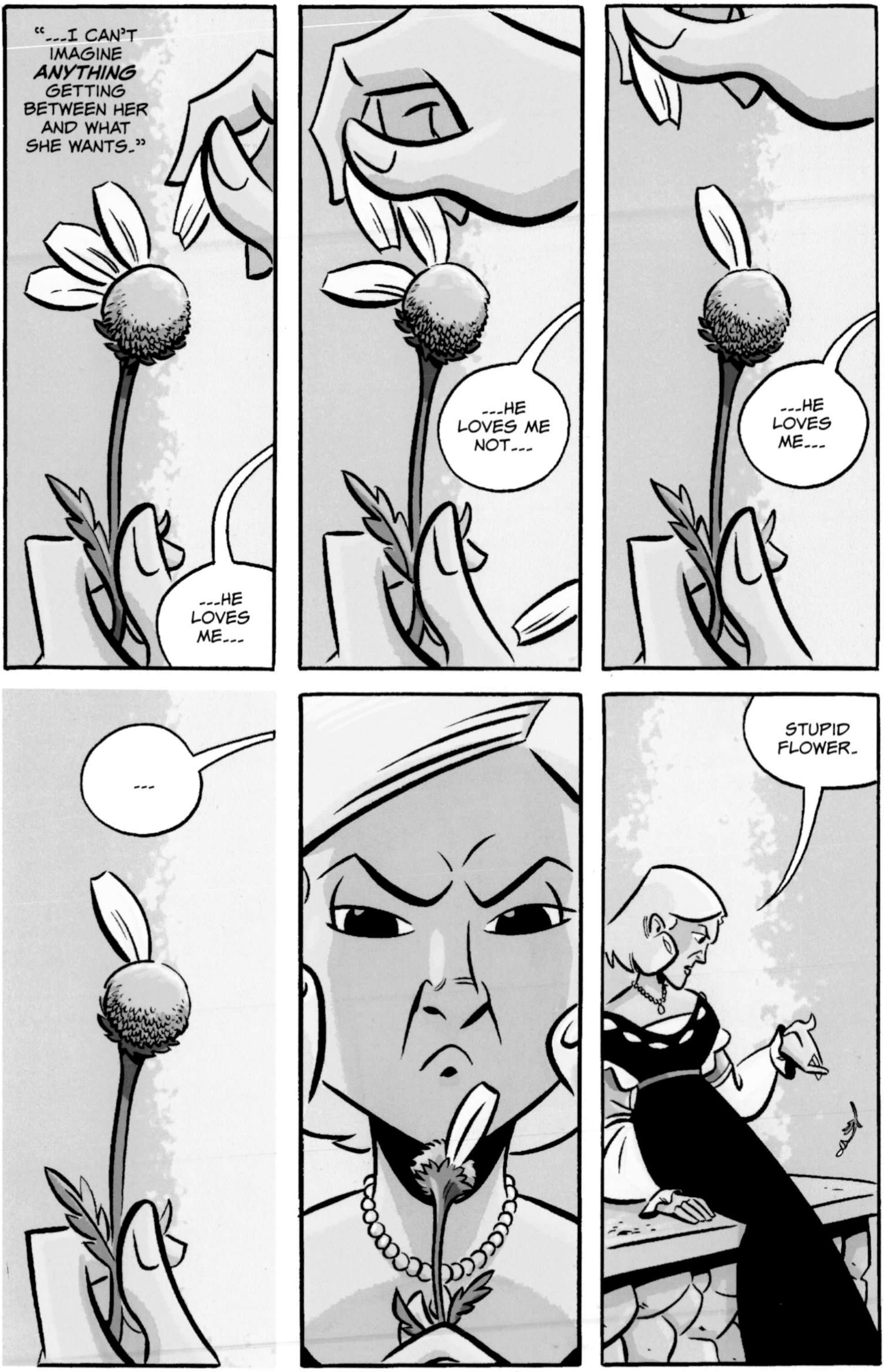
"...I CAN'T IMAGINE ANYTHING GETTING BETWEEN HER AND WHAT SHE WANTS."
...HE LOVES ME...
...HE LOVES ME NOT...
...HE LOVES ME...
...
STUPID FLOWER.

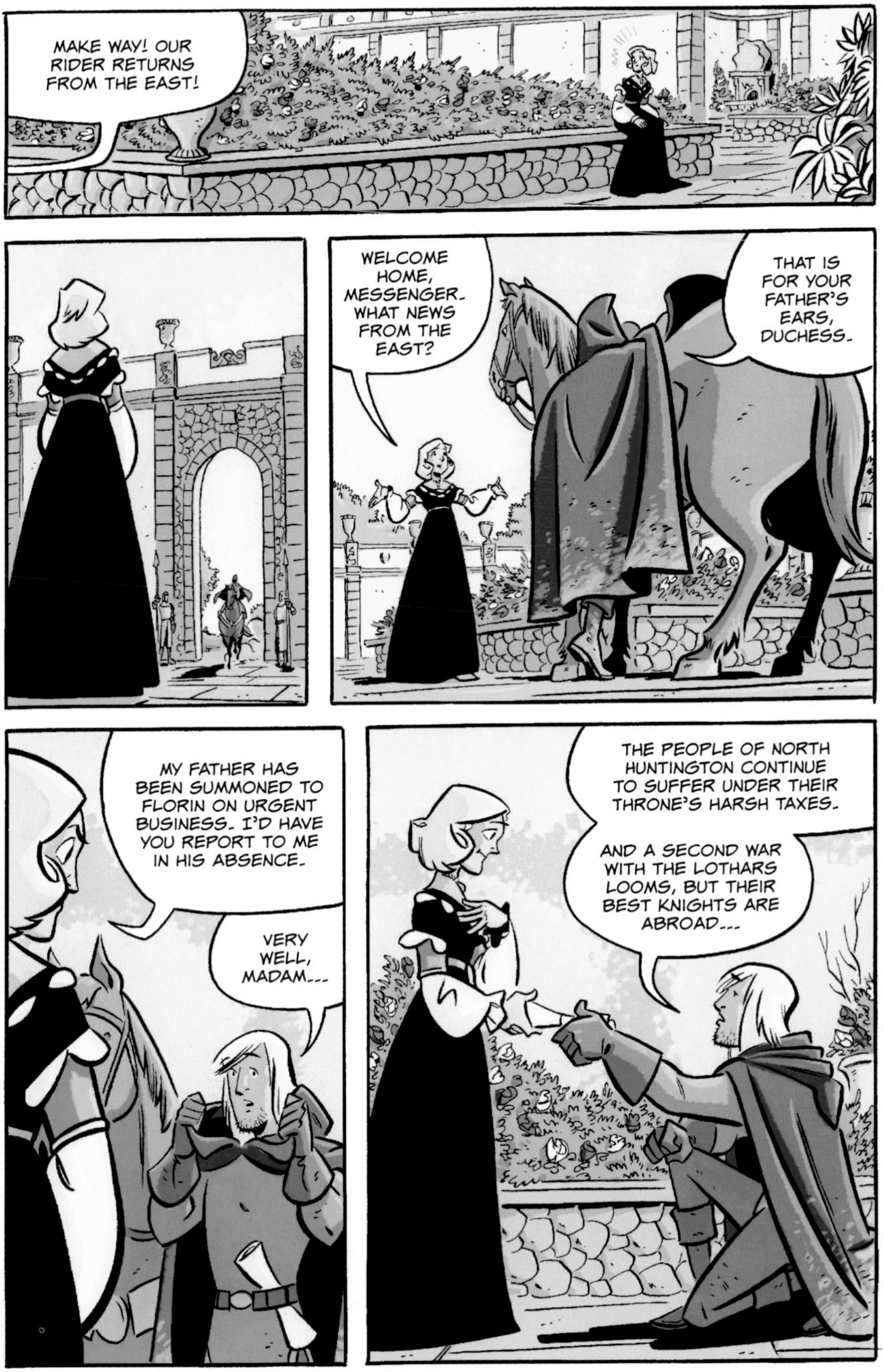
MAKE WAY! OUR RIDER RETURNS FROM THE EAST!
WELCOME HOME, MESSENGER. WHAT NEWS FROM THE EAST?
THAT IS FOR YOUR FATHER'S EARS, DUCHESS.
MY FATHER HAS BEEN SUMMONED TO FLORIN ON URGENT BUSINESS. I'D HAVE YOU REPORT TO ME IN HIS ABSENCE.
VERY WELL, MADAM...
THE PEOPLE OF NORTH HUNTINGTON CONTINUE TO SUFFER UNDER THEIR THRONE'S HARSH TAXES.
AND A SECOND WAR WITH THE LOTHARS LOOMS, BUT THEIR BEST KNIGHTS ARE ABROAD...

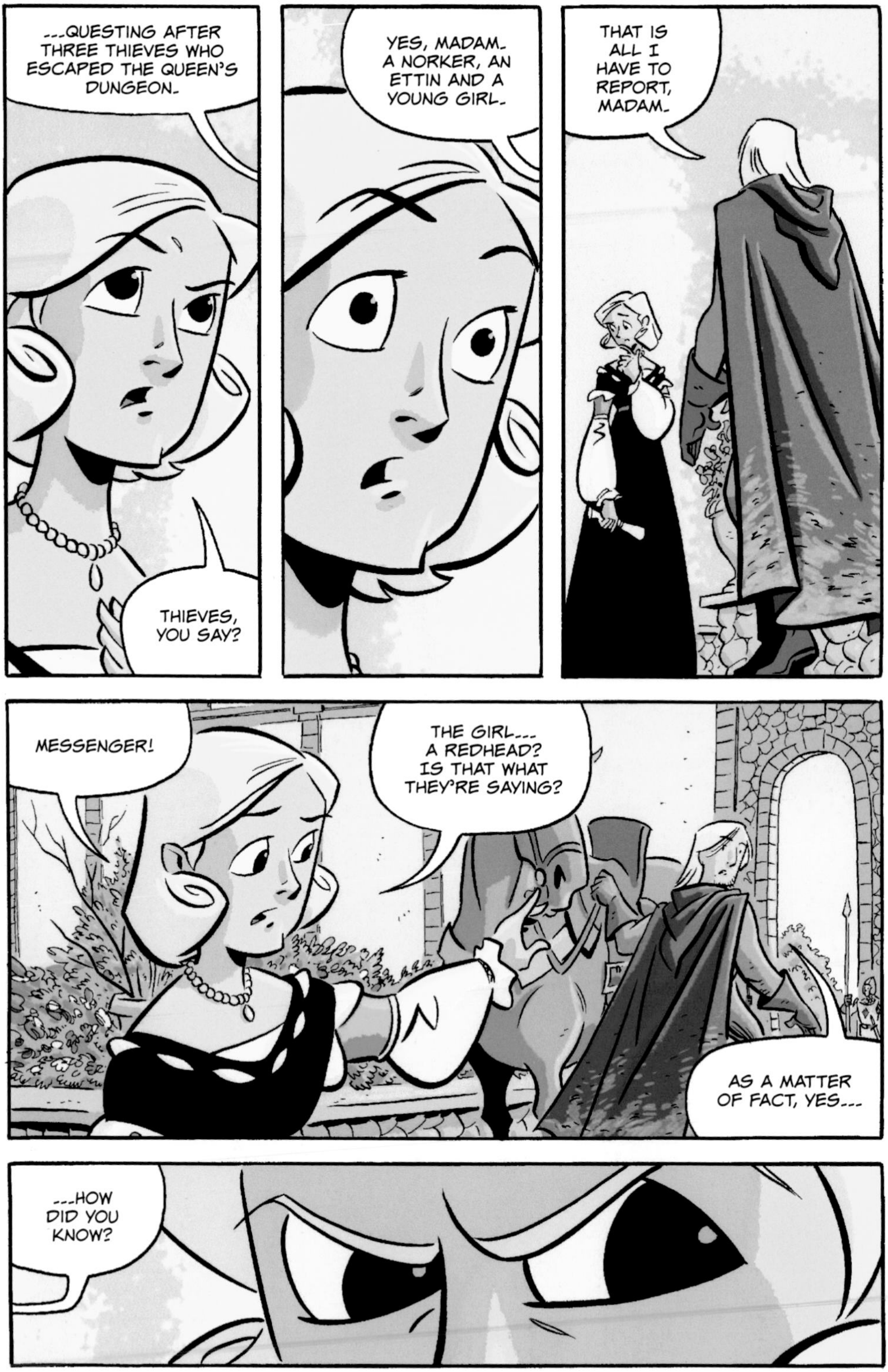
...QUESTING AFTER THREE THIEVES WHO ESCAPED THE QUEEN'S DUNGEON.
THIEVES, YOU SAY?
YES, MADAM. A NORKER, AN ETTIN AND A YOUNG GIRL.
THAT IS ALL I HAVE TO REPORT, MADAM.
MESSENGER!
THE GIRL... A REDHEAD? IS THAT WHAT THEY'RE SAYING?
AS A MATTER OF FACT, YES...
...HOW DID YOU KNOW?

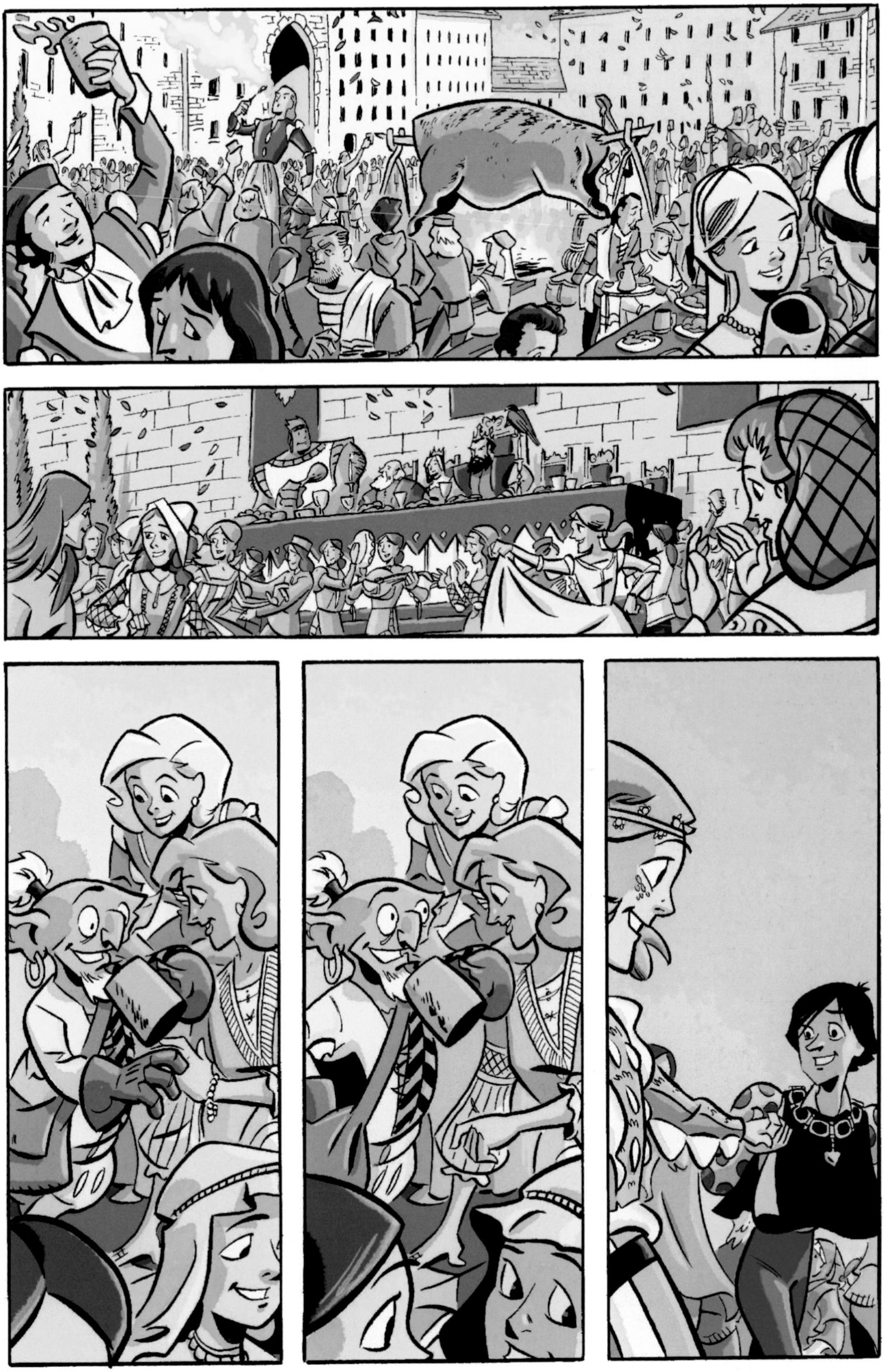

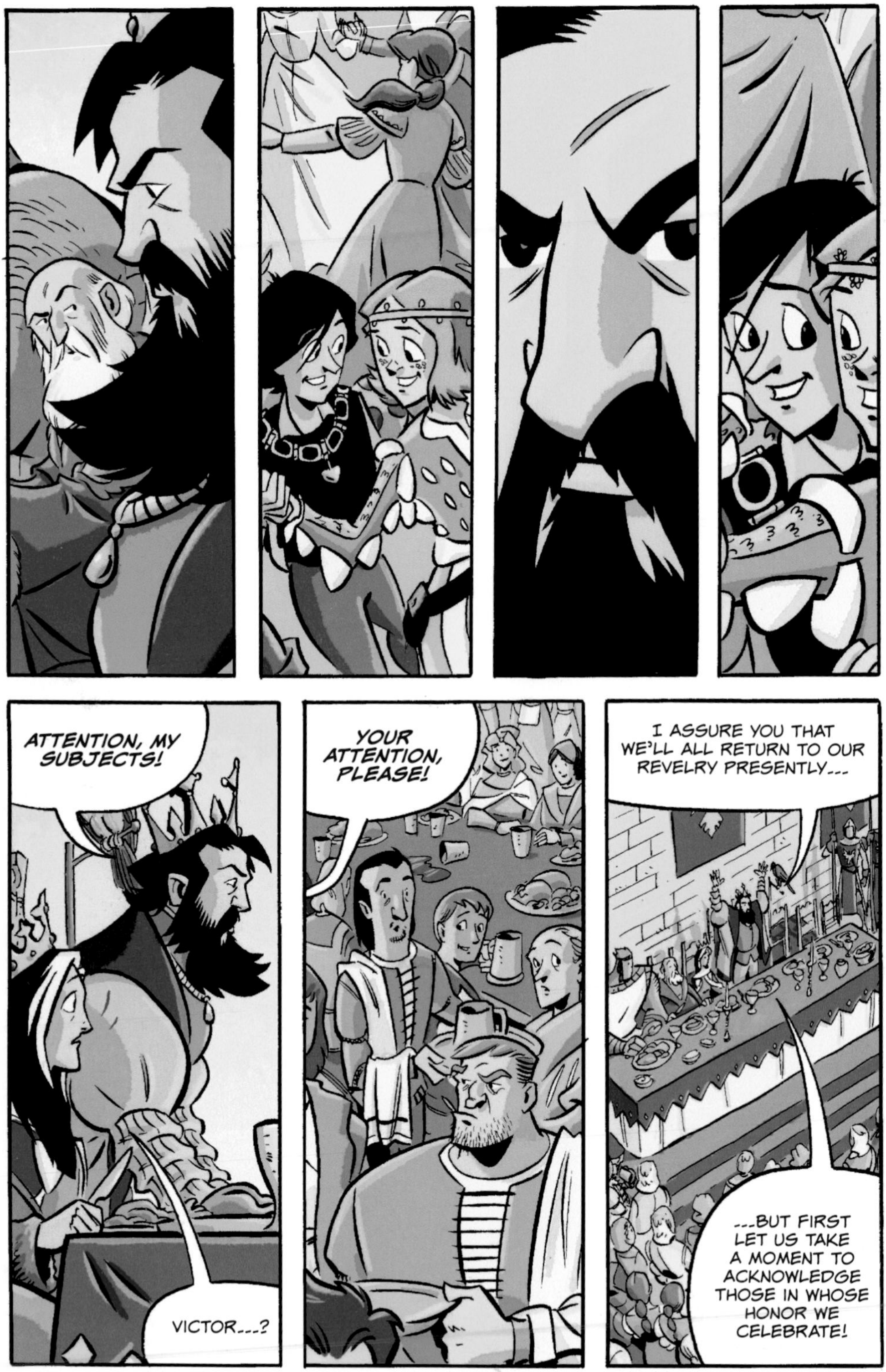
ATTENTION, MY SUBJECTS!
VICTOR...?
YOUR ATTENTION, PLEASE!
I ASSURE YOU THAT WE'LL ALL RETURN TO OUR REVELRY PRESENTLY...
...BUT FIRST LET US TAKE A MOMENT TO ACKNOWLEDGE THOSE IN WHOSE HONOR WE CELEBRATE!

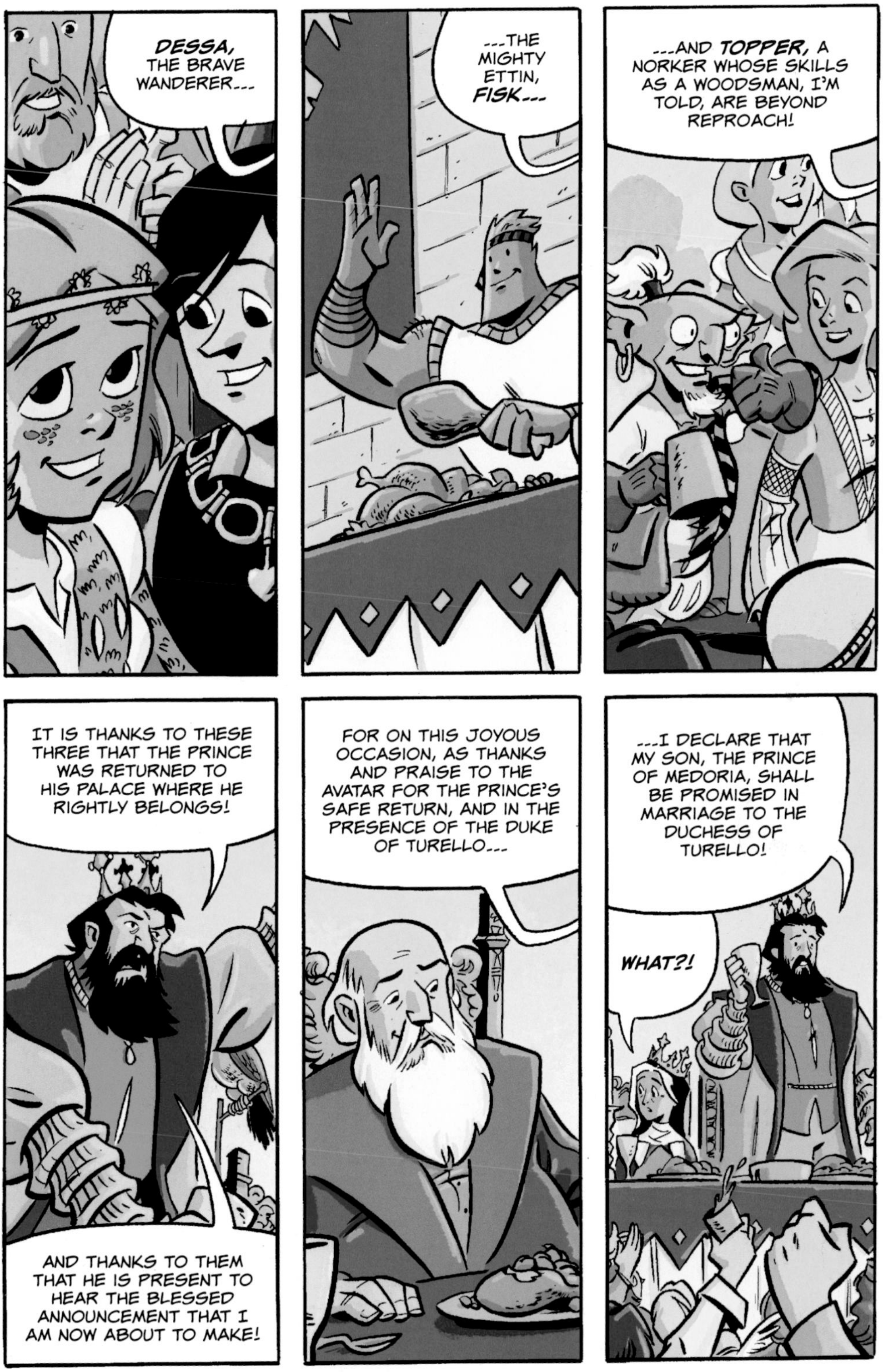
DESSA, THE BRAVE WANDERER...
...THE MIGHTY ETTIN, FISK...
...AND TOPPER, A NORKER WHOSE SKILLS AS A WOODSMAN, I'M TOLD, ARE BEYOND REPROACH!
IT IS THANKS TO THESE THREE THAT THE PRINCE WAS RETURNED TO HIS PALACE WHERE HE RIGHTLY BELONGS!
AND THANKS TO THEM THAT HE IS PRESENT TO HEAR THE BLESSED ANNOUNCEMENT THAT I AM NOW ABOUT TO MAKE!
FOR ON THIS JOYOUS OCCASION, AS THANKS AND PRAISE TO THE AVATAR FOR THE PRINCE'S SAFE RETURN, AND IN THE PRESENCE OF THE DUKE OF TURELLO...
...I DECLARE THAT MY SON, THE PRINCE OF MEDORIA, SHALL BE PROMISED IN MARRIAGE TO THE DUCHESS OF TURELLO!
WHAT?!

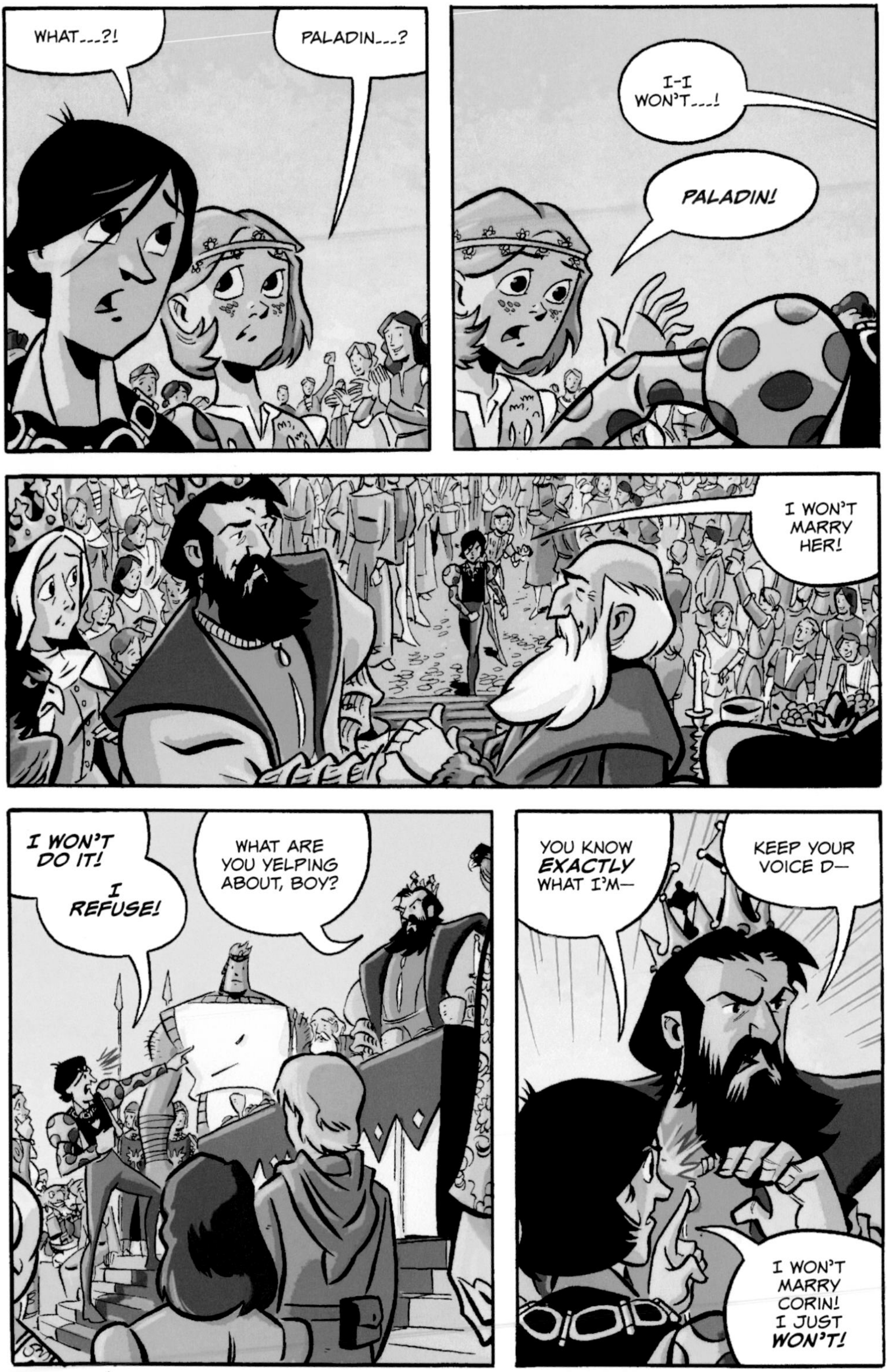
WHAT...?!
PALADIN...?
I-I WON'T...!
PALADIN!
I WON'T MARRY HER!
I WON'T DO IT!
I REFUSE!
WHAT ARE YOU YELPING ABOUT, BOY?
YOU KNOW EXACTLY WHAT I'M—
KEEP YOUR VOICE D—
I WON'T MARRY CORIN! I JUST WON'T!

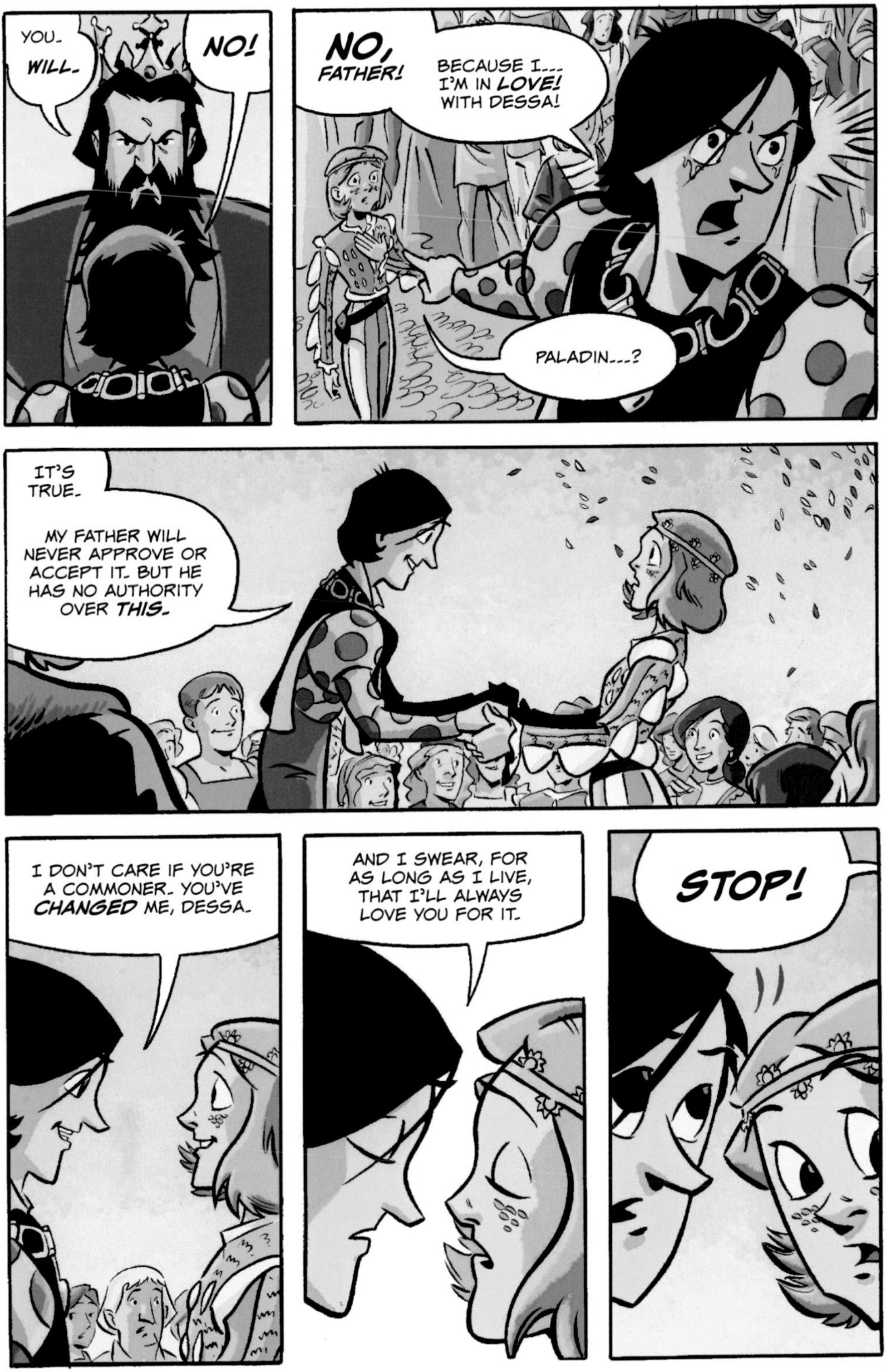
YOU... WILL...
NO!
NO, FATHER!
BECAUSE I... I'M IN LOVE! WITH DESSA!
PALADIN...?
IT'S TRUE.
MY FATHER WILL NEVER APPROVE OR ACCEPT IT. BUT HE HAS NO AUTHORITY OVER THIS.
I DON'T CARE IF YOU'RE A COMMONER. YOU'VE CHANGED ME, DESSA.
AND I SWEAR, FOR AS LONG AS I LIVE, THAT I'LL ALWAYS LOVE YOU FOR IT.
STOP!

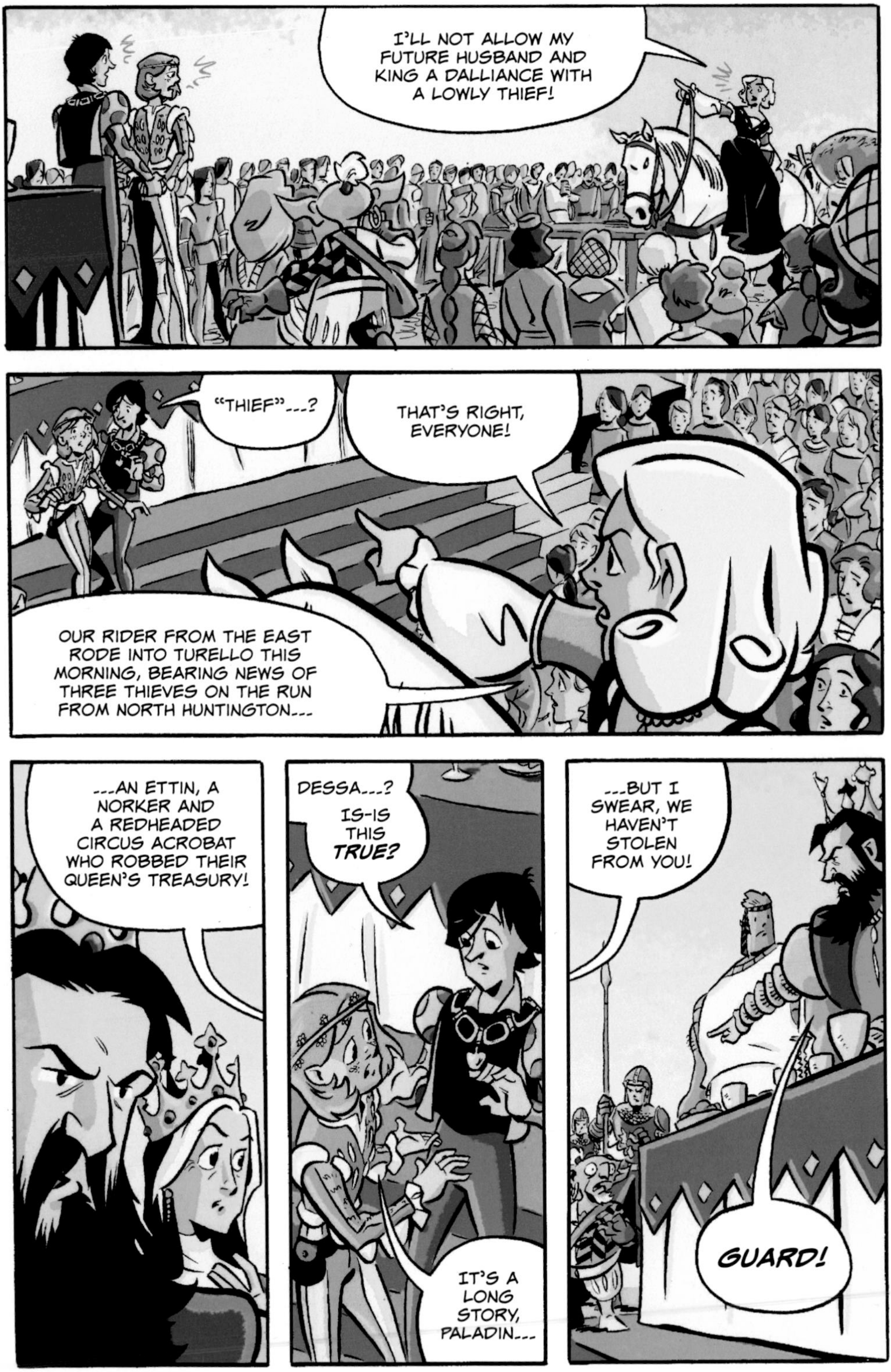
I'LL NOT ALLOW MY FUTURE HUSBAND AND KING A DALLIANCE WITH A LOWLY THIEF!
"THIEF"...?
THAT'S RIGHT, EVERYONE!
OUR RIDER FROM THE EAST RODE INTO TURELLO THIS MORNING, BEARING NEWS OF THREE THIEVES ON THE RUN FROM NORTH HUNTINGTON...
...AN ETTIN, A NORKER AND A REDHEADED CIRCUS ACROBAT WHO ROBBED THEIR QUEEN'S TREASURY!
DESSA...?
IS-IS THIS TRUE?
IT'S A LONG STORY, PALADIN...
...BUT I SWEAR, WE HAVEN'T STOLEN FROM YOU!
GUARD!

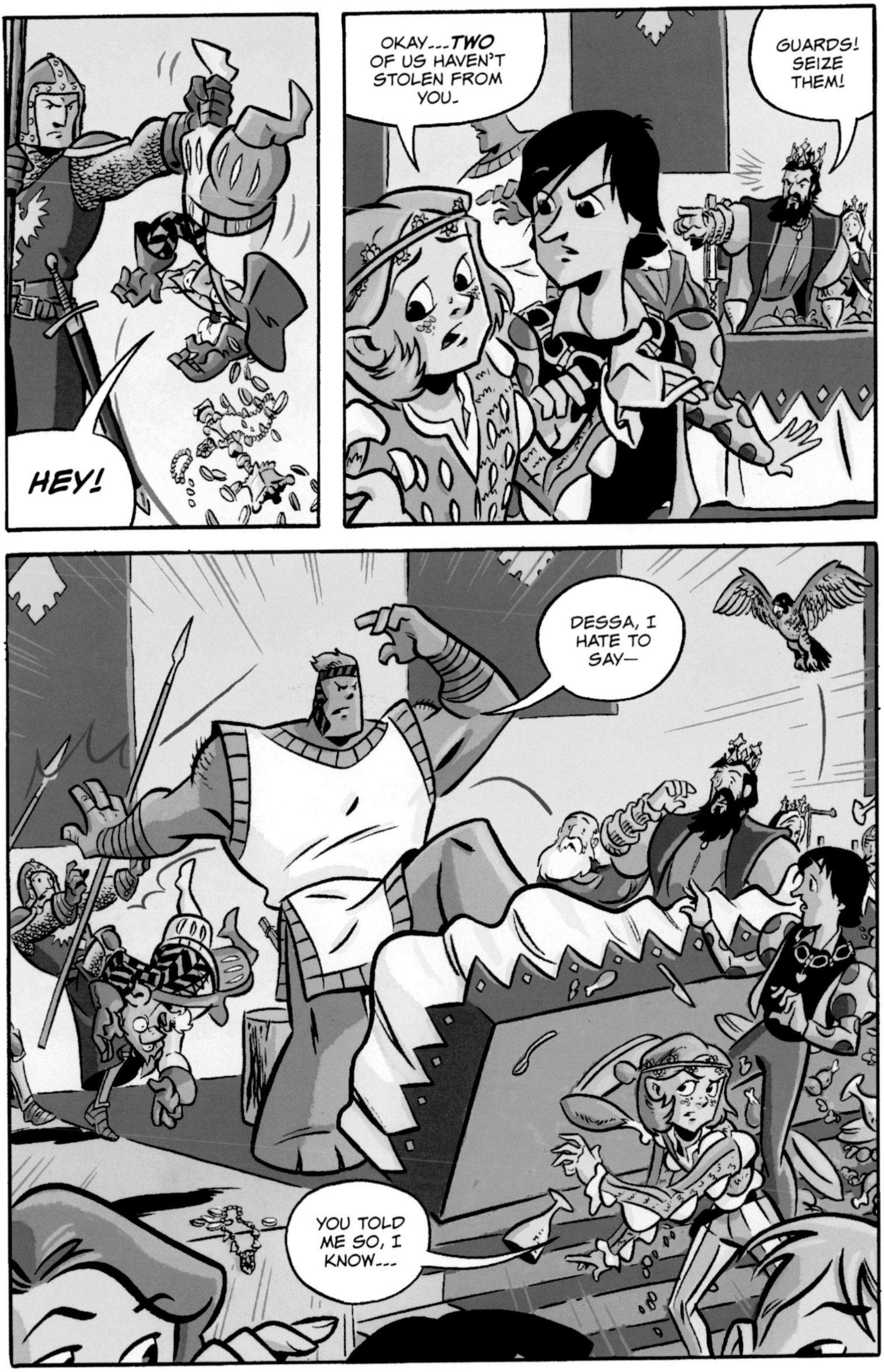
HEY!
OKAY...TWO OF US HAVEN'T STOLEN FROM YOU.
GUARDS! SEIZE THEM!
DESSA, I HATE TO SAY—
YOU TOLD ME SO, I KNOW...

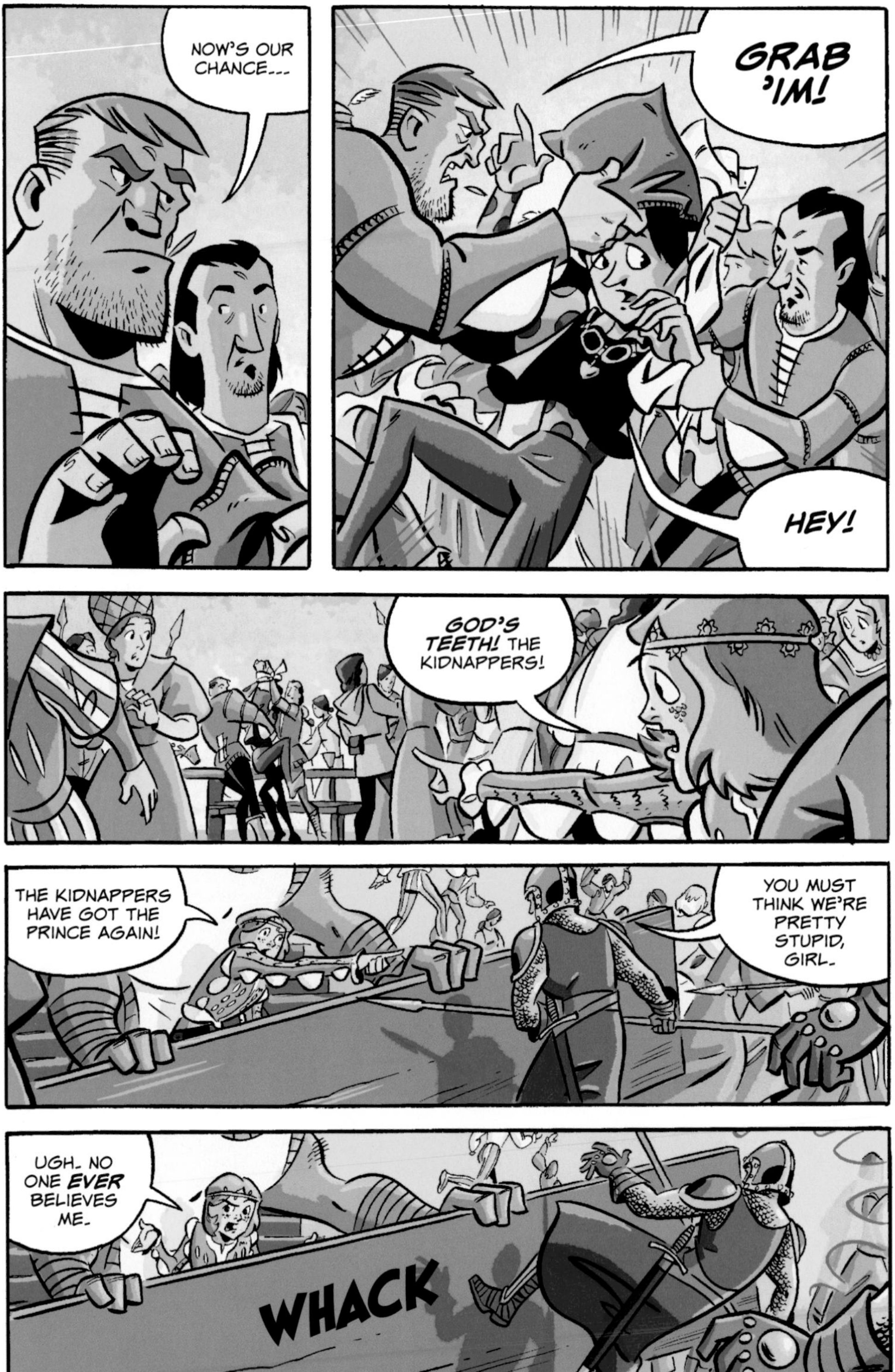
NOW'S OUR CHANCE...
GRAB 'IM!
HEY!
GOD'S TEETH! THE KIDNAPPERS!
THE KIDNAPPERS HAVE GOT THE PRINCE AGAIN!
YOU MUST THINK WE'RE PRETTY STUPID, GIRL.
UGH. NO ONE EVER BELIEVES ME.
WHACK

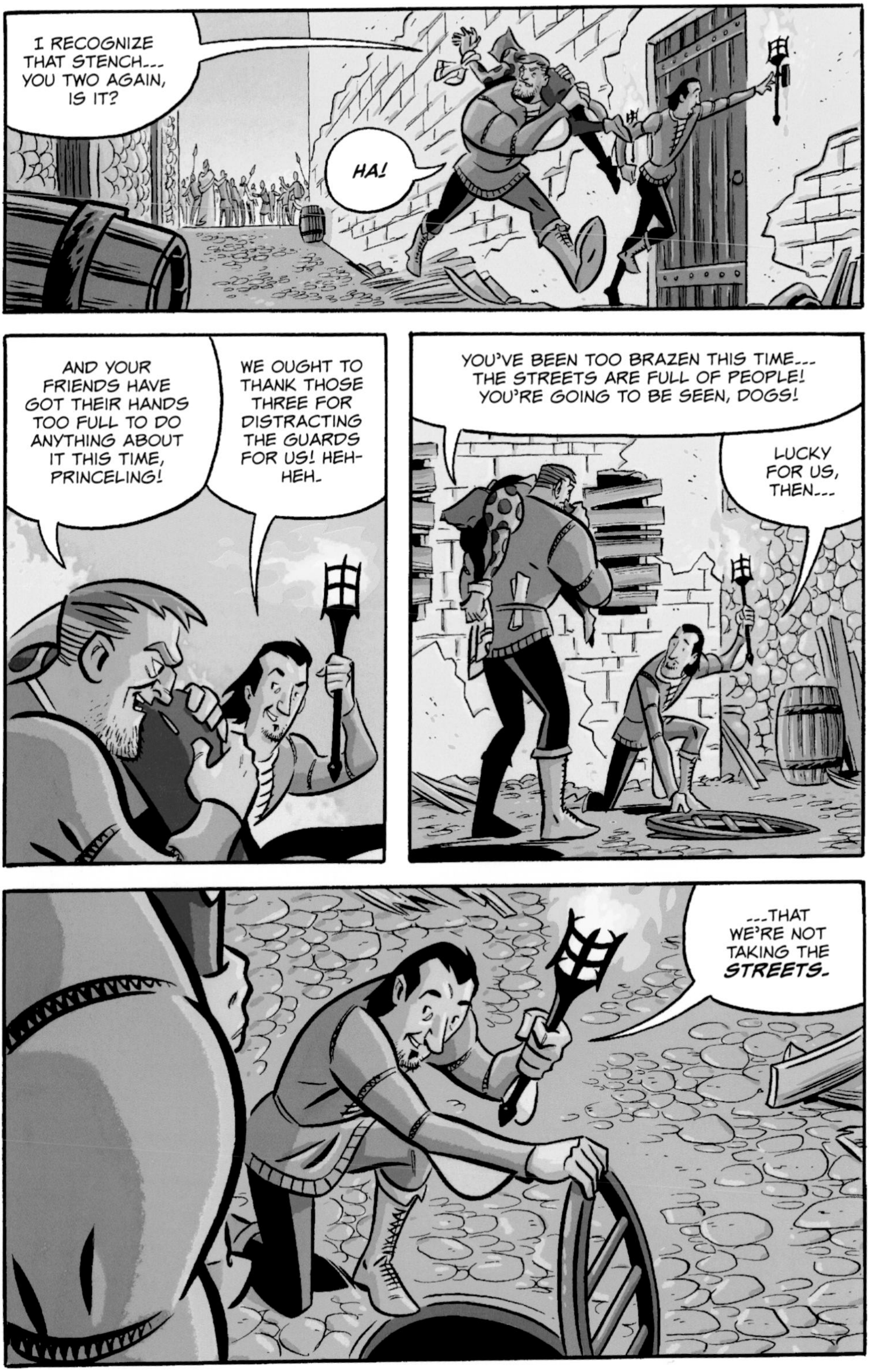
I RECOGNIZE THAT STENCH... YOU TWO AGAIN, IS IT?
HA!
AND YOUR FRIENDS HAVE GOT THEIR HANDS TOO FULL TO DO ANYTHING ABOUT IT THIS TIME, PRINCELING!
WE OUGHT TO THANK THOSE THREE FOR DISTRACTING THE GUARDS FOR US! HEH-HEH.
YOU'VE BEEN TOO BRAZEN THIS TIME... THE STREETS ARE FULL OF PEOPLE! YOU'RE GOING TO BE SEEN, DOGS!
LUCKY FOR US, THEN...
...THAT WE'RE NOT TAKING THE ***STREETS***.

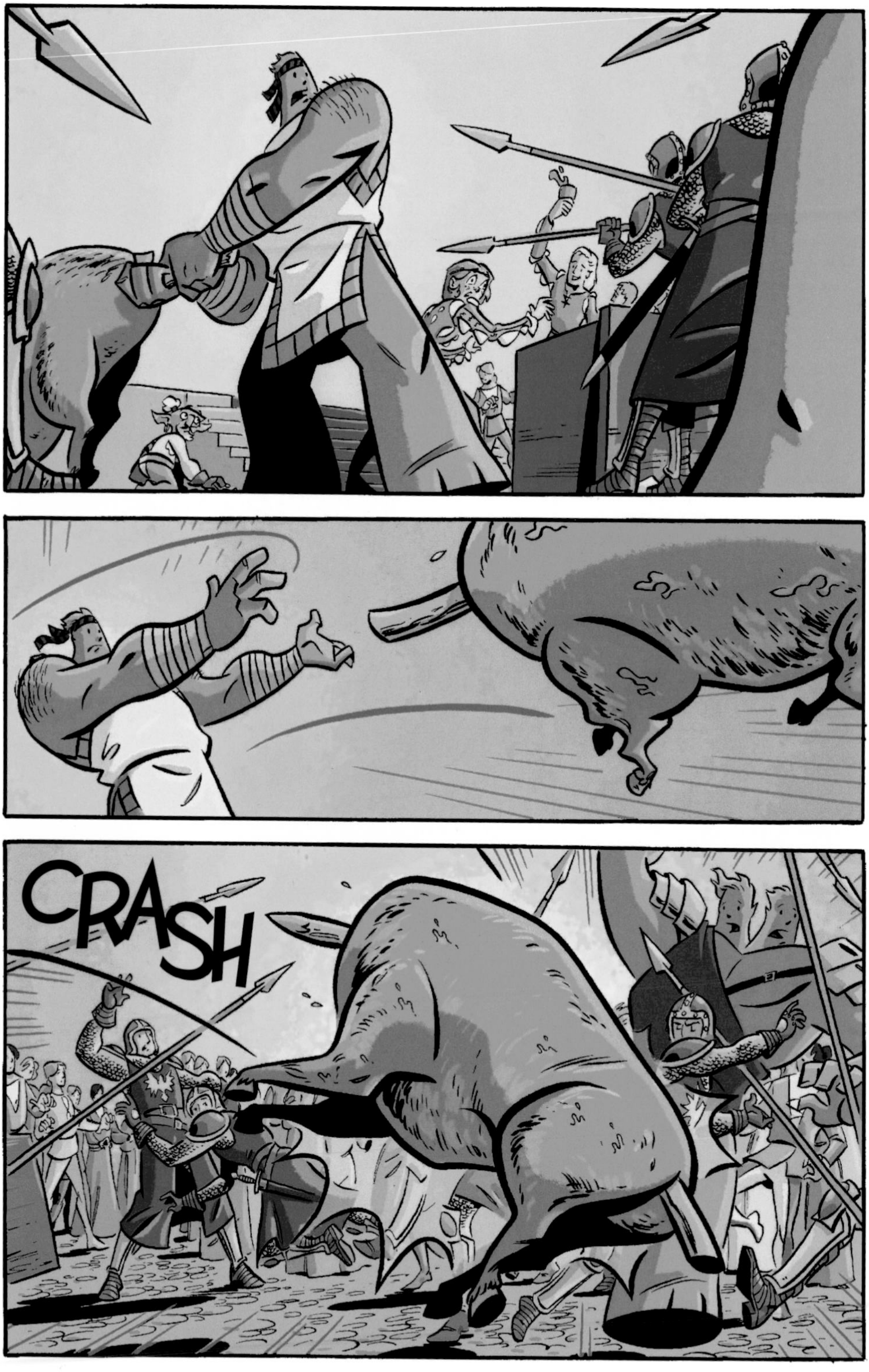
CRASH

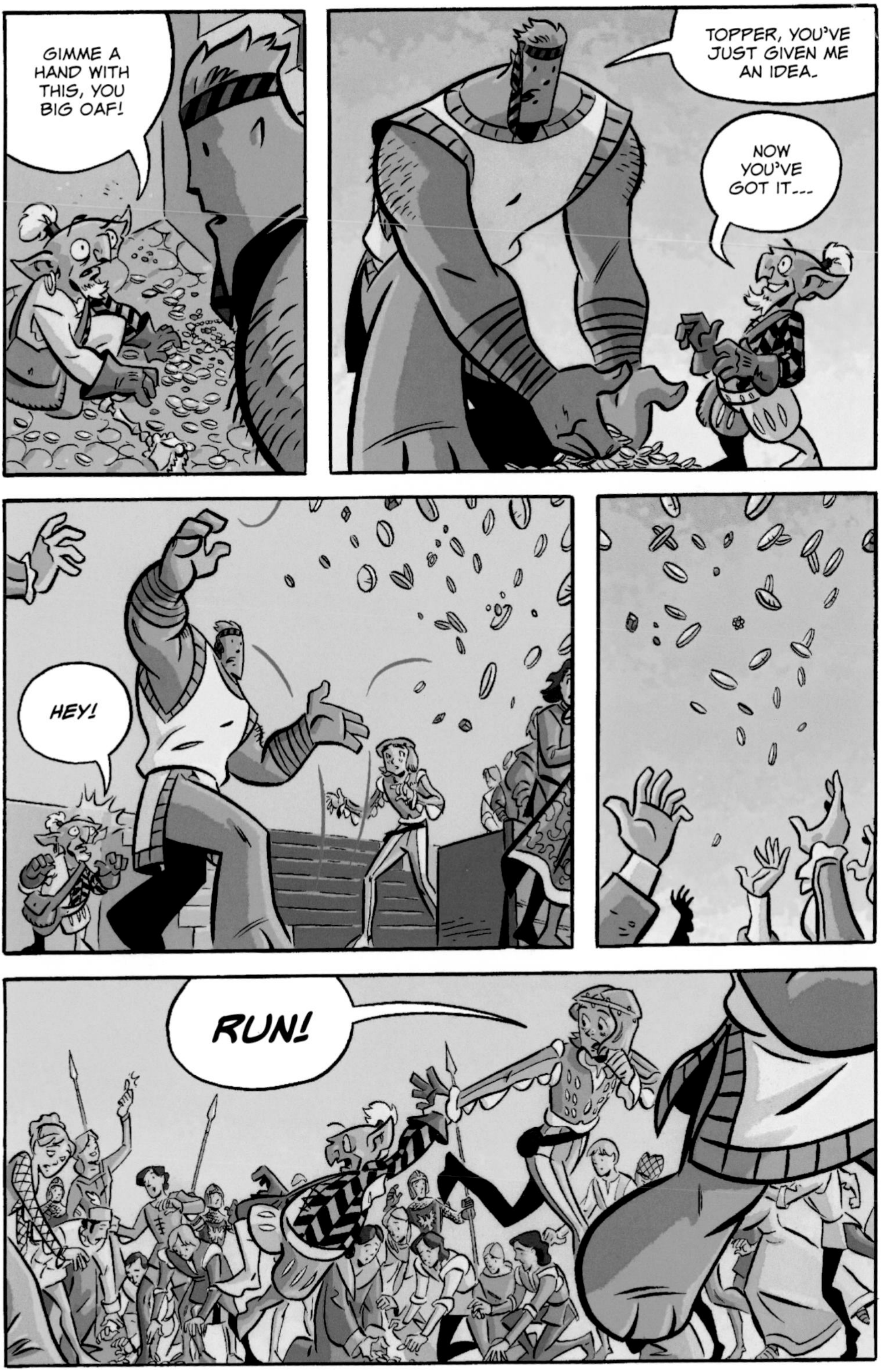
GIMME A HAND WITH THIS, YOU BIG OAF!
TOPPER, YOU'VE JUST GIVEN ME AN IDEA.
NOW YOU'VE GOT IT...
HEY!
RUN!

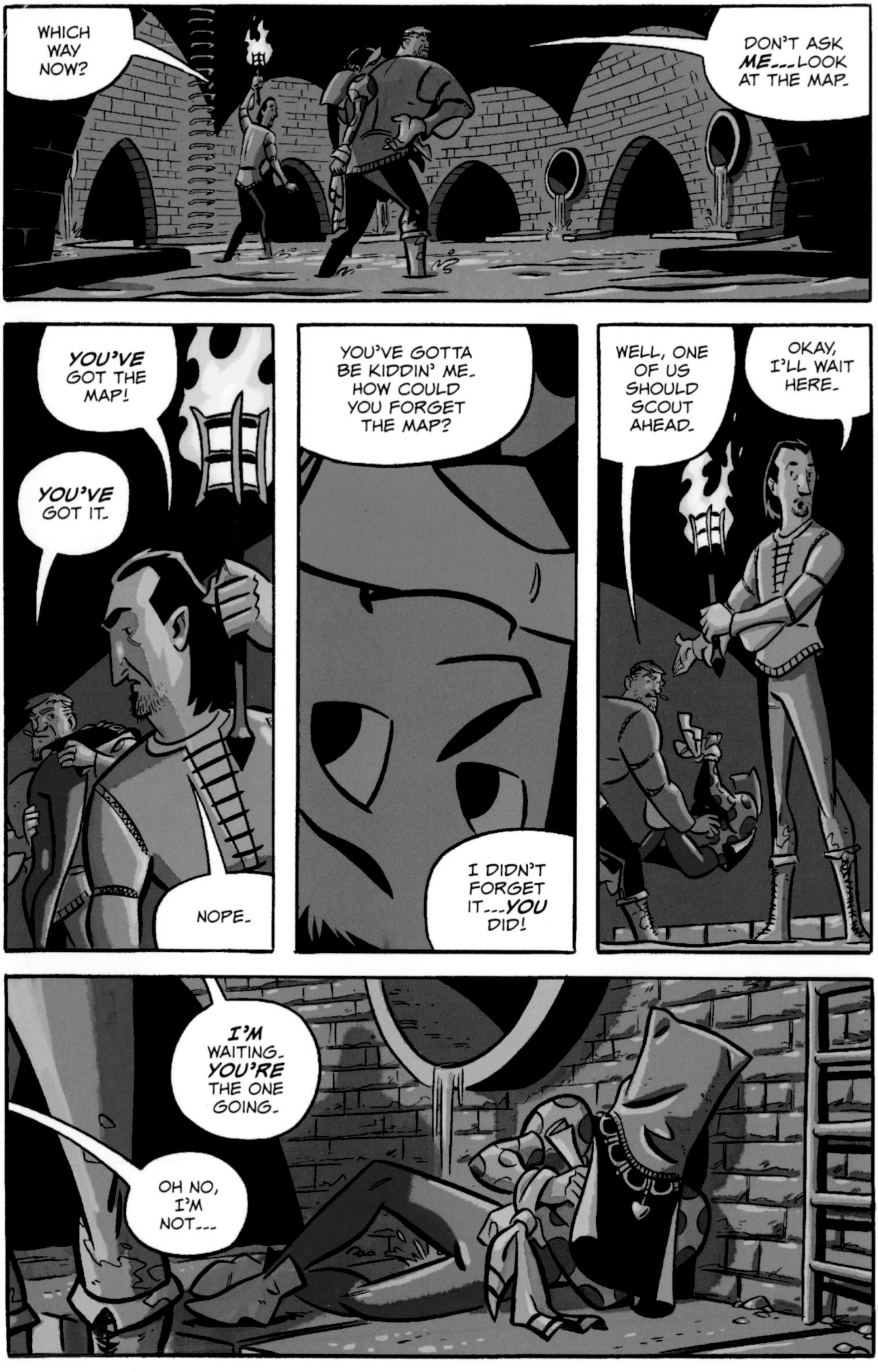
WHICH WAY NOW?
DON'T ASK *ME*...LOOK AT THE MAP.
YOU'VE GOT THE MAP!
YOU'VE GOT IT.
NOPE.
YOU'VE GOTTA BE KIDDIN' ME. HOW COULD YOU FORGET THE MAP?
I DIDN'T FORGET IT...*YOU* DID!
WELL, ONE OF US SHOULD SCOUT AHEAD.
OKAY, I'LL WAIT HERE.
I'M WAITING. *YOU'RE* THE ONE GOING.
OH NO, I'M NOT...

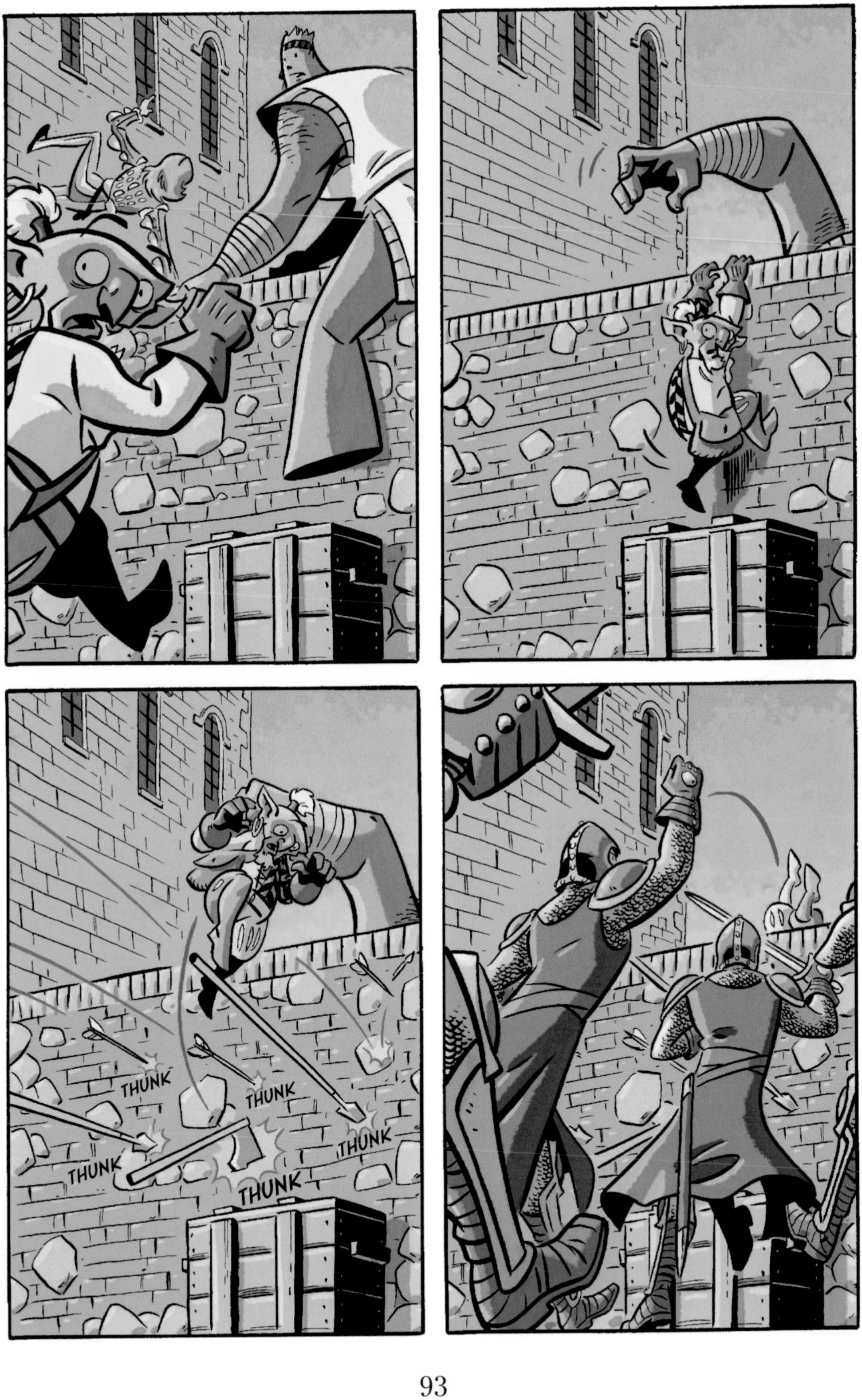
THUNK
THUNK
THUNK
THUNK
THUNK

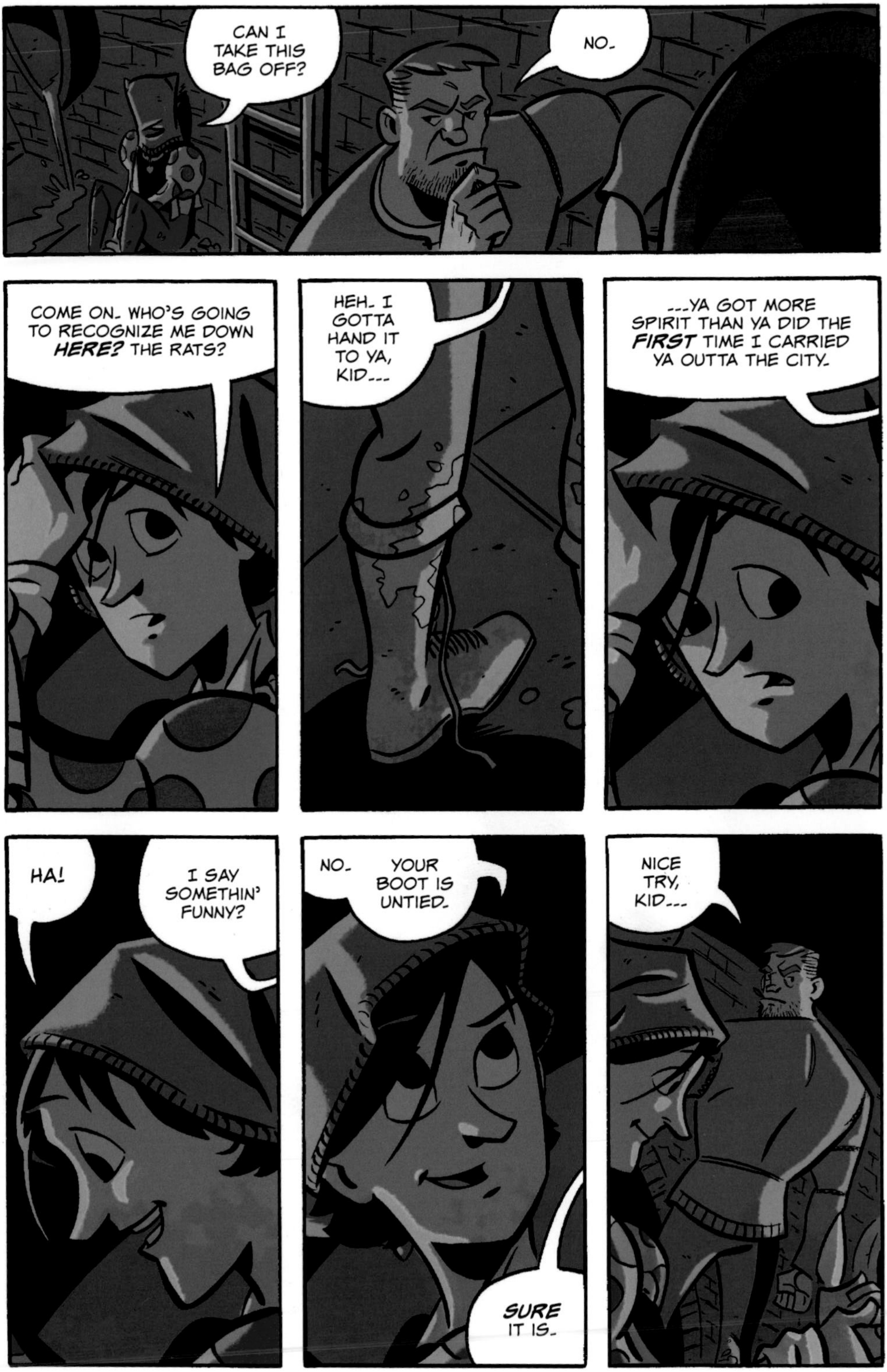
CAN I TAKE THIS BAG OFF?
NO.
COME ON. WHO'S GOING TO RECOGNIZE ME DOWN *HERE?* THE RATS?
HEH. I GOTTA HAND IT TO YA, KID...
...YA GOT MORE SPIRIT THAN YA DID THE *FIRST* TIME I CARRIED YA OUTTA THE CITY.
HA!
I SAY SOMETHIN' FUNNY?
NO.
YOUR BOOT IS UNTIED.
SURE IT IS.
NICE TRY, KID...

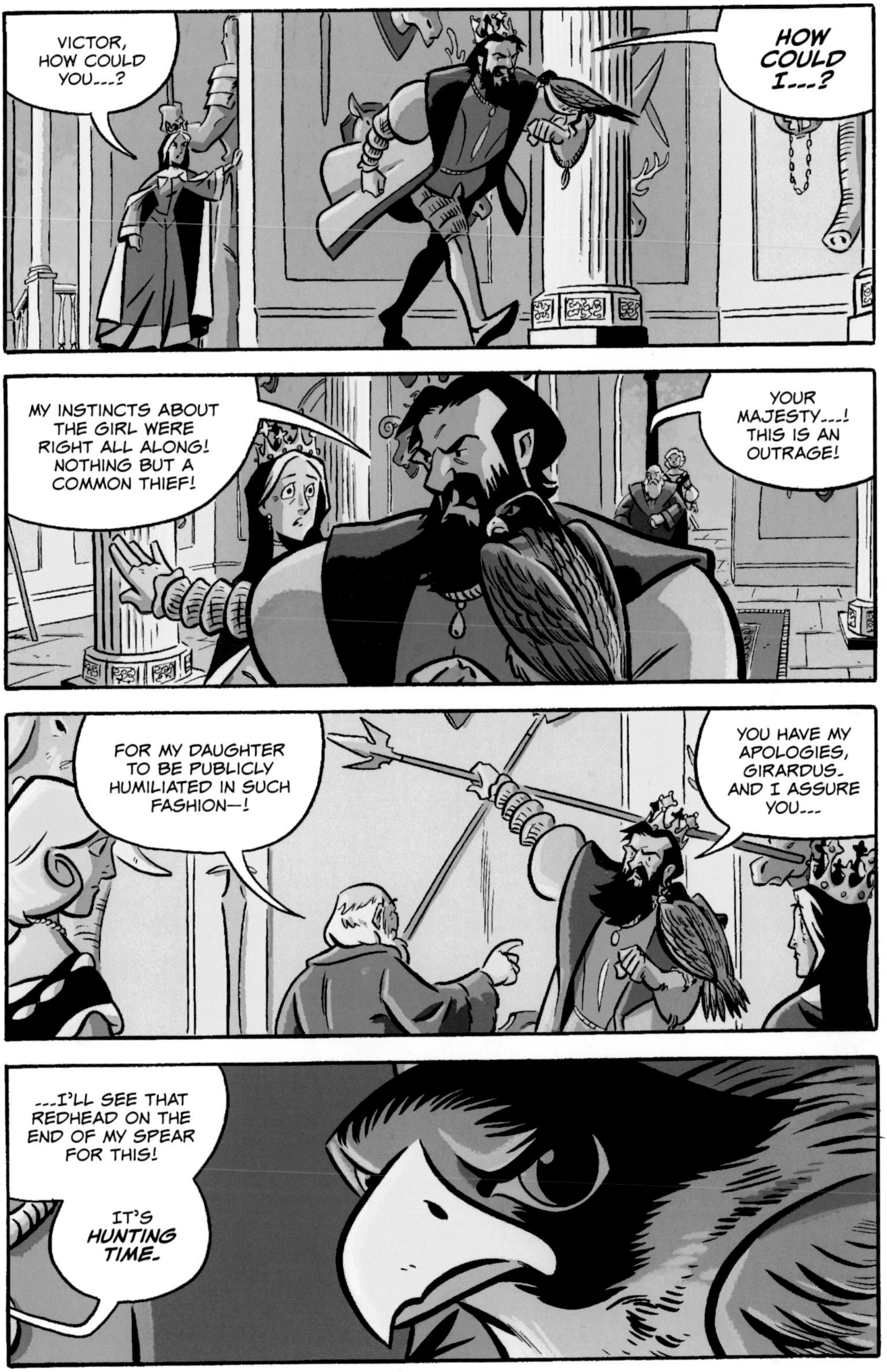
VICTOR, HOW COULD YOU...?
HOW COULD I...?
MY INSTINCTS ABOUT THE GIRL WERE RIGHT ALL ALONG! NOTHING BUT A COMMON THIEF!
YOUR MAJESTY...! THIS IS AN OUTRAGE!
FOR MY DAUGHTER TO BE PUBLICLY HUMILIATED IN SUCH FASHION—!
YOU HAVE MY APOLOGIES, GIRARDUS. AND I ASSURE YOU...
...I'LL SEE THAT REDHEAD ON THE END OF MY SPEAR FOR THIS!
IT'S HUNTING TIME.

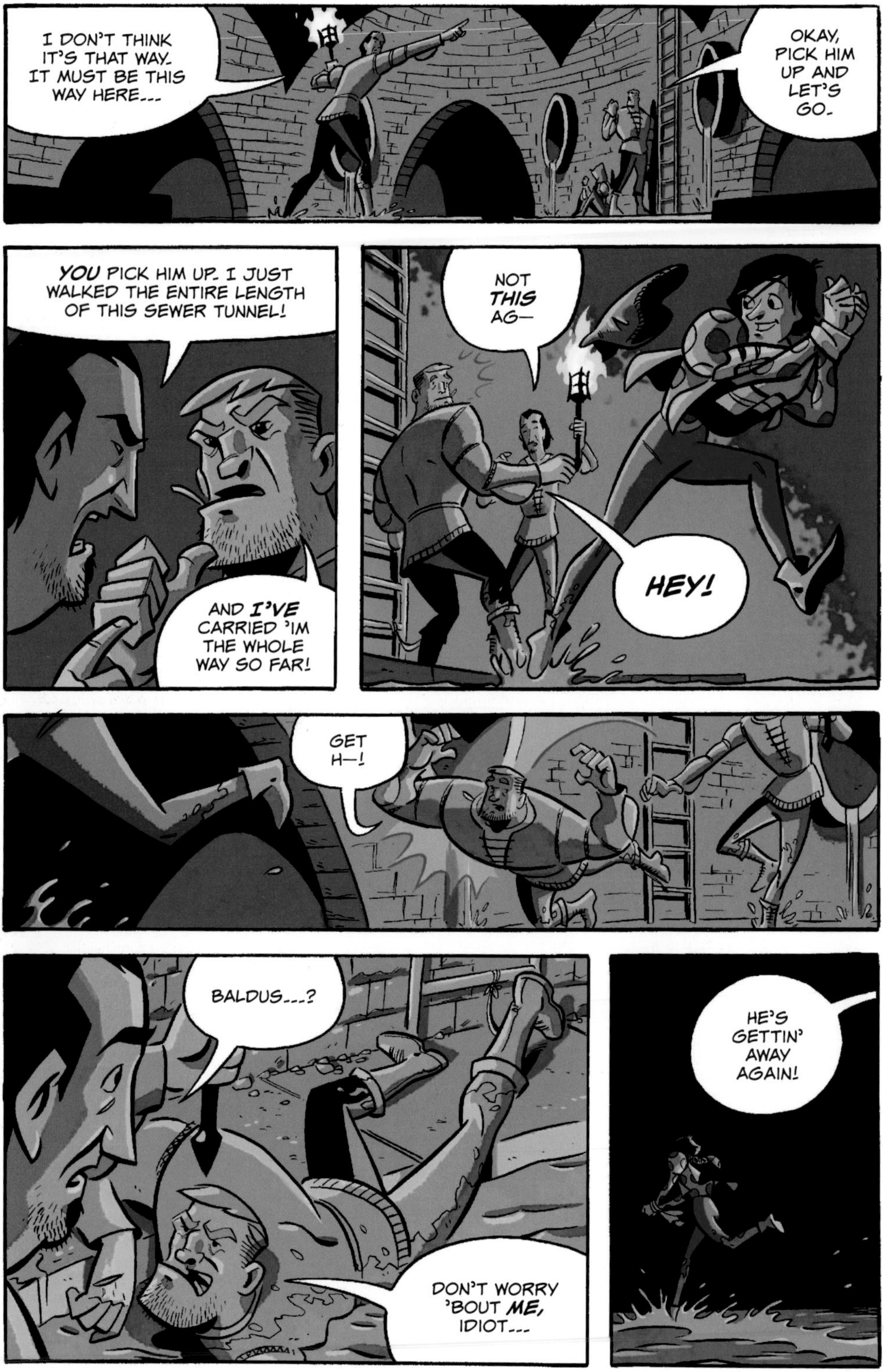
I DON'T THINK IT'S THAT WAY. IT MUST BE THIS WAY HERE...
OKAY, PICK HIM UP AND LET'S GO.
YOU PICK HIM UP. I JUST WALKED THE ENTIRE LENGTH OF THIS SEWER TUNNEL!
AND I'VE CARRIED 'IM THE WHOLE WAY SO FAR!
NOT THIS AG—
HEY!
GET H—!
BALDUS...?
DON'T WORRY 'BOUT ME, IDIOT...
HE'S GETTIN' AWAY AGAIN!

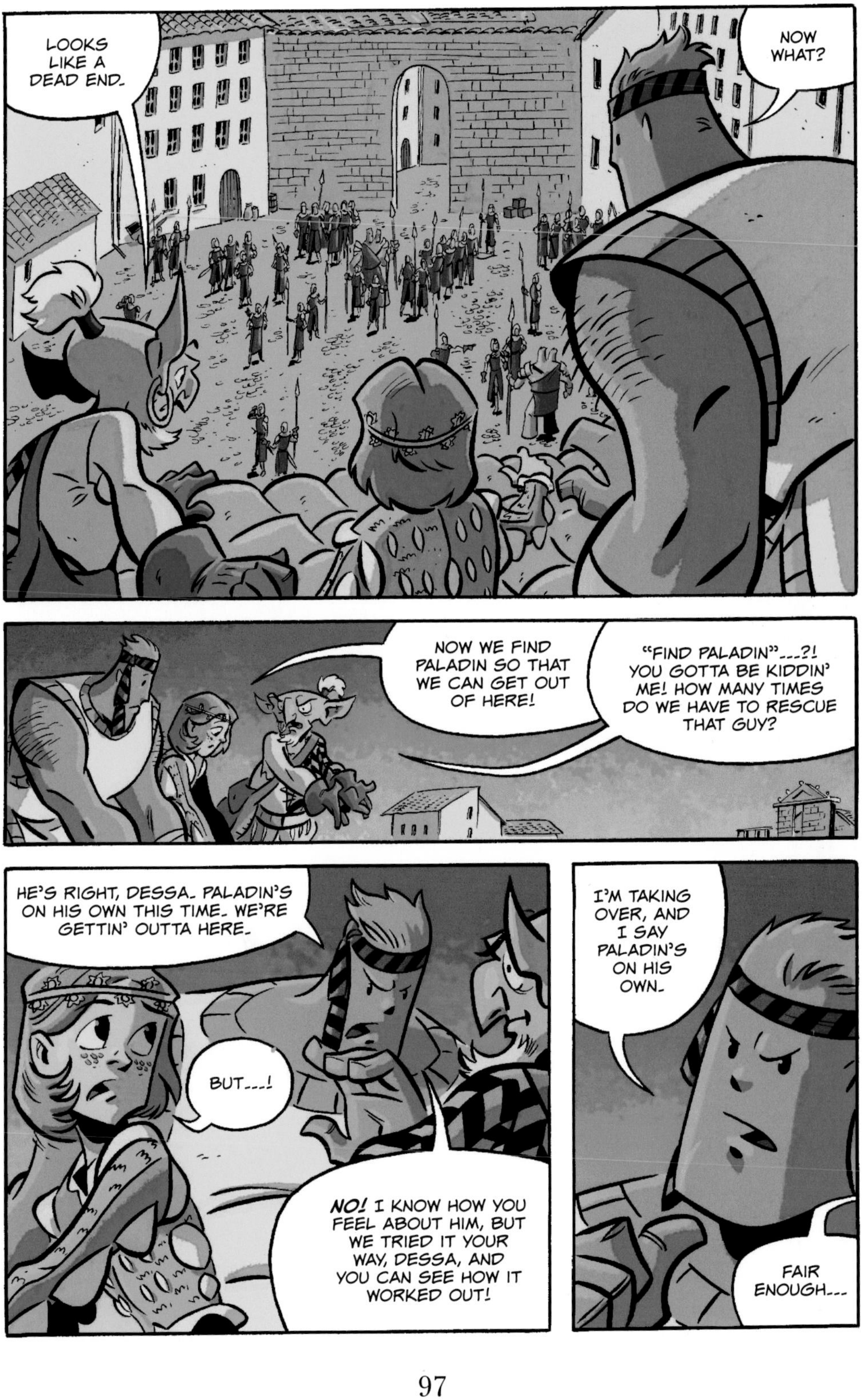

LOOKS LIKE A DEAD END.
NOW WHAT?
NOW WE FIND PALADIN SO THAT WE CAN GET OUT OF HERE!
"FIND PALADIN"...?! YOU GOTTA BE KIDDIN' ME! HOW MANY TIMES DO WE HAVE TO RESCUE THAT GUY?
HE'S RIGHT, DESSA. PALADIN'S ON HIS OWN THIS TIME. WE'RE GETTIN' OUTTA HERE.
BUT...!
NO! I KNOW HOW YOU FEEL ABOUT HIM, BUT WE TRIED IT YOUR WAY, DESSA, AND YOU CAN SEE HOW IT WORKED OUT!
I'M TAKING OVER, AND I SAY PALADIN'S ON HIS OWN.
FAIR ENOUGH...

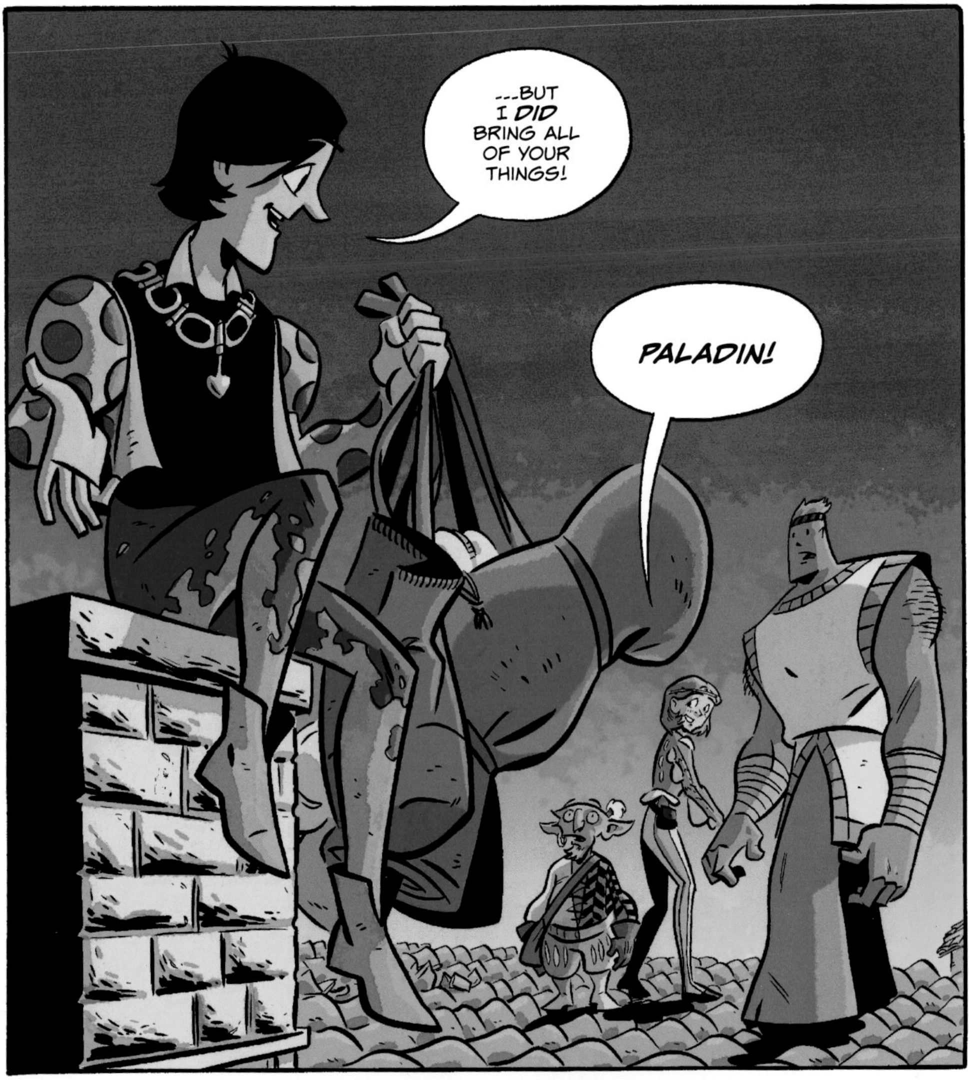
...BUT I *DID* BRING ALL OF YOUR THINGS!
PALADIN!

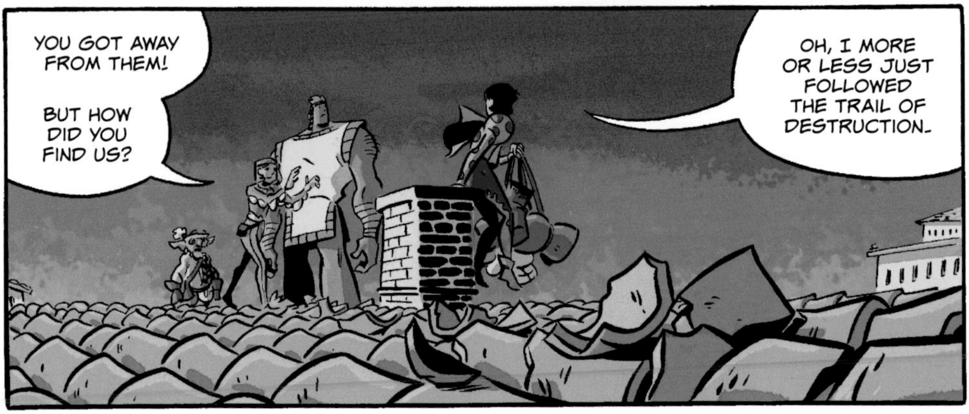
YOU GOT AWAY FROM THEM!
BUT HOW DID YOU FIND US?
OH, I MORE OR LESS JUST FOLLOWED THE TRAIL OF DESTRUCTION.

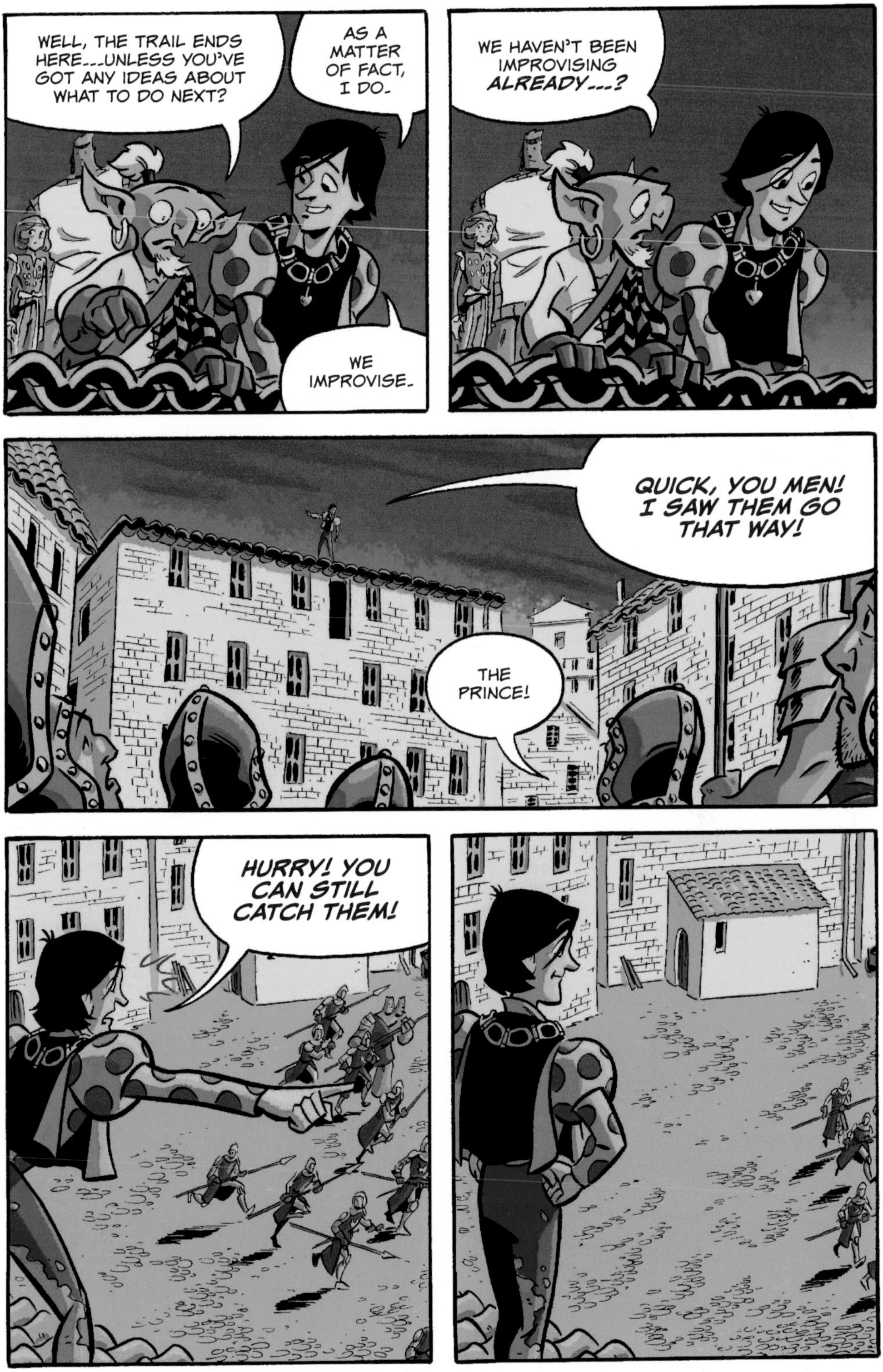
WELL, THE TRAIL ENDS HERE...UNLESS YOU'VE GOT ANY IDEAS ABOUT WHAT TO DO NEXT?
AS A MATTER OF FACT, I DO.
WE IMPROVISE.
WE HAVEN'T BEEN IMPROVISING ALREADY...?
QUICK, YOU MEN! I SAW THEM GO THAT WAY!
THE PRINCE!
HURRY! YOU CAN STILL CATCH THEM!

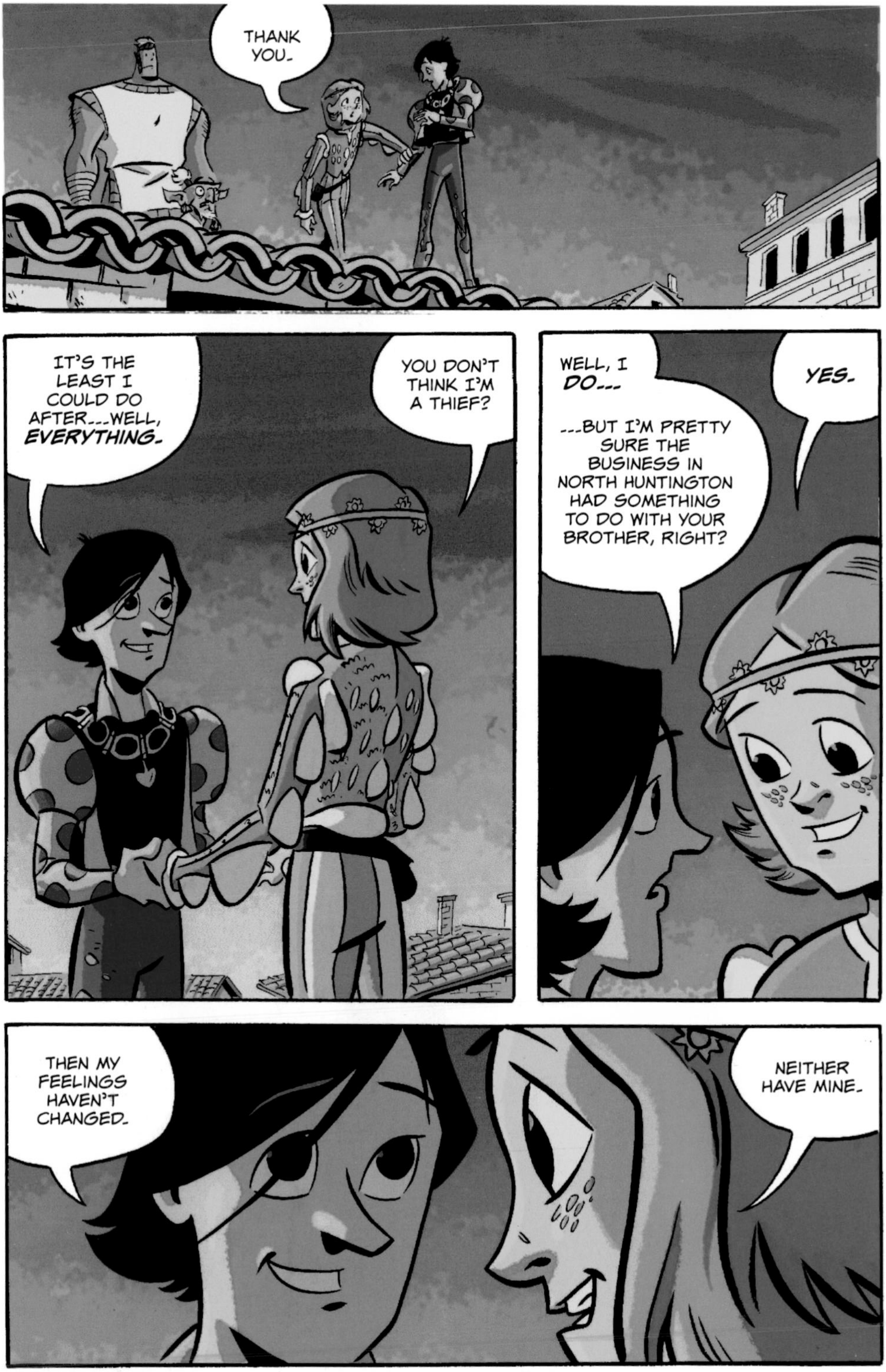
THANK YOU.
IT'S THE LEAST I COULD DO AFTER...WELL, *EVERYTHING.*
YOU DON'T THINK I'M A THIEF?
WELL, I *DO...*
...BUT I'M PRETTY SURE THE BUSINESS IN NORTH HUNTINGTON HAD SOMETHING TO DO WITH YOUR BROTHER, RIGHT?
YES.
THEN MY FEELINGS HAVEN'T CHANGED.
NEITHER HAVE MINE.

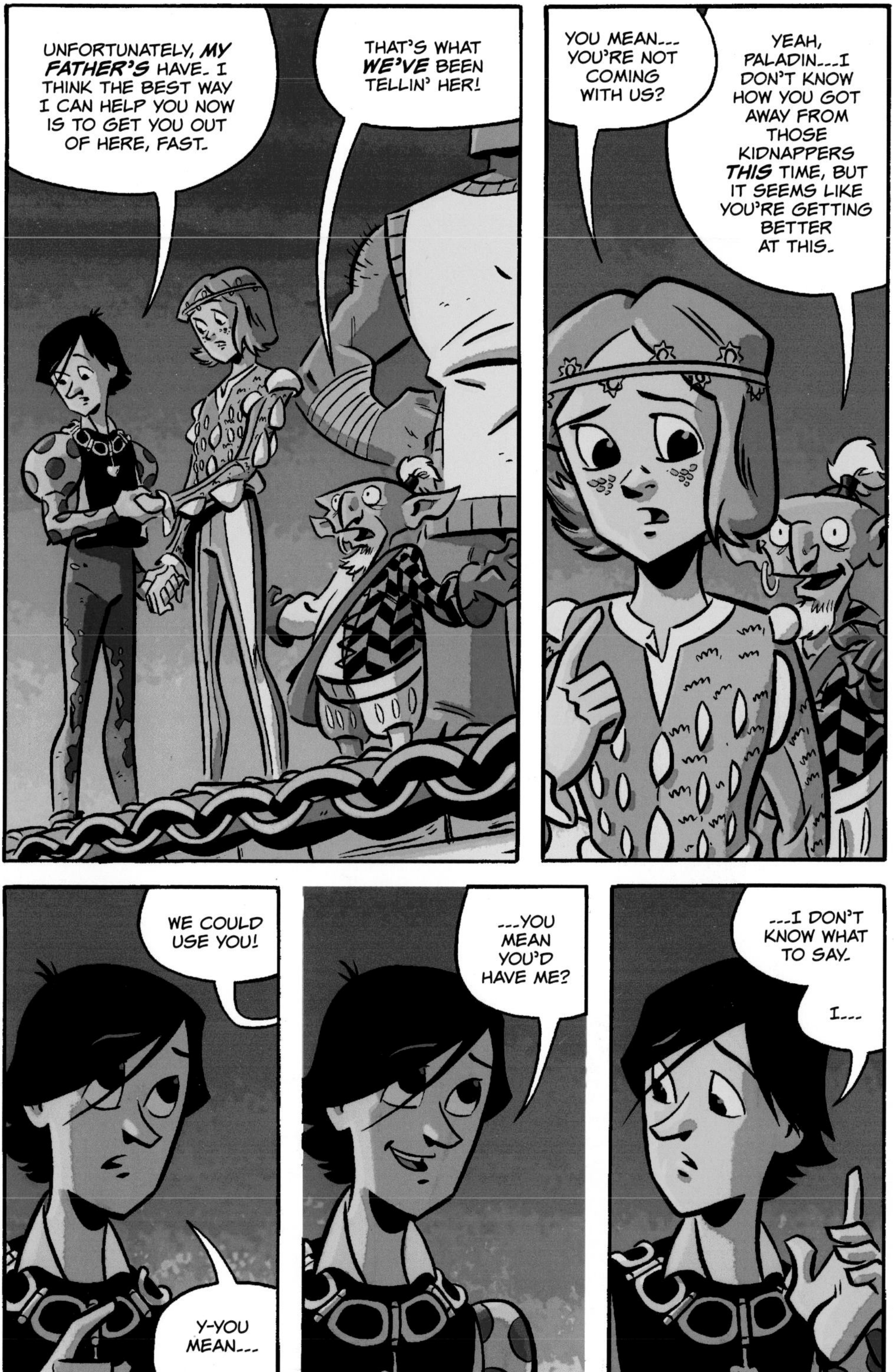
UNFORTUNATELY, **MY FATHER'S** HAVE. I THINK THE BEST WAY I CAN HELP YOU NOW IS TO GET YOU OUT OF HERE, FAST.
THAT'S WHAT **WE'VE** BEEN TELLIN' HER!
YOU MEAN... YOU'RE NOT COMING WITH US?
YEAH, PALADIN...I DON'T KNOW HOW YOU GOT AWAY FROM THOSE KIDNAPPERS **THIS** TIME, BUT IT SEEMS LIKE YOU'RE GETTING BETTER AT THIS.
WE COULD USE YOU!
Y-YOU MEAN...
...YOU MEAN YOU'D HAVE ME?
...I DON'T KNOW WHAT TO SAY.
I...

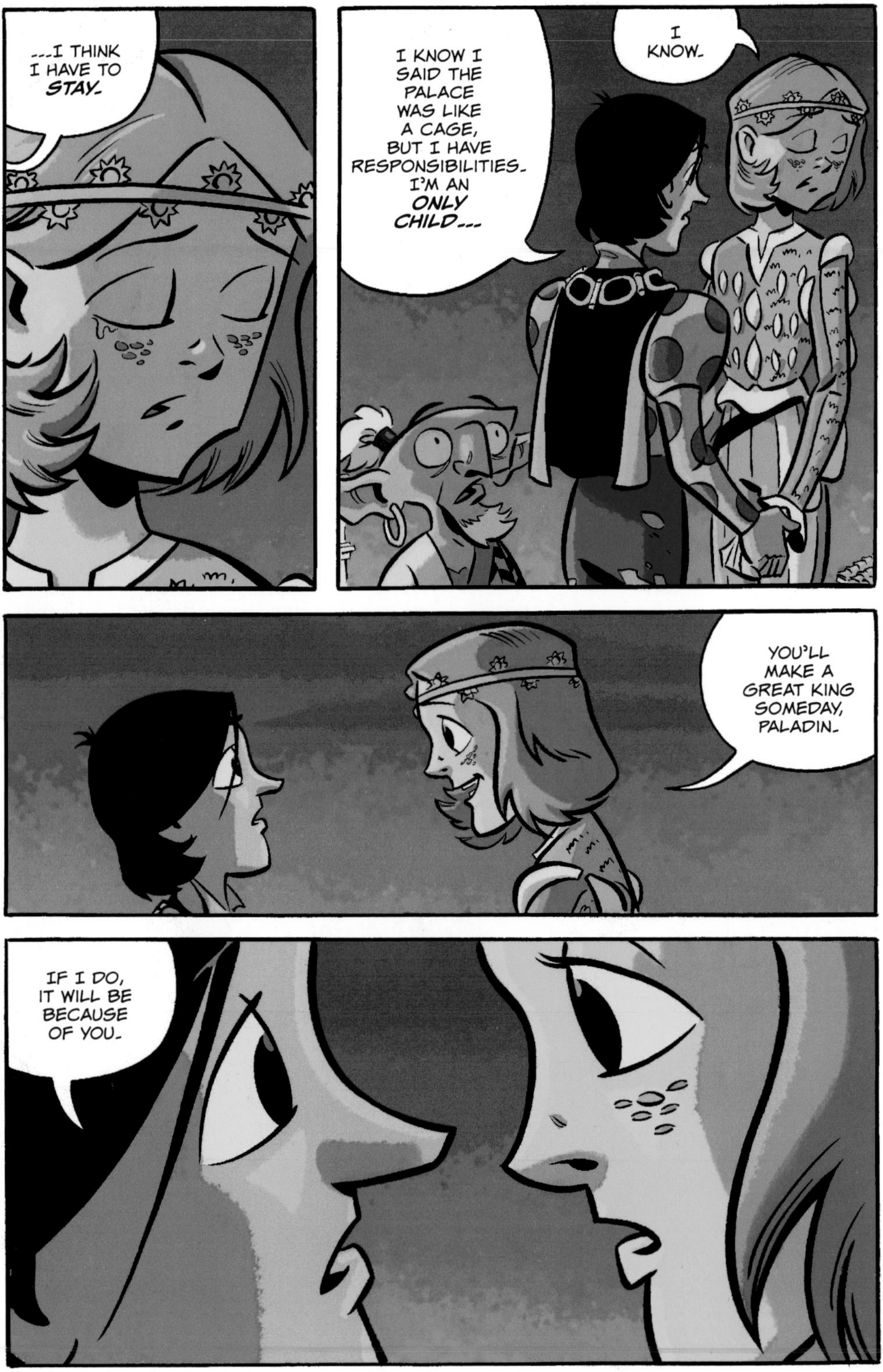
...I THINK I HAVE TO STAY.
I KNOW I SAID THE PALACE WAS LIKE A CAGE, BUT I HAVE RESPONSIBILITIES. I'M AN ONLY CHILD...
I KNOW.
YOU'LL MAKE A GREAT KING SOMEDAY, PALADIN.
IF I DO, IT WILL BE BECAUSE OF YOU.

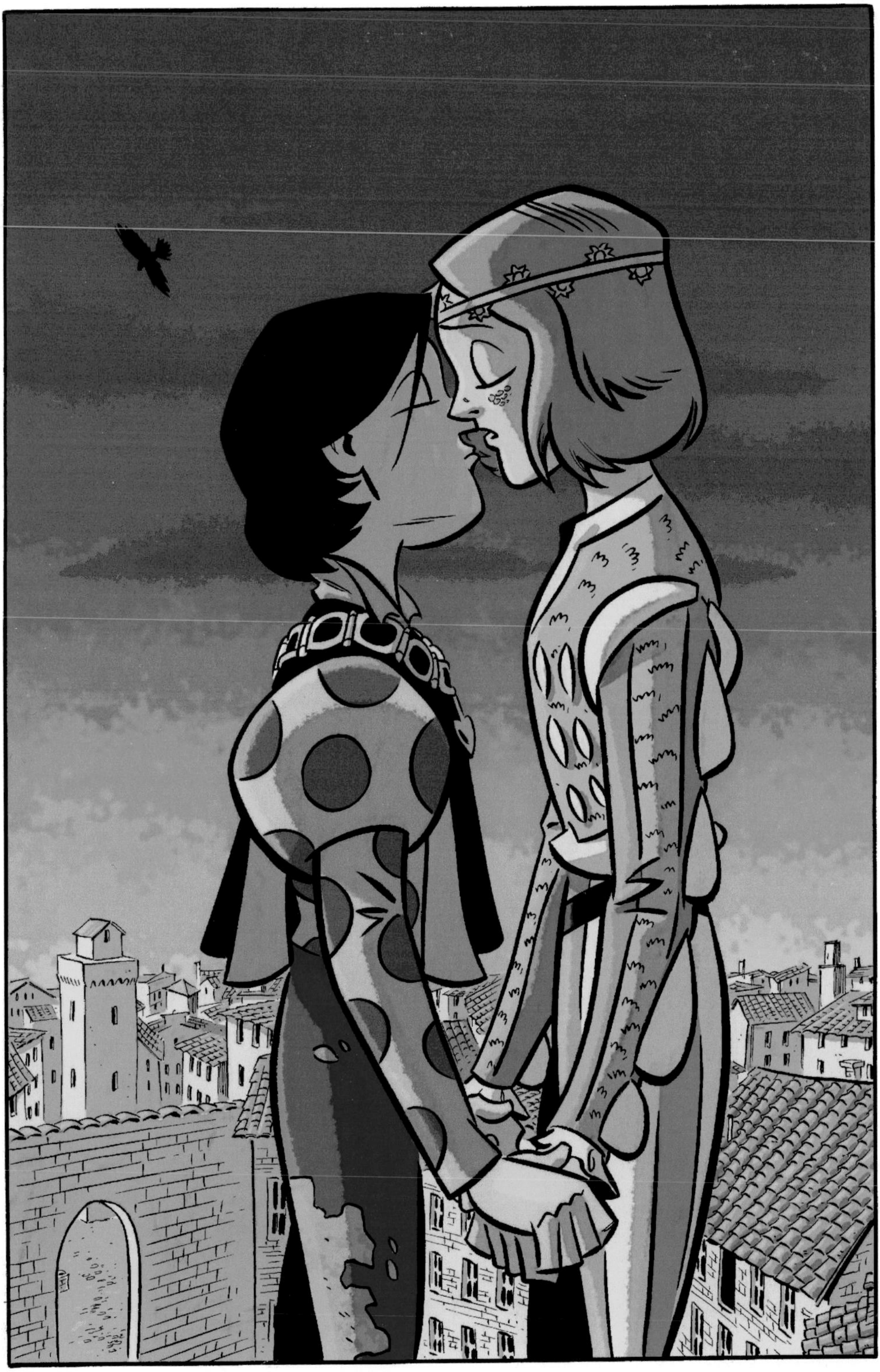

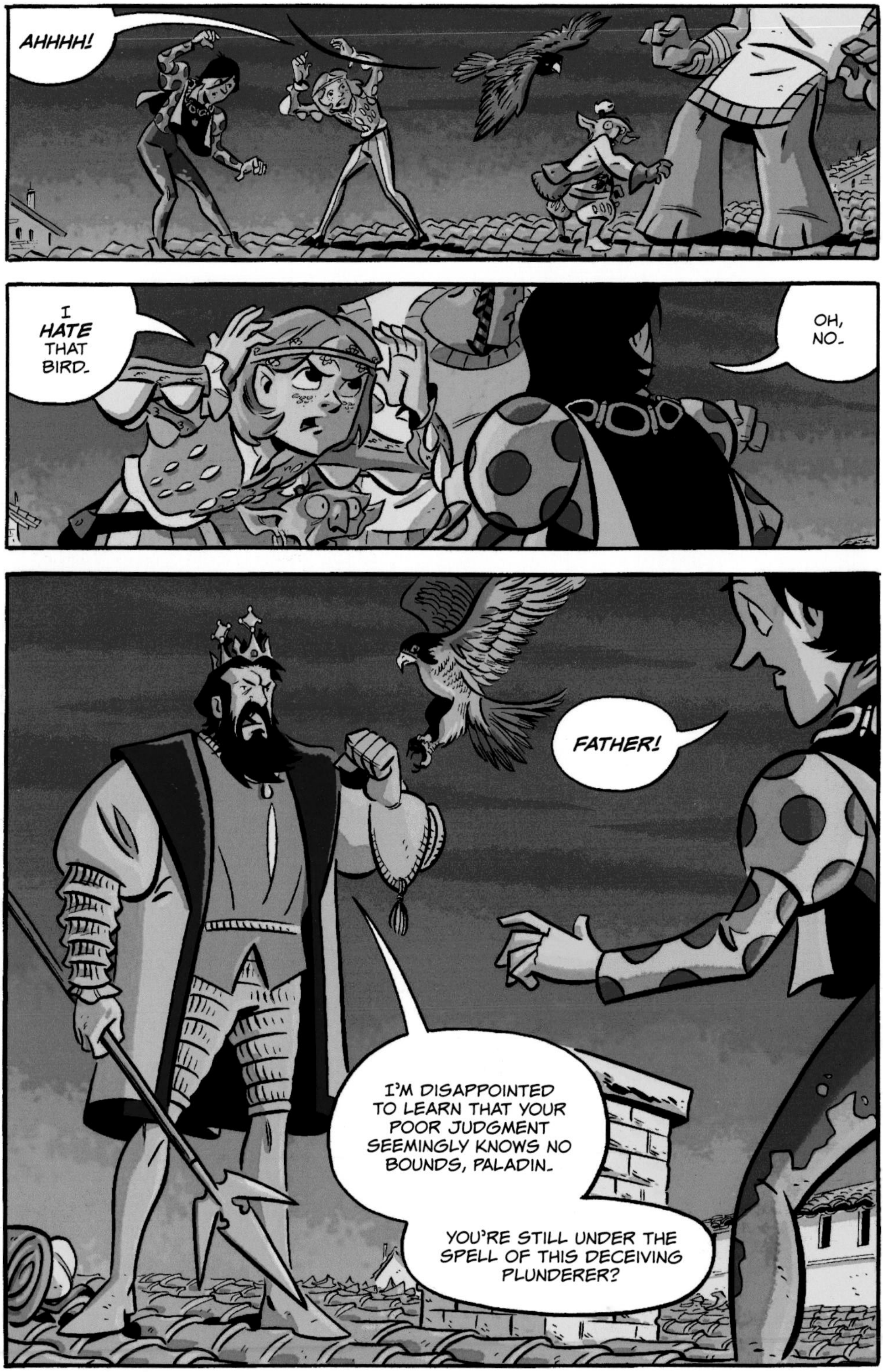
AHHHH!
I HATE THAT BIRD.
OH, NO.
FATHER!
I'M DISAPPOINTED TO LEARN THAT YOUR POOR JUDGMENT SEEMINGLY KNOWS NO BOUNDS, PALADIN.
YOU'RE STILL UNDER THE SPELL OF THIS DECEIVING PLUNDERER?

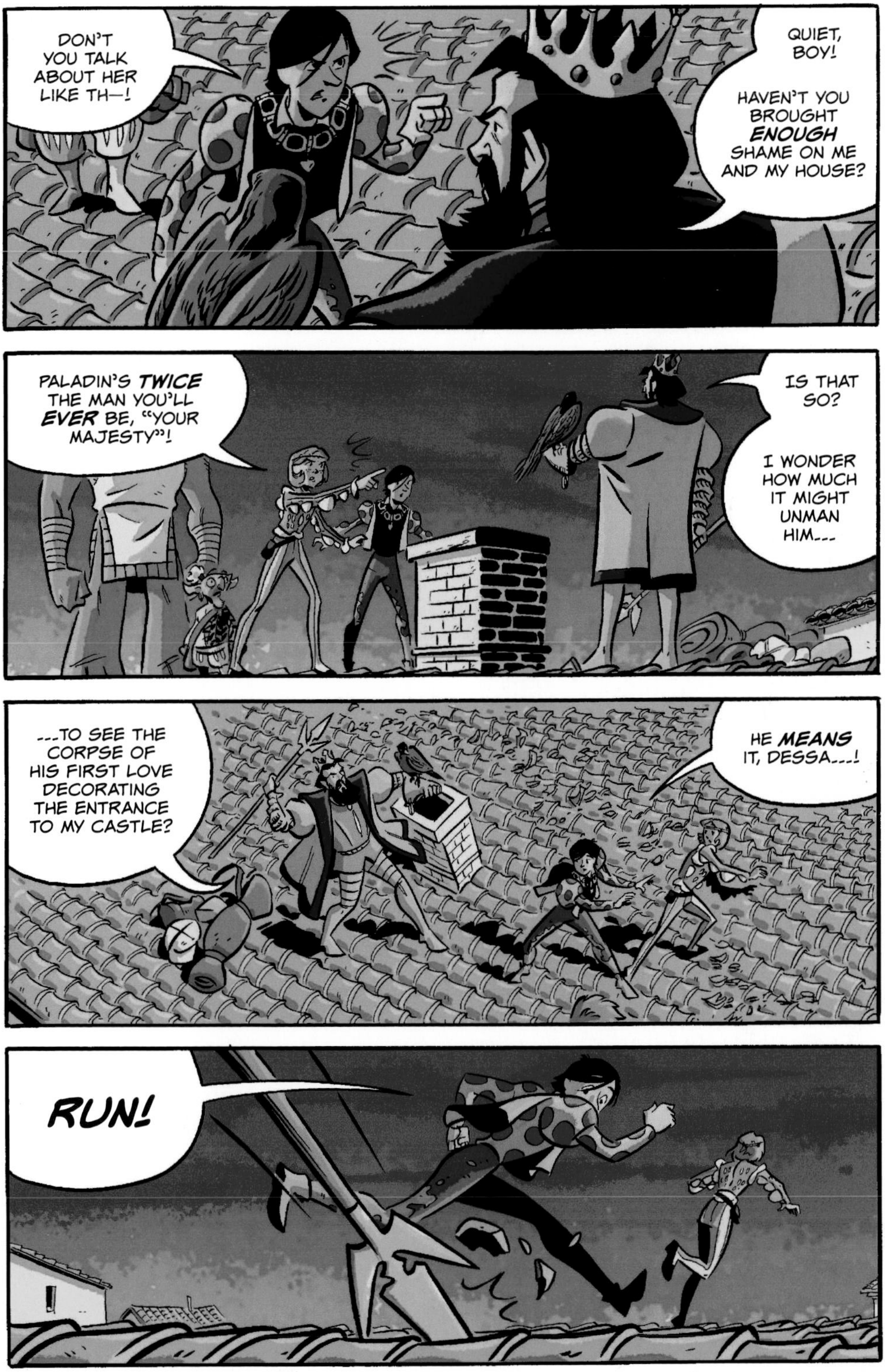
DON'T YOU TALK ABOUT HER LIKE TH—!
QUIET, BOY!
HAVEN'T YOU BROUGHT *ENOUGH* SHAME ON ME AND MY HOUSE?
PALADIN'S *TWICE* THE MAN YOU'LL *EVER* BE, "YOUR MAJESTY"!
IS THAT SO?
I WONDER HOW MUCH IT MIGHT UNMAN HIM...
...TO SEE THE CORPSE OF HIS FIRST LOVE DECORATING THE ENTRANCE TO MY CASTLE?
HE *MEANS* IT, DESSA...!
RUN!

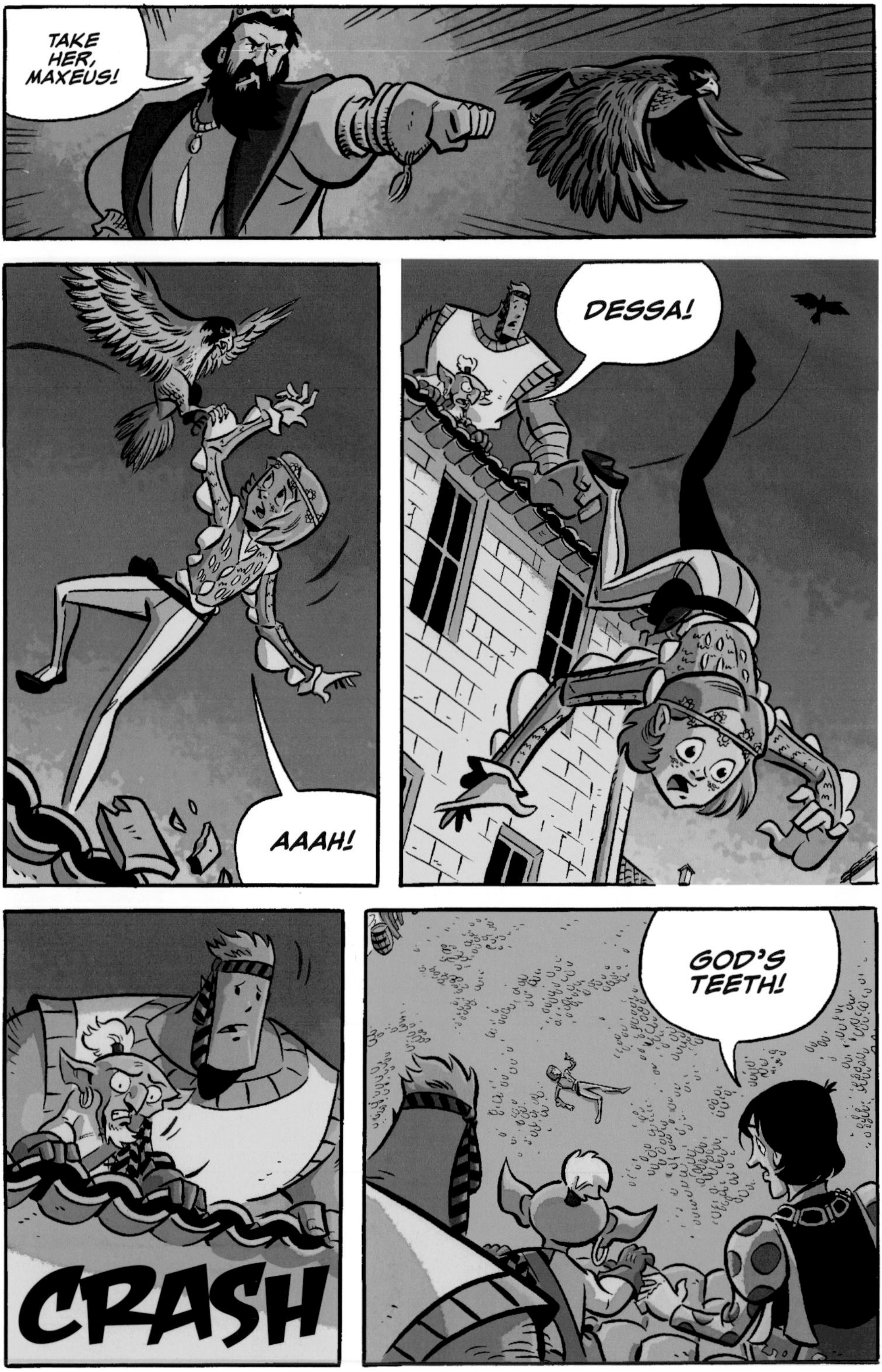
TAKE HER, MAXEUS!
AAAH!
DESSA!
CRASH
GOD'S TEETH!

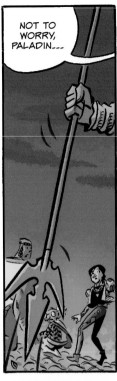

NOT TO WORRY, PALADIN...

...I'LL PUT HER OUT OF HER MISERY.

KRAK

MAXEUS...!

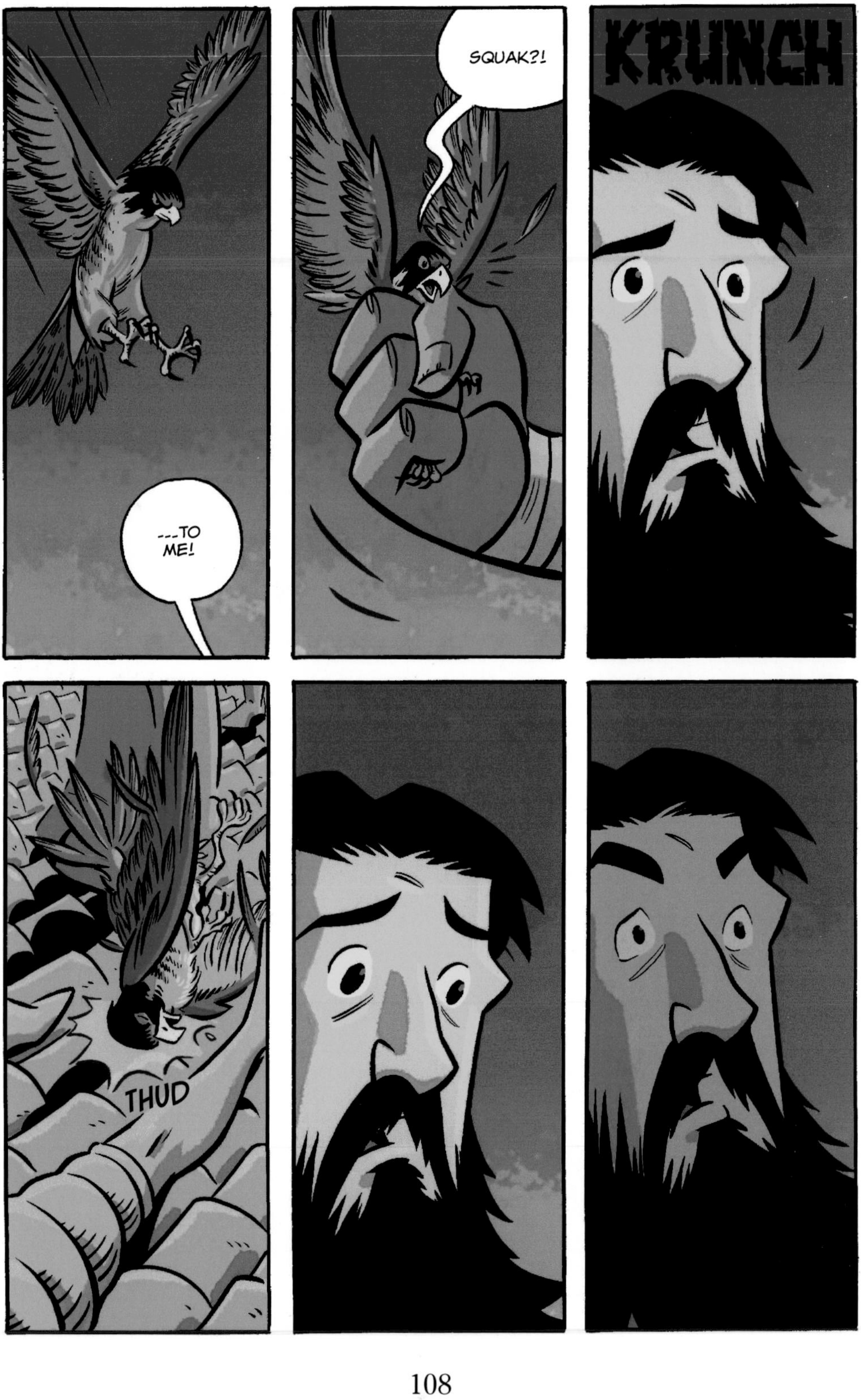
---TO ME!
SQUAK?!
KRUNCH
THUD

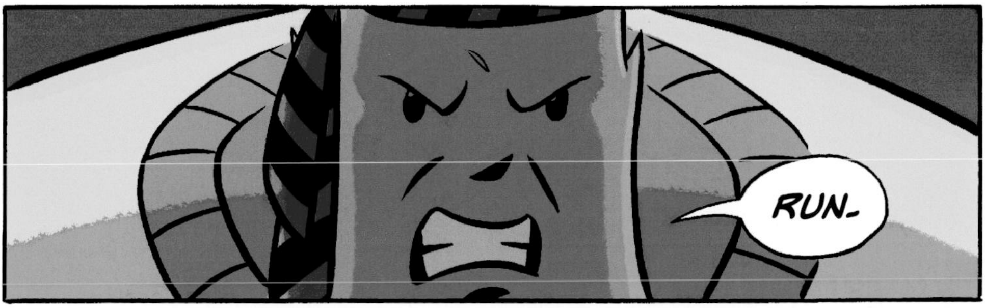
RUN.

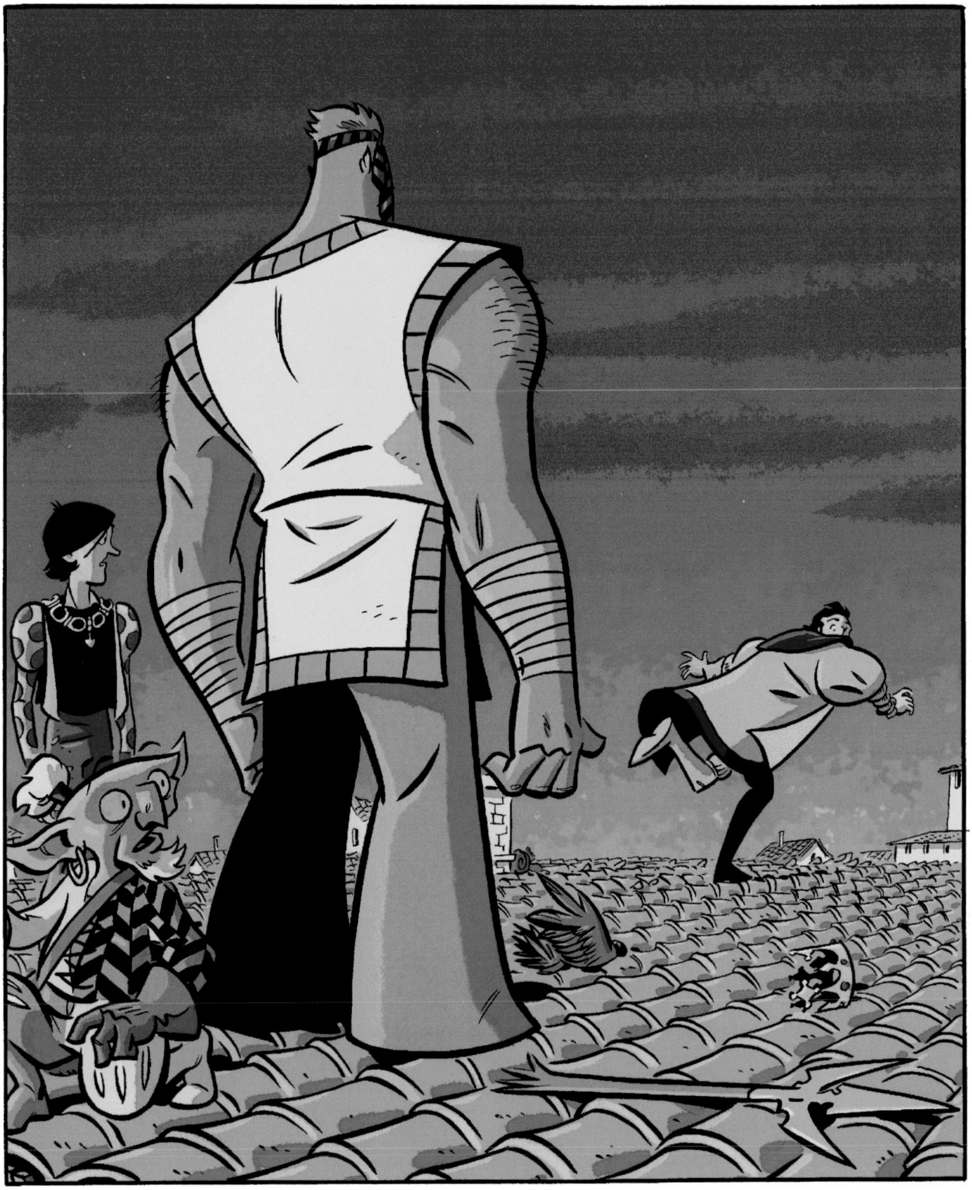

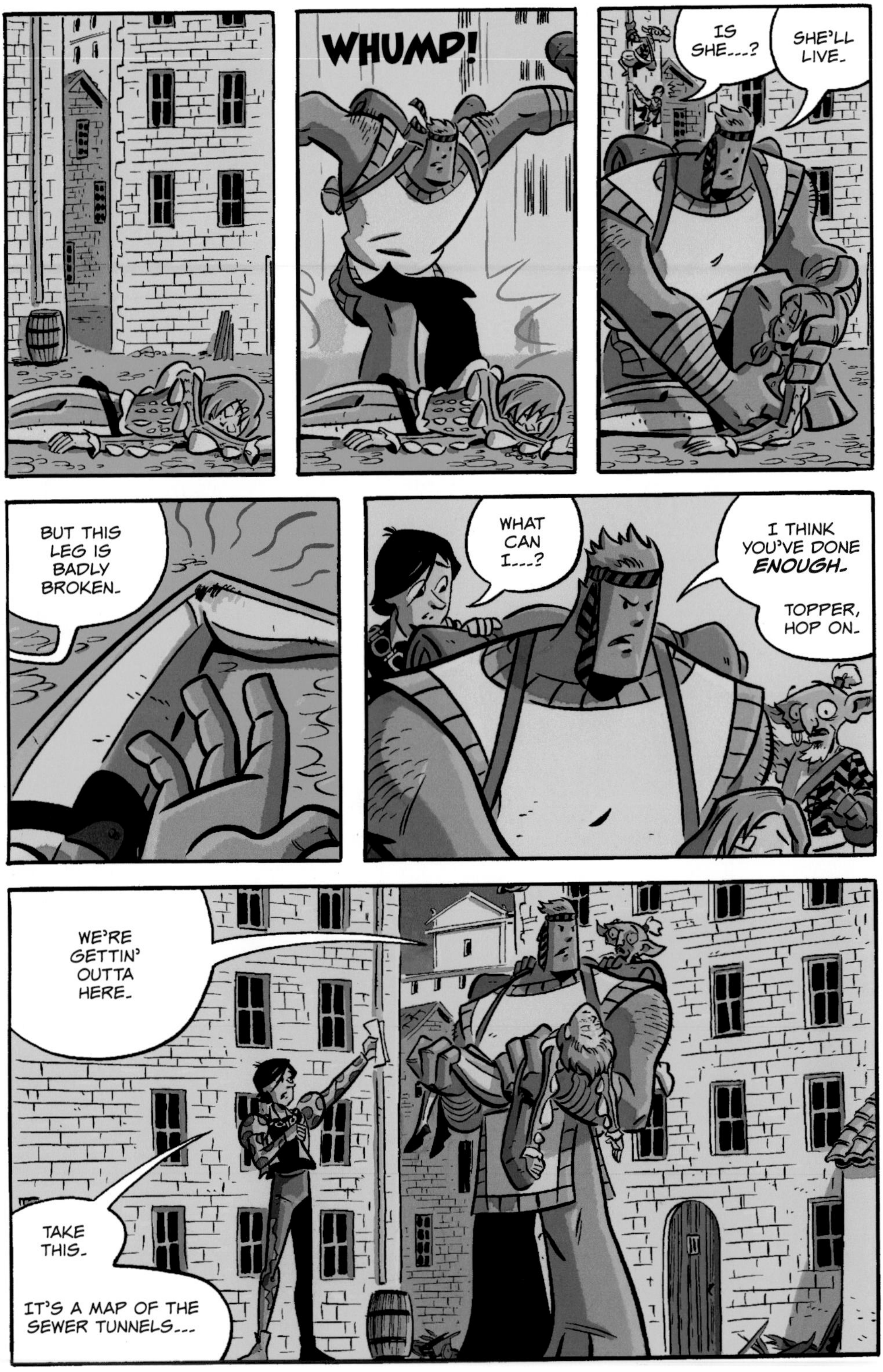
WHUMP!
IS SHE...?
SHE'LL LIVE.
BUT THIS LEG IS BADLY BROKEN.
WHAT CAN I...?
I THINK YOU'VE DONE ENOUGH.
TOPPER, HOP ON.
WE'RE GETTIN' OUTTA HERE.
TAKE THIS.
IT'S A MAP OF THE SEWER TUNNELS...

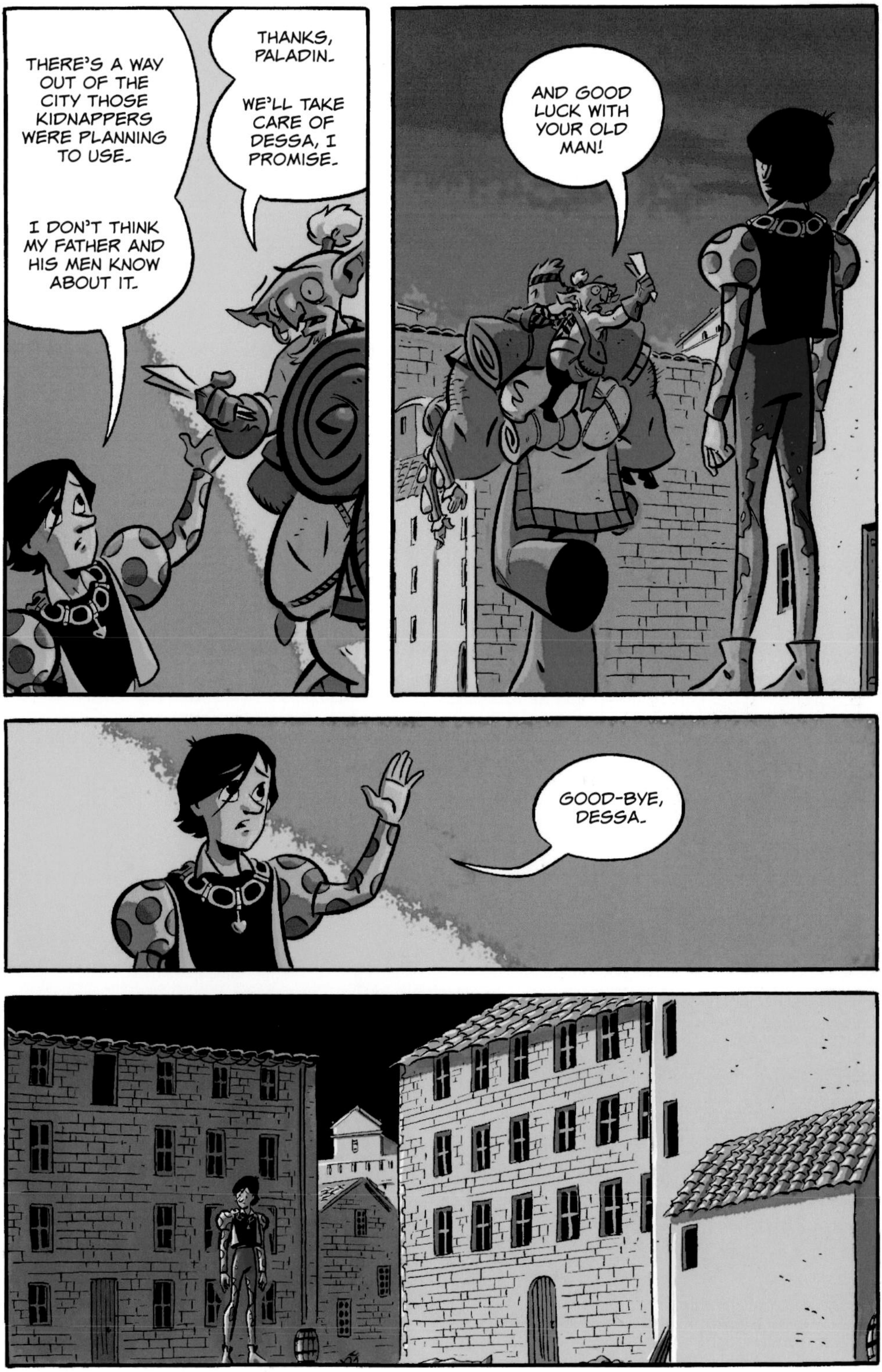
THERE'S A WAY OUT OF THE CITY THOSE KIDNAPPERS WERE PLANNING TO USE.
I DON'T THINK MY FATHER AND HIS MEN KNOW ABOUT IT.
THANKS, PALADIN.
WE'LL TAKE CARE OF DESSA, I PROMISE.
AND GOOD LUCK WITH YOUR OLD MAN!
GOOD-BYE, DESSA.

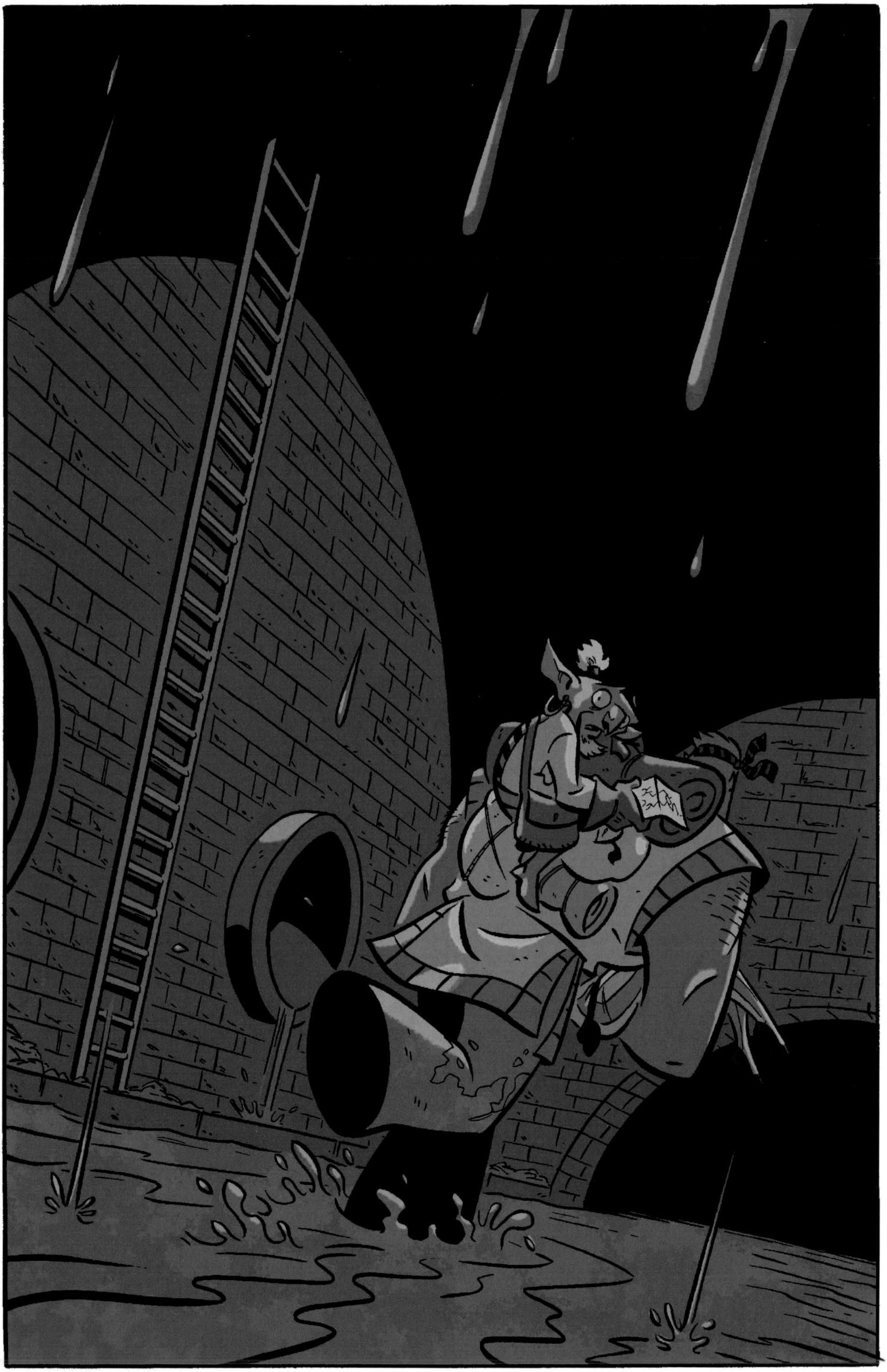

EPILOGUE

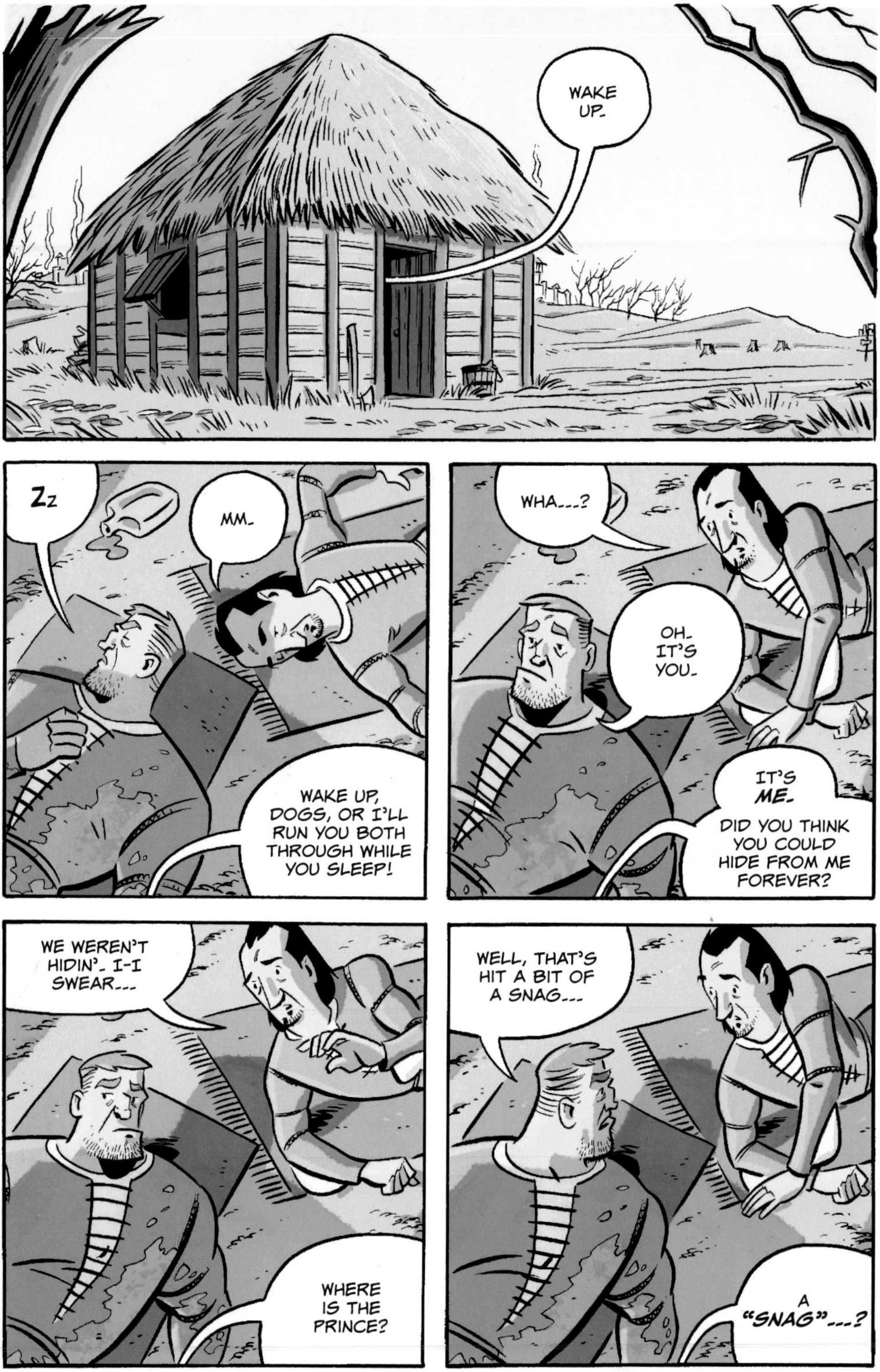
WAKE UP.
Zz
MM.
WAKE UP, DOGS, OR I'LL RUN YOU BOTH THROUGH WHILE YOU SLEEP!
WHA...?
OH. IT'S YOU.
IT'S ME.
DID YOU THINK YOU COULD HIDE FROM ME FOREVER?
WE WEREN'T HIDIN'. I-I SWEAR...
WHERE IS THE PRINCE?
WELL, THAT'S HIT A BIT OF A SNAG...
A "SNAG"...?

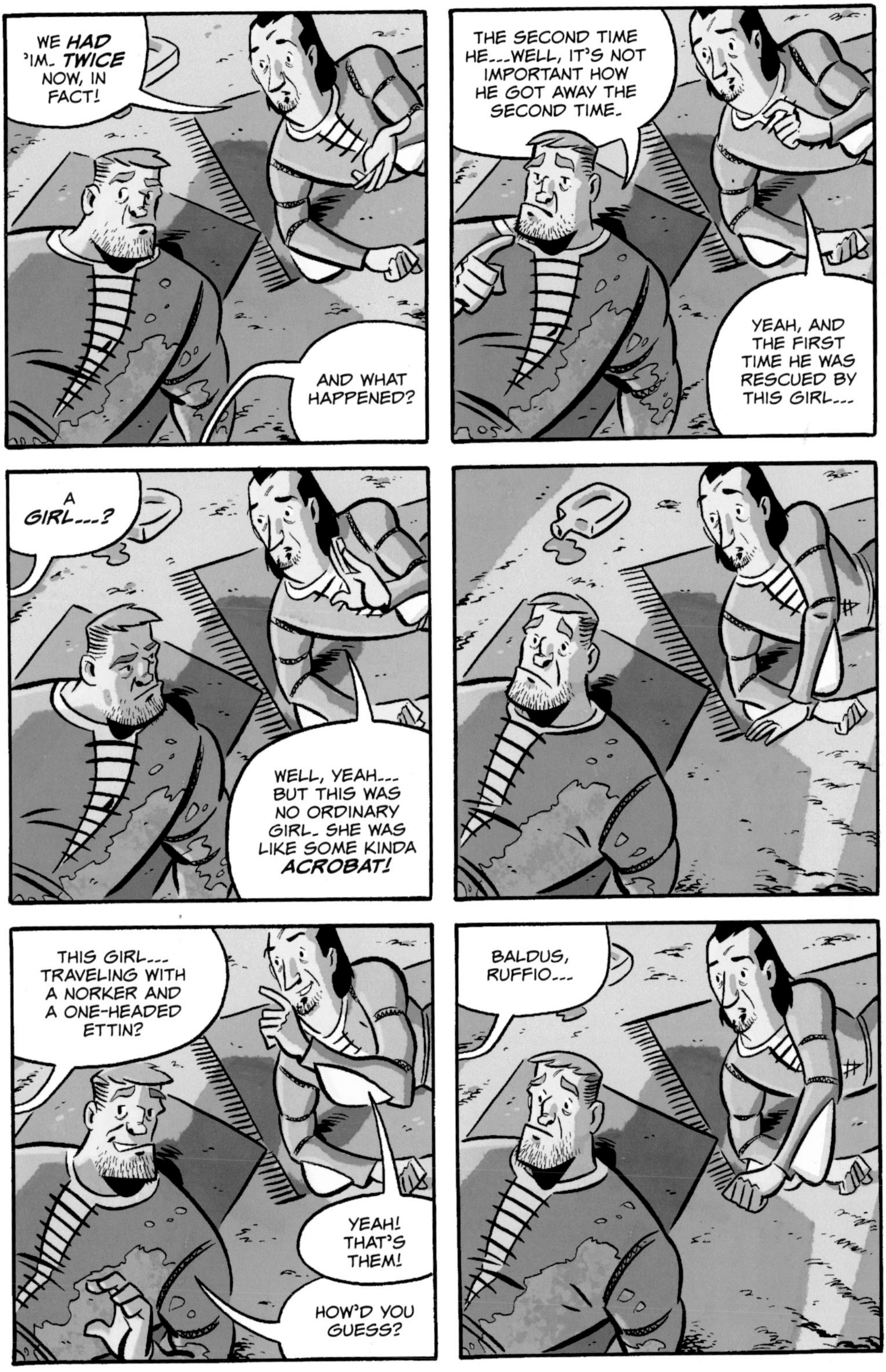
WE HAD 'IM. TWICE NOW, IN FACT!
AND WHAT HAPPENED?
THE SECOND TIME HE...WELL, IT'S NOT IMPORTANT HOW HE GOT AWAY THE SECOND TIME.
YEAH, AND THE FIRST TIME HE WAS RESCUED BY THIS GIRL...
A GIRL...?
WELL, YEAH... BUT THIS WAS NO ORDINARY GIRL. SHE WAS LIKE SOME KINDA ACROBAT!
THIS GIRL... TRAVELING WITH A NORKER AND A ONE-HEADED ETTIN?
YEAH! THAT'S THEM!
HOW'D YOU GUESS?
BALDUS, RUFFIO...

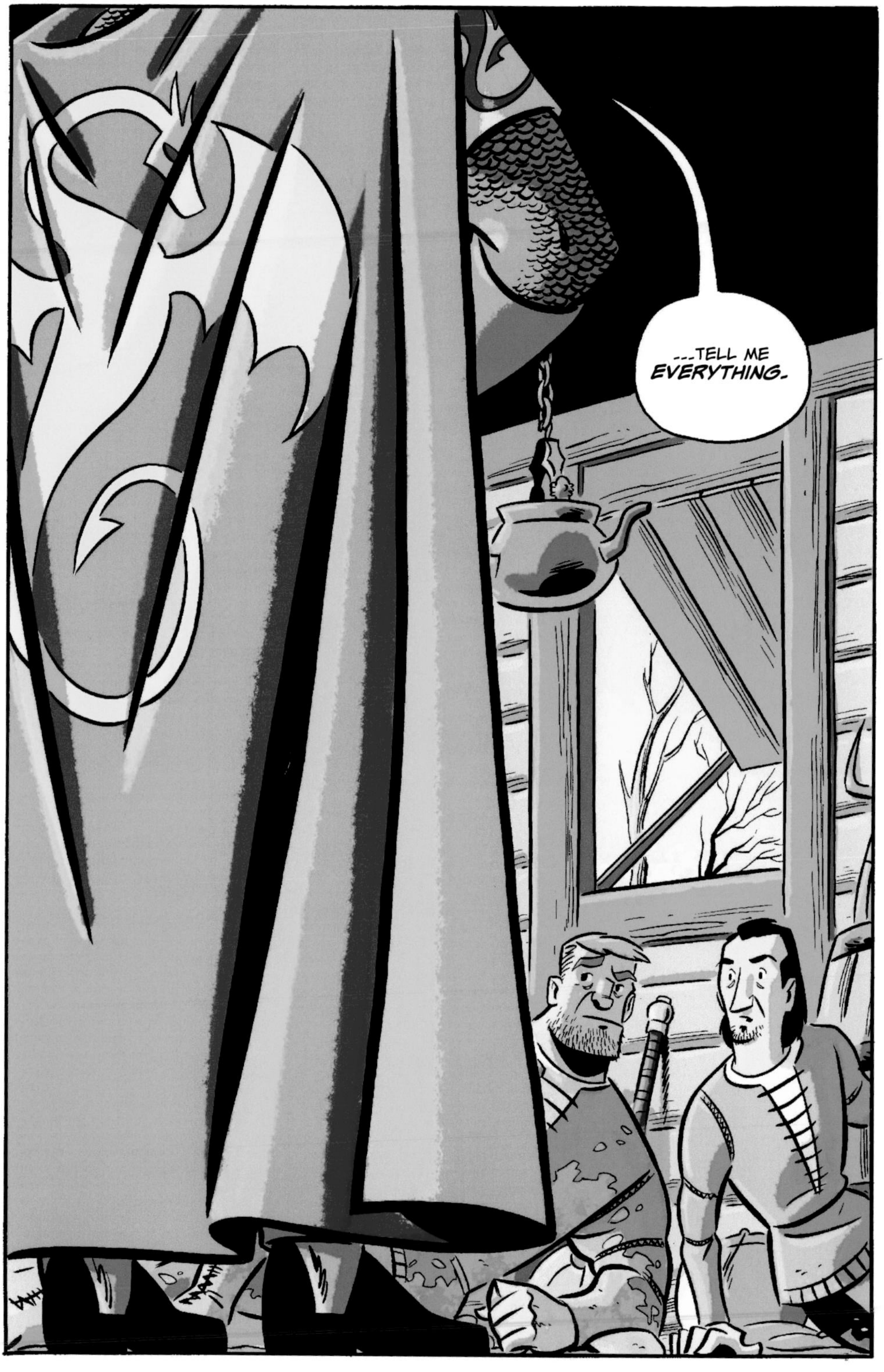
...TELL ME EVERYTHING.